Four

Calling

Burds

Also by Vincent Meis

Eddie's Desert Rose

Tio Jorge

Down in Cuba

Deluge

Four Calling Burds

Vincent Meis

Printed in The United States of America

FIRST EDITION
Fallen Bros. Press
29403 N Enrose Ave
Rancho Palos Verdes, CA 90275

ISBN-13: 978-0-9976728-4-8
ISBN-10: 0-9976728-4-6

For

Brothers and Sisters

1: Augie

In small, pigeon-toed steps, a boy abandoned his family and propelled himself to the base of a pedestal. With his eyes uplifted, he gazed at a statue of a child about the same age riding a giant seahorse. The statue boy, naked except for a sombrero hanging at his back, raised one hand in a triumphant wave. Delight spread across the real boy's face as he raised his hand to mimic the statue. He pivoted on one foot toward his parents as if to say, "*Adios!* This is my destiny." The parents looked bewildered, and the boy giggled. He turned his attention back to the seahorse just as a giant wave pounded against the seawall, sending up spray that doused a group of screaming teenagers playing chicken with the waves.

Under the last light of day hanging like a purple cloak over the carnival of Puerto Vallarta's Malecon, my sister, M, and I stood in the middle of the flurry of activity and yet not part of it. We were both drawn to the boy gazing up at the boy riding the seahorse. I was pleased to see a smile take over M's face while I squeezed my brow, wracking my brain for something clever to say.

"In seahorses, it's the males who carry the babies to term," I said.

M turned toward me as if startled, not because my comment was peculiar—she was quite used to my quips plucked from a brain file she had labeled UBEFs (useless but extraordinary facts)—but because they were the first words I had uttered since we left the Miramar Restaurant a half hour before. During the seaside walk back to the hotel, I had been using great restraint to keep my tongue in check. At a loss how to address what had happened at dinner, I thought it best to let M start the conversation.

God knows I had about a million opportunities to point out an absurdity or rattle off an inane fact to get a little dialogue going: families with double strollers and other kids in tow contributing to the overpopulation of the world; teenagers wearing shiny colors and looking like parrots while screeching in similar fashion; trinkets sold at the souvenir stalls made in China rather than Mexico; dessert sellers pushing very un-Mexican items like red velvet cakes and lemon meringue pies.

However divergent our points of view, M and I did share a great love of people watching, and I was normally able to spark laughter in her with my observations. But since the torched-earth dinner earlier that evening, with its painful revelations, mini betrayals, and frustrating reactions, nothing had been normal.

M is a child psychiatrist and prone to symbolism, so her response to my comment showed little interest in the role reversal of seahorse child bearing. "I see a boy riding high on a particularly exotic marine creature, a calm but persistent seahorse swimming through life, staying true to its unusual self, not changing to adapt to its environment," she said. I was amazed how she came up with these observations. But she wasn't done. "Its lower half is tailored to the sea, and its upper half is a caricature of a land animal. The statue boy has attached his fate to the fanciful beast, riding it into the future, and the real boy has inclinations to do the same."

"Oh," I said. But I liked to stick to facts. "They mate for life, you know."

She tilted her head in the form of a question. "Really?" She always looked for some hidden meaning in the things I said, as if I was trying to steer the conversation in a particular direction, as if I might have been making an offhand reference to her relationship with her husband or my own relationship with Ruben.

"They do," I said.

"Good for them," M mumbled without sarcasm. Her attention was clearly focused on the parents.

After several increasingly loud verbal attempts to bring the boy back into the brood, the father resorted to a heavy-handed approach, grabbing the child by the arm. The boy mounted a vigorous protest, but the father managed to corral him. M frowned at the parent's interruption of the boy's flight of wonder. She turned to me, no doubt to express her analysis of the parents' behavior, but I gave her a look that it was really none of our business. Besides, my attention had already been captured by another young daddy carrying his son on his shoulders. I stared wistfully at the father and son, remembering when Colton was that age. I wished I had insisted Ruben and Colton come with us, M's mandate of only the siblings be damned.

An uneasy quiet frustrated the force that normally brought us together as if we were the north and south poles of a magnet. Still only halfway to our hotel, we came to a large plaza dominated by the church of Our Lady of Guadalupe, the tower topped by a magnificent wrought iron crown lifted up by a circle of iron angels. The art of even a mediocre church such as this was made to inspire, to draw one's attention to the heavens. In more modern times, the town expressed its art in more modest projects, the series of sculptures along the malecón of which "The Seahorse" was the most famous. Just at the opposite end of the plaza was another called "Dance of the Dolphins." Two dolphins hovered above a large round fountain, entwined in what looked more like an embrace than a dance.

"I wonder how dolphins do it," I said.

"You mean you don't know?" said M in feigned shock. As we got closer, she added, "I guess they've already done it. There's a baby dolphin near the base. It's family rated: mom, pop, and baby dolphin."

"And all *is* right with the world."

As we approached the Rio Cuale, a sort of dividing line between the more Mexican center of Puerto Vallarta and the heavily touristy area to the south, the incongruous sounds of a grunge band playing what sounded like a Pearl Jam cover assaulted my ears. The music came from a cement platform where the river met the sea.

We started over the pedestrian overpass that crossed the river, and then stopped to watch the out-of-place, long-haired pale boys wailing on their guitars. A brief stop, I thought, might give our two younger siblings, Lio and AJ, a chance to catch up. The four of us had left the restaurant together, but they had fallen behind. M and I leaned on the railing, sporting expressions of bewilderment at the music. Surrounding us were Mexican families eating mayonnaise-smeared corn on the cob, seemingly oblivious to the music while drunk tourists awkwardly tried to move with the erratic beat.

A young man standing next to me along the railing turned to me and said in a Midwestern twang, "I just stuck my feet in a tub of piranhas." Of all the eleven thousand or so tourists on the streets of Puerto Vallarta, a mathematical calculation I made based on yearly visitor numbers, he had chosen me as the recipient of this astounding revelation.

The girl standing on the other side of the man burst into laughter. "You mean Garra rufa fish, you dufus." Leaning forward, she shouted to me over the young man who now nodded to the music as if in a trance. "It's a sort of foot spa. They eat away the dead skin on your feet."

"Oh," I said.

"My boyfriend's got a ton of it."

"Gee."

I turned to M. "Travel is so enlightening. I can't imagine what other changes an influx of tourists brings to a town like this."

There was a tiny break in the ice, and M almost smiled.

"Maybe tomorrow we should venture out to one of the nearby towns, see something real," I said.

"Do you think AJ and Lio passed us?"

"I doubt it. They were pretty far behind."

When the squealing guitars and pounding percussion reached a level of discomfort, we looked at each other and nodded that it was time to move on. I was anxious to have a real conversation, but was it the proper place? M couldn't have meant what she had said at dinner. It must have been a function of the truth-or-dare ambience brought on by the tequila and the ungroundedness of being a long distance from home. I had no idea if the evening would live in infamy or be quickly and conveniently forgotten. All four siblings had revealed things we'd probably like to take back, though M's had been the most jarring.

I loosened my tie, removed my jacket, slung it over my shoulder, and hooked it on my thumb. I felt as if I was choking on the damp heat. Thanks to M, we were the only people on the boardwalk dressed in formal attire. Before we left for Mexico, she had ordered her siblings, in her inimitable way, to bring at least one change of dress clothes for a night out in Puerto Vallarta's best restaurant. We would toast our recently departed mother and reminisce.

"Why Puerto Vallarta?" I had asked with a scrunched-up nose the day she suggested the trip. I had traveled all over Mexico, climbing the pyramids at Teotihuacan, visiting Mayan ruins in the jungles of Yucatan, riding the Copper Canyon railroad in Chihuahua, and sunning on Mexico's only semi-official nudist beach of Zipolite, Oaxaca. But one place I had avoided was the so-called Mexican gay Mecca, Puerto Vallarta. I had always been lukewarm on the concept of a gay holiday. Now that I was married with a kid, traveling to gay party destinations made even less sense.

"I want to get away for a few days," said M. "No spouses. No kids. Just the four of us together for the first time in ages. We deserve it. The last few months have been tough." We had devoted countless hours to our mother, watching her waste away day by day. "And besides, Puerto Vallarta is where Mom and Dad honeymooned, very possibly where I was conceived."

"Now that's a sobering thought," I said.

M chuckled. "Can you imagine?"

"I'd rather not." And then a juicy tidbit popped into my head. "It was in Puerto Vallarta where Elizabeth Taylor and Richard Burton had a torrid affair during the filming of *The Night of the Iguana.* They ended up buying a house, or two houses actually, connected by a bridge over the street. There was a big scandal with the other stars and the director."

"How do you know all this stuff?"

"It's in the UBEF file. Remember, I work in a library."

M laughed knowingly. "It's all coming back to me now. Mom told me she wanted to honeymoon down there because she thought she might run into Elizabeth Taylor."

We had this kind of breezy exchange so easily back in normal times. Had the dinner changed things between us? Could we get back to where we had been?

The dinner to honor our mother had begun with shots of tequila, and it quickly spiraled into unchartered territory. A death in the family can have that effect. The memories of our mother started sweet and funny, but before we knew it, we ventured into the more bizarre and confusing things she had done.

"Viva the Spanish language," I said, and we all toasted. Mom had spent half her life trying to learn Spanish and barely reached a high beginner level.

"We should have been more supportive," said Lio.

We reflected on Lio's thought a moment, and then abandoned the topic of our mother altogether, delving instead into our individual crises, each one trying to outdo the others in detailing the complexities of what we were going through.

AJ was the first to spin the whine wheel. "No, but wait," AJ shouted in the noisy restaurant. "You won't believe what he said the other night." But we wouldn't have to stretch our imaginations to believe just about anything AJ reported about her husband, Bart.

"One of his co-workers was complaining about Jews, so he reminded him the president's daughter married one. I guess he thought he was being clever. So I asked him if he mentioned he had married a Jew. He looked at me dumbfounded as if he had forgotten. Then he said his personal life was nobody's business." We all tried to be appropriately sympathetic. If any sense of competition existed in our gripe session, everyone might expect AJ to be the winner. Her husband had become unbearable in his defense of the president, and she was forced to fight her battles in the distant outpost of Modesto. After Bart's house-flipping business in the Bay Area failed during the financial crisis of 2008, he had insisted on moving AJ and their two boys back to his hometown.

On my fourth Margarita, I brought up the time the four-year-old Lio let little AJ slip from his arms to the floor as if any damage to her head might explain her choice in a husband. It was my favorite sibling taunt because I could zing both Lio and AJ at the same time. M and I were known to gang up on the two younger ones in a lopsided battle.

Most of the family acknowledged a gradual decrease in IQ following birth order. Our maternal grandmother, a health food aficionado before it was *de rigueur*, blamed it on change in diet as with each pregnancy our mother, Gloria, ate more processed food. As compensation, Lio and AJ were given unimpeachable beauty, which they were discreet enough not to throw back in our faces. Our grandmother was silent on that phenomenon. The physical differences between the two older and the two younger siblings were striking enough that we used to tease our mother, saying she must have had an affair during the years Lio and AJ were conceived.

"I most certainly did not," said Gloria. "Each one of you is attractive in your own way," she said to my moans of protest. And then Gloria continued with one of her annoying non-sequiturs. "You know, my sister, your Aunt Sarah, was nominated for homecoming queen in high school. AJ looks just like her."

After my three siblings mercilessly admonished me for bringing up the baby-dropping story, dessert was served. M banged on her water glass with a knife. She began in a trembling voice that made me feel an immediate knot in my stomach.

"I have something I want to share with you guys." Normally a good public speaker, she struggled to form the words. When they finally came out, it was as if a bomb had been dropped from a very high place and only became apparent when it took the air out of the room. My brother, sister, and I wandered in the wasteland of our silence before coming to the collective conclusion, communicated by furtive glances, that the only way out was to imagine she had invented it. As the oldest and natural leader, she always had to win even if it was a race to construct the most startling revelation.

But then with a brief consideration, I realized that she was not only serious, but it made sense. Throughout our growing up, M had on numerous occasions come to my rescue when other boys were picking on me, which had been both an embarrassment and a relief. M had gotten all the macho genes that should have been mine. She liked motorcycles and sports and being a bit of a bully in conversations where she was clearly the smartest participant.

AJ sat with a death grip on the stem of her wine glass, her face going through its repertoire of emotions before finally settling on something resembling a feeling of abandonment, her eyes welling up with tears. Just as AJ was forming her words, the mariachis tooted their final chords and fell silent. "M, you can't mean that!" Her lament came out much too loud and hung in the air, vibrating as crisp as the neon palm tree on the sign across the street. Several people in the restaurant looked over at our table.

Lio jumped in to save his sister. "That could change everything, I mean…" He couldn't quite articulate what we must have all been thinking. How would it work in terms of M's relationship with her husband? She and Arnold had always been an unusual couple, but they were by far the most successful in the family. Professionals, though not slaves to their professions, they owned a stunning four-bedroom home in Piedmont, drove nice cars, and traveled to Europe often. More than that, they genuinely seemed to love each other.

M produced an odd sound, part nervous chuckle, part agonizing groan, registering her complete lack of surprise at how AJ and Lio reacted. She then turned to me, her dear brother, for a sympathetic ear. All she got was my chin falling to my chest in deep contemplation of my half-eaten flan. I shaved off a lump of the custard with my spoon and let it plop into the caramel as if it were me drowning in the sticky bath.

"Well, it was just something I've been thinking about," M finally said. "I haven't actually started, you know, the process or anything."

I pushed my flan aside, feeling like I had to say something. I should have stayed silent. I should have known it is better to say nothing after four drinks. "Well, there's Aunt Ida," I said. Aunt Ida used to wear mannish hats and dress in the baggy, layered style of her idol, Gertrude Stein.

"Aunt Ida?" M's voice screeched like a creaky door. "What are you talking about?"

"Oh, God!" I said, suddenly remembering Ida's later years when she abandoned all decorum and walked around in food-stained sweats, claiming she was her father reincarnated.

M took out her credit card and slapped it on top of the bill. "I don't know about anybody else, but I need some air." No one fought her over the check.

Just when M and I had achieved enough distance from the grunge band that we might have a conversation, a fire-eater flipped on a battered boombox in front of us and started his performance to a Donna Summer track. Again, we stopped to watch. I chanced a glance at M, still with that awful feeling churning my gut since dinner. In the light from the fire batons, I felt the pain the way a twin might.

Turmoil lined her face but also highlighted the way she had aged. Too caught up in the confusion of my own life these last few years, I had failed to notice. She had a face people described as handsome rather than pretty. At forty-seven she was hardly old, but her face drooped in a way even the night could not soften. Just two years younger, I wondered how I must look. I touched my face, hot from the sun I had absorbed watching young men play Frisbee on the beach that afternoon. Mesmerized by the flying disc and the men's bodies, along with the consumption of several margaritas, I had spent way too much time in the sun without sunblock. I worried one afternoon in the blazing Mexican sun had reversed all the years I had religiously applied a moisturizer for men that promised to awaken and uplift dull, fatigued skin.

I had the habit of engaging in my moisturizing ritual behind closed doors, but one evening I had neglected to close the bathroom door, thinking my husband, Ruben, was sound asleep in front of the living room TV as was his custom. Intently rubbing in the cream, I looked up and saw Ruben leaning into the doorjamb, staring fixedly at me and shaking his head.

"What?" I said. "Not everyone has been blessed with perfect brown skin that never seems to age like yours."

"Oh, Augie, your lines, and I mean the few you have, give you distinction."

"Yeah, right."

I felt I was fighting a losing battle. No cream could diminish the hawk nose I had inherited from my father. Rogaine had done nothing for the encroaching bald spot at the top of my head. The hair that no longer grew on my head sprouted in great quantities on my back. I had given up on the hair displacement, but still had hopes for my face.

M and I got the gist of the fire-eater's act in a few minutes. M leaned her head in one direction and we started to move. I stopped and looked back. "It really seems we have lost Lio and AJ."

"They'll catch up."

"Lio has a terrible sense of direction."

"But AJ doesn't," M reminded me.

The previous night I had been the one who lingered behind after our taco dinner. I wandered off, imagining the other siblings would note my absence at some point and probably roll their eyes, but they had asked no questions the next day. I had stood outside a stripper bar and watched through the open window as patrons stuck pesos into the waistbands of the dancer's trunks. I was just drunk enough now that I wouldn't mind returning to the bar and making a fool of myself by approaching the dancers with sweaty bills in my fists. Perhaps this was why I had avoided Puerto Vallarta all these years. But when in Rome... The thought of indulging my fantasies sent a bubbly excitement from my navel down to my crotch. But I couldn't leave M alone, especially after my failure to support her at dinner.

I loosened my tie and unstuck the shirt collar from the sweat around my neck. I cleared my throat. "It's not that I—"

"Not now, Augie. Obviously you think I'm out of my mind."

"No, I was in shock. You never told me about any of this. I always told you everything." I remembered all the times I had recounted my gay escapades in the years before I met Ruben, holding back nothing. She would be supportive, non-judgmental, at times offering advice, but all the while I wondered if she was analyzing me.

"Do you have any idea how hard it is? I'm not surprised at Lio and AJ, but I expected better from you."

"But you don't just lay something like that on us in the middle of drunken celebration of Mom's life."

"When *is* the right time?" said M bitterly.

I looked down at the pavement. "You're standing on a Huichol peyote sun."

M's eyes blazed with frustration. "What?"

"The symbol in the sidewalk. It represents male energy that comes down so the corn will grow." All along the Malecon, Native American symbols were embedded in the pavement using little pebbles. "Look over there, the shaman. And over there, corn."

"You're impossible." She started walking at a fast pace as if whatever made my brain so bizarre might be contagious, and she needed to get away.

I felt bad. I really did. But that didn't stop me from wandering both mentally and physically as we continued to make slow progress back to the hotel. I noticed a golden angel suspended in the air. The living statue gripped a sword attached to the ground, the only thing that kept him from ascending up into the heavens. I approached him. M turned around, realizing I was no longer by her side. I motioned for her to come back and take a photo of me with my arm around the waist of the celestial creature. I felt the most lovely radiant warmth along my arm. M snapped the picture.

When I reluctantly withdrew my arm from the angel's waist, it was damp. Enthralled by the titillating image of a sweaty angel, I turned, smiled at the young man, and made a small donation in his cup. As soon as I was outside of the heavenly orbit of my angel, several others jumped to take my place. The whole town, with its inflated population of tourists, seemed to be out walking the Malecon. Before rejoining M, I turned around once more to see if Lio and AJ were anywhere in sight. I made a grunt of irritation that they had fallen so far behind.

"Don't worry about it," said M. "We'll see them back at the hotel."

From the rooftop of a nearby hotel, I heard pounding dance music and high-pitched laughter. Visions of go-go boys entered my head. I noticed a group of young men with tank tops and shorts clinging to their gym bodies, marching like zombies toward the beat. They spoke in the high decibels of inebriation as they passed by. One of them bumped into me, and I automatically said, "Sorry." At the same moment, I wondered why I had apologized when the young man had run into me. I stopped and shouted, "I said sorry."

The youth turned around with a confused smile that emphasized his dimples. He had a golden tan and exaggerated pecs. "What's your problem?"

My protest withered as if the other's beauty gave him license to be excused for anything. Embarrassment caused me to color. All I could think about was my own scrawny torso and how a few years back, I had made a brief, miserable attempt at having a body with definition. Lio, who had started working out, had encouraged my venture into the realm of gym rats. After only a few months, Lio already had enough musculature that he felt compelled to shave his chest to best show it off. When he insisted on taking off his shirt and showing me his developed pectorals and corrugated stomach, I repeated the question I had uttered so many times, "Now which one is the gay brother?"

"That's what I'm saying, Augie. You could have all the guys after you." The implication was that Lio did, and he quite liked the attention. M had gotten the manliness, Lio the beauty, and AJ the charm. What had I gotten to survive gay life? Nothing. Life was full of injustices.

M and I sat in flower-print rattan chairs in the lobby with fresh cocktails, waiting for Lio and AJ.

"What should we do tomorrow? Whale watching?" asked M.

My inclination was to chill at the beach and appreciate the eye candy. I hadn't been able to indulge without Ruben looking over my shoulder in years. But I felt embarrassed to express such a desire especially after my drunken revelation at dinner about a one-night stand at a writing workshop. "Whale watching. That sounds cool," I said.

"They're avoiding me, aren't they? They can't handle it. Maybe I should just go to bed. When they get back, you could talk to them. Tell them I was drunk. Didn't know what I was saying." It was unusual to see her so unsure, so vulnerable.

"Of course they're not avoiding you. If I know Lio, he probably wanted to stop and listen to that band."

"It's been nearly an hour."

"I sent Lio a text. I'm sure Mr. Economical is not responding because he thinks it costs too much."

M took the last sip of her drink, shook the ice around, and managed another few drops. "That's it. I'm going to bed."

M got up, and I listened to her sandals slap down the hall. Everything about her was now seen through a new filter. I shuddered, imagining what the new M might look like. Her door opened and closed rather forcefully. Finally alone, I exhaled a sigh of relief. If I hurried, I could get out the door and take the long way around to the go-go bar so I wouldn't run into AJ and Lio. Instead, I ordered another drink.

2: M

I watched Martina Navratilova win the Australian Open on TV in 1981. The next day, I picked up a racket and began a daily routine of practicing at the tennis courts near my house. I entered a tournament that summer and won my first trophy. A local pro with a beaming smile approached me in the clubhouse while I mopped the victorious sweat from my brow. He wanted to coach me in pursuing a tennis career.

"Do I have to wear those silly little dresses and put the second serving ball up into my panties?" I was a sassy eleven-year-old girl.

"It's what most of the girls do," answered the bemused coach.

"I'll think about it," I said.

By the luck of the genetic draw, I not only received athletic ability, but a good brain and an inexplicable drive no one else in the family had. My science projects won awards at school. I was always at the top of my class, and I was elected class president in my senior year of high school. I enjoyed being a leader, and from an early age, I was at the helm, charting the choppy waters for my three younger siblings, even playing a significant role in raising them. This was not to say our parents had fallen short of their duties. Both our parents had careers and were more than happy to let me take some of the responsibilities.

People always asked why Arnold and I didn't have children. The blame falls on me. The thought of bearing children frightened me. Before Arnie and I got married, I told him of my doubts. If he felt disappointment, it fluttered away like a butterfly as he mumbled, "Who wants to bring children into this screwed-up world anyway?"

Any motherly instincts I had were certainly being fulfilled by my role in the family. Even as we navigated our forties, I took on the role of giving advice to my brothers and sister. And my chosen profession, a psychiatrist specializing in children, had me in constant contact with kids. Of course, none of it was a replacement for having my own offspring, but I was at peace with that.

I solidified my parental position in the family the day our mother returned to her job at the university library after a ten-year hiatus. A bossy ten-year-old, I called a meeting that changed history and was always referred to as the renaming meeting.

Our parents confessed that they really hadn't planned on having a big family, so naming four children had provided a challenge. Traditional family names were definitely out. Gloria had brought home a stack of baby naming books from the library, which proved unhelpful. After Gloria's doctor determined the due date of her first daughter, me, she dutifully marked it on her calendar as if it were the return of a library book.

She glanced at the top of the page and felt inspired. May. She thought the name light and precise as well as hopeful. A few years later when Augie was born in August, she thought, well, why not?

"August is a strong name," said our father.

Lio was born in July at the beginning of what everybody called our mother's Spanish phase due to her infatuation with Julio Iglesias and all things Spanish. Thanks to her enrollment in a Spanish course at the local adult school, she was able to explain to her husband that *julio* meant July. Ira seldom challenged his wife's whims. Julio it was. When AJ was born in April, they decided it was too late to cease with the month nomenclature and saddled her with April June.

The name May had always sounded too prissy to me, though the last straw prompting the renaming meeting could be blamed on our mother's penchant for musicals and her constantly playing the soundtrack from *Camelot*, a particular favorite. Whenever Augie heard it, he danced around the house singing along with Julie Andrews, "Tra la, it's May, the lusty Month of May." He was insufferable at times. The combination of my name with lusty drove me crazy, which made Augie sing all the louder though he hadn't the foggiest idea what lusty meant. I cornered him one day by the new avocado side-by-side refrigerator and threatened to cut off his private parts if he didn't stop. So, the day Gloria left me in charge, I called the meeting.

"From now on, I will be called M, like the letter. Anyone who forgets will be locked in the basement with the lights turned off." The look of terror in their eyes was classic. They *would* remember. "And August will be called Augie."

"But…" said Augie.

I made the scissor sign and he shut up.

"What about Julio?" said Augie.

"I want to be Hoo," said Julio.

I rolled my eyes. "Really? Everyone will be saying: Who is Hoo? Where is Hoo? How is Hoo?"

"What about Joo then?" said Julio.

I sighed. "Do you know what a Jew is?"

"Huh?" said Julio, looking like he had said a bad word.

Augie and I were the only ones old enough to understand we actually were Jewish despite the fact it was rarely talked about. Our last name, Burd, didn't have an obvious Jewish association, and very little in our lives suggested our background. No celebration of the holidays, bar or bat Mitzvahs. Only the grandparents on our father's side were religious. They lived in New York and rarely visited. Gloria's parents, though they occasionally went to temple, made little fuss about our heritage.

"Your new name is Lio," I declared.

"And what about April?" said Augie.

"AJ, of course."

I knew I could count on Augie to use the new names, especially when I made the cutting motion pointing at his crotch. We easily got the four-year-old Lio to promise to use the new names by presenting it as a game where he might win a prize. And baby AJ was barely talking, so she didn't have much say on the matter. Our parents resisted at first, and Gloria was particularly upset about Julio. "Such a beautiful name. *Que nombre más lindo!*" she declared. She had kept up with her Spanish by hiring a Salvadoran house cleaner with whom she insisted on speaking Spanish. Sometimes Conchita would look dumbfounded at Gloria's barrage of mismatched phonemes. Nevertheless, Gloria persisted.

Like my mother, I was stubborn. Born under the sign of Taurus, I refused to answer to May and forbade the other children to answer to their given names. In less than a week, my first revolution was a success. Everyone started using the nicknames and had ever since.

The boy only filled a small portion of the armchair on the other side of my desk, seeming at the same time fragile and princely. A condescending scowl distorted his delicate features. The mother sat at his side, stiffly on the edge of her seat in a well-tailored jacket and skirt, her hands folded in her lap.

The child was a new client, and the mother had been vague on the phone, something about problems at school, aggressive behavior. In our conversation, I thought I remembered the woman saying "her daughter." The chart said he had knocked down a schoolmate in a recent fight. I looked at the boy and had a hard time imagining it. I glanced down at my notes and thought I might have grabbed the wrong file. The name read Cynthia Mason, which neither fit the Asian features of the mother nor the apparent sex of the child. But the woman had distinctly introduced herself as Mrs. Mason.

The woman broke the silence as I continued to shuffle through the papers on my desk. "My daughter, Cynthia, is confused," she said softly.

"I'm not confused," the child said, holding his emotions in check so he could keep his register low. "And my name's Sid."

The mother sighed and looked from the hands in her lap to the brass orb on my desk, a gift from Arnie. "You see, Doctor, she refuses to respond to her name." She spoke with only a hint of an accent.

"I am *not* a girl," Sid growled. Her mother flinched. "She the one confused. Ain't never been a girl."

I experienced a strange flutter under my ribs and wondered if it might be the beginning of a heart attack. I imagined cutting the interview short, shakily buzzing my receptionist and gasping for her to call an ambulance. But the sensation passed, leaving me with a slight nausea. I looked at Mrs. Mason and forced a smile. "Would you mind if I talked to…uh… your child alone for a few minutes?" Normally, I liked a longer time with the parent and child in the first interview before separating them, but the painful expression on Sid's face appeared to have taken over his whole body, and I couldn't bear to see him explode.

I had avoided taking gender identity cases, telling myself it wasn't my area of expertise. I had been tricked into this interview by Mrs. Mason's vagueness on the phone. I decided I would talk to the child a few minutes, and then apologize to the mother for not being able to take Sid as a patient.

With the mother out of the room, Sid stared at me in a way no other child had. A wry smile bloomed on his face.

I met the boy's stare. "How did you come up with the name Sid?"

"Read it in a book." His speech inflections mimicked those of an inner city black child, incongruous coming from someone whose mother was Asian and whose father I guessed was Caucasian.

"The name change, was it recent?"

"A few months ago."

"Oh, so these feelings of being a boy are new?"

"No way." He continued to stare at me as if he could see right through me. I was completely unsettled but tried not to show it. "Always been a boy. Do I got to spell it out for you?"

"I see." I was having a hard time breathing. The flutter now seemed to have taken the form of a burning bubble rising within my rib cage. I took a deep breath and reminded myself that some people, including children, didn't identify with the gender on their birth certificate. I had read case studies, but I had to admit I was unprepared to confront a child who was so sure of his identity. "You know boys and girls are born with different bodies."

Sid gave me a sideways look and squinted. "Oh my God."

"I'm assuming you were born with female parts."

Sid slouched and spread his legs. He wore brown corduroy jeans and a *Star Wars* T-shirt. "You wastin' my time."

I tried to snuff the smile I felt coming on. I no longer wanted to rush him out the door. If I revealed something about myself, perhaps I could get through to the child.

"When I was a little girl, I liked boy things. I begged my mother for cowboy pajamas and didn't care much for the dolls people gave me. Sometimes little girls like boy things and little boys like girl things. There's nothing wrong with that."

"I ain't gay."

"That's not what I meant."

"I like boy things because I'm a boy."

"Tell me about your father."

"Uh-huh. Everybody wants to know what I am. People's always looking at me with big ol' question marks in they eyes. He white, but pretty cool. A few weeks ago, he lemme shop in the boy's department."

"Do you think he is okay with you being a boy?"

"Look, I got two older sisters. My dad wanted a boy."

"But your mother is obviously not happy about it."

"They's a lot a things about reality she don't wanna accept. She want a world all tied up in neat little packages."

I had several sessions with Sid, and he never once wavered from the certainty he was a boy. Mrs. Mason called one day to say they were discontinuing the therapy. No explanation. But long after the sessions ended, Sid's words played in a loop in my brain and he would creep into my dreams at night, leaving me no peace.

Augie and I sat out on the balcony with Puerto Vallarta's frigate birds soaring overhead, high in the air rising off the hot land, gliding on currents. They did not flap their wings, seemingly confident they could go on forever while looking down on the humans below, pitying us for being earthbound. Augie was entranced by the slow, monotonous motion of the birds. On the edge of my consciousness was a notion that something was wrong, out of balance, that at any moment bad news might arrive.

I couldn't take it anymore, the birds increasing my anxiety. An occasional screech from a seagull would make me shudder. I stood up with sweat trickling down the sides of my face. Before I went back to my room, I paused, looking down at Augie with disbelief. He slouched in his chair as if he hadn't a care in the world. We had always had different ways of dealing with crisis, Augie drifting, avoiding, longing to be a bird in flight while I was more a bull rushing toward a red cape.

"You know you actually burn less calories in times of stress, contrary to what you'd think," Augie said, as if speaking from a trance.

"Oh, shut up, Augie!" Anger shook me, and I wasn't quite sure if it was more the lingering disgust for his lack of support the evening before or his seeming ambivalence in a time of crisis. Lio and AJ had never returned from the dinner. Both their cell phones went unanswered. I wanted to grab and shake him, but instead I retreated to my room. I feared something had happened and I had failed in some way, keeping my family together, protecting them.

From inside my room, I watched Augie gazing down at the street where people in bathing gear plodded toward the beach. It was only eight in the morning. Out over the sea, four brown pelicans glided in a V formation with one bird clearly at the apex.

I reached for my glass of water, but it slipped from my fingers and crashed to the floor. That brought Augie out of his stupor. "Everything okay in there?"

I stepped back out on the balcony. "That's it. We're going to the police."

"You're right. It's time." He reached down to pick up his phone from the side table but as soon as he touched it, the screen lit up with a message notification. "Hey, wait! There's something from AJ."

"What? When? Haven't you been checking your phone? I didn't get anything."

Augie looked at the screen. "Just got it." I had a feeling he was lying. He opened the message and was knocked back into his chair. I looked over his shoulder. It was a video message, but even in the still frame of the video I could see something was terribly wrong. AJ was sitting in a rusty chair in a dark room with bare walls.

I grabbed the phone and tapped the play arrow. "Hey, guys," AJ began in a surprisingly unemotional voice. Her makeup looked freshly applied, and her hair was neatly pulled back. "Major bummer. These guys want money. Lio's okay. He's over there." The camera quickly panned to a brown sofa on the other side of the room where a terrified Lio sat. He gave a brief wave. "They think we have money. Well, I guess compared to them we do, but really...how much can we scrape together? I mean, we're okay for now, but the place where they're holding us sucks. You should see the toilet!"

They heard an accented voice in the background say, "That's enough. We contact you. Don't go to police or else."

The video ended.

Augie and I were frozen, stunned. I tapped the arrow and we played it again. "What the fuck?" said Augie. "This can't be happening. Didn't I tell you about that restaurant kidnapping I read about online just weeks before we came down here?"

I was not surprised Augie was putting the blame on me. That's the downside of being the leader. "But that was gang stuff," I said. "They don't kidnap tourists. Not in Puerto Vallarta."

"Well, obviously they do. Christ, M, what do we do now?" Augie was in full panic mode, his hands alternating between covering his face and slicing through the air. I still held the phone aloft as if it would provide us an answer.

My mind began to function, analyze, seek answers. "They want money. We've got money from Mom. I mean, we don't actually have it yet, but—"

"Our inheritance? This is how we spend our inheritance?" Each quarter of the inheritance wasn't a huge amount of money, but Augie already knew what he was going to do with his. With the money, he would be able to quit his job and pursue his writing full time. When he first mentioned his dream to Ruben, before they knew about the inheritance, it caused a major uproar. Ruben reminded him they had a killer mortgage after buying a house they really couldn't afford, and they still had Colton's education to consider.

I knew it had always been Augie's dream to write seriously instead of just dabbling at it, start publishing all the stories he had been working on for ages. Both Ruben and I had reminded him nobody could realize all of his dreams. We pointed out how many dreams Augie *had* brought to life: being a husband, a father, a homeowner. All at the expense of his desire to write, Augie lamented to me but didn't say in front of Ruben. Ruben had sufficiently shamed him into putting his dreams on hold. But when we learned about the inheritance, Augie's heart had leapt. At least it would give him a year he could dedicate to writing.

At the Puerto Vallarta dinner, all four of us had laid out our plans for the money we were going to inherit, each of us thinking it would be the tool to claw his or her way out of a midlife crisis.

"You're crying about our inheritance when our brother and sister's lives might be at stake?" I screamed. "You want to take the chance they'll let them go if we just say we don't have any money?"

"No, no. Of course not. But what if they want everything Mom left us or more?"

My brother's selfishness had always bothered me. It blinded him to the seriousness of the situation. "Give it a rest, Augie. If we have to lose all the money, that's the way it is. But that might not even be possible. We don't have it yet."

Augie rose up out of the chair as if an unseen force lifted him by his hair. "Didn't AJ seem unusually calm for the situation?"

At first unnerved by his sudden shift, I quickly followed his train of thought. "Hah! Maybe because she's used to being a prisoner?"

Augie sniggered. "Yeah, she seemed more upset about the bathroom thing than being kidnapped."

"You're right. It's weird. Why wasn't she more shaken up?"

3: Augie

Family barbeques at the Rockridge house were always filled with drama, but the tension level was particularly high one Sunday late in May. Gloria was in the hospital after a fall, and we had gathered to discuss what to do about her failing health. She couldn't stay in the house alone, so we four children, along with spouses, hashed out a care plan that worked around all our erratic schedules and current crises.

Except for Bart, who drank beer, we all sipped Ruben's homemade sangria and shooed bees away from the remnants of our lunch. Thanks to the sangria, conversation shifted to funny family stories. A short distance away, Colton played with his cousins, Jason and Elijah, AJ's boys. One was a year older and the other a year younger than Colton. Bart stayed out of the conversation and focused on the cell phone in his lap. We ignored him, guessing he was watching a sports event or scrolling through Breitbart News. From time to time, he would glance over at the boys as if he were a playground monitor anticipating one of the boys wouldn't play fair.

The boys played horseshoes, a game their grandfather had introduced them to. It was the only physical activity Ira had engaged in that might be considered a sport, and it was fitting his fatal heart attack had occurred just after he had made a ringer.

I turned to M. "I've got a bone to pick with you."

"I know where this is going," said Ruben. "The other night Colie came home from school and said we should all watch the Warriors game. A horrified Augie said, 'What's that? Basketball?'"

Everyone laughed, and even Bart raised his eyes from the screen with a smile.

"So," I said. "I had to ask my son why in the world he thought our family time should be spent watching a sports event. And then it comes out that the last time he spent the night at Aunt M's, they had watched a game and he liked it. M, how could you? That's subversion!"

"Have you ever watched a game?" said M. "It's fun."

"Yeah, Augie," said AJ. "It's like ballet except all men, beautiful muscular bodies twirling and leaping in the air." Bart snorted and went back to his phone.

"Ballet?" I shrieked. "Next you're going to tell me boxing is like tango dancing."

Just as the laughter died down, a commotion broke out among the boys and the N-word rang out from the older of AJ's sons. Technically, Colton was only half black. His surrogate mom was African American, a friend of Ruben's from college. We had used both Ruben's and my sperm, and we didn't know whose spunk had been more vigorous in the race to fertilize. And at least for the moment, we didn't want to know. Possibly we would do a genealogy test some day to find out if Colton was half-Jewish or half-Latino, but did it matter?

I jumped up. "What the hell, AJ?"

AJ looked as if she might burst into tears, shocked both by what her son had said and then being yelled at by her brother.

I rushed over and grabbed Colton by the hand. "We're leaving."

Colton seemed more frightened by my anger than the slur. "It's okay, Dad."

"No, it's not okay," I said, fixing my gaze on Bart, who had positioned himself behind Jason with a hand on his shoulder. Jason's initial panic that he had screwed up changed to a sneer.

"Chill, man," said Bart. "You're making a big deal out of nothing. They're just kids."

"Nothing? How can you say it's nothing? It's a sickness that people still use that word, and it seems to be getting worse lately."

AJ now stood next to me. "Jason, tell Colton you're sorry."

"April, stay out of this," said Bart. In his eyes was the resentment that everyone in the family hated him. He stood tall, one man against the world, as if it was up to him alone to defend his son. "Probably something Jason just heard at school."

I took a step forward, still with Colton in tow. "Just as likely he heard it at home."

"You calling me a racist?"

M jumped up and joined the fracas. "Hey," she shouted loud enough to shut everyone up. "Everybody calm down." Her words carried the weight of being the oldest, and even Bart tended to steer clear of her. "I'll handle this." She extracted Colton's hand from mine and motioned for AJ's two boys to follow her, taking them a distance from the crowd that had formed around Bart.

All eyes drifted to the new circle formed by M and the boys. We could hear her explaining how calling people names is hurtful, and some names packed more of a punch than others thanks to history.

"It's not okay to call someone out because they look different. When I was little, other kids used to call me Big Foot because I was bigger than everybody else." The three boys giggled and she joined in. "Now that's one thing. All kids do it. But it's *never* okay to call someone a name because of the color of his or her skin. You got it?"

"Yes, Aunt M."

"Now, Jason shake hands with Colton." The boys did what they were told while Bart stood at a distance with his arms crossed. I appreciated what M was doing, but I was still furious. I entered the circle, nodded a perfunctory thanks to M, and took Colton by the hand again.

I pulled Colton toward the gate and Ruben followed after us, stopping briefly to turn and give a brief, apologetic wave to the group. Outside the gate, Ruben caught up with us and put a hand on Colton's shoulder. "I don't think Jason meant to be mean."

I gave Ruben a dirty look. "That's where parenting comes in. Even when AJ tried..."

"Don't," said Ruben, nodding at our son.

"Why does she stay with him?"

"Augie! Later."

When we got to the car, I was still shaking. Ruben took the keys out of my hand. "I'd better drive." He eased the car onto the Bay Bridge and toward the fog that awaited us, a healing fog that rolled over the city, a fog that cooled nerves.

On the new, wide-open part of the bridge, traffic glided as swiftly and smoothly as the sailboats on either side, but as we got to the tunnel, brake lights lit up in rapid succession. I groaned as if the traffic jam was created just for me, as if the world was out to get me. It wasn't my best moment.

"It wasn't the first time," said Colton matter-of-factly from the back seat.

"What?" I said.

"Jason said stuff like that before."

Ruben took one hand off the steering wheel and placed it on my leg, pleading for calm. "You should always tell one of us," said Ruben sweetly, "when something like that happens."

Colton thought a minute. "I don't want to be a tattletale."

I squirmed in the front seat. I took deep breaths. I tried to absorb the calmness coming through Ruben's hand. "That's not the same as...as telling on a friend who steals a piece of candy. When someone uses a racial slur, we need to know."

"What's that mean?"

"When someone says something bad about you just because of the color of your skin."

"Am I ever going to meet my mother?"

Ruben glanced at me with a here-we-go look. "Here's the deal, Colie. Your daddy and I wanted a child, but we needed a woman to carry you in her tummy for nine months, you know, like we talked about. The woman who carried you—"

"My mother," Colton corrected.

I let Ruben handle it. He's a much better man than me. "Yes, technically she's your mother. She wasn't at a point in her life where she was ready to take care of a child, but she was happy to help us." That part was true. But what we were hesitant to mention was she also liked the idea of making money to pay for studio time and musicians for a demo tape.

"Why wasn't she ready?" asked Colton.

"She has dreams of being a singer," I said.

We had reached the tricky part where we didn't know how much to tell our son. Joy's singing career had floundered and she hadn't taken it well. There was talk of alcohol abuse and drugs.

"Can I find her on YouTube?"

"Not yet," I said. "Making it in the music business is really hard."

"Yeah," Ruben added. "Like any career in the arts. Like being a writer for instance." I felt the sting. My husband wasn't perfect. He got his licks in when he could.

"What's her name?" said Colton.

"Joy," I said. "We had an agreement Papi and I would be your only parents so it wouldn't be confusing to you."

Colton turned quiet, and I twisted around to give his leg a reassuring squeeze. "Maybe it doesn't make sense to you, but Joy thought if she couldn't be around all the time, maybe it was better to stay out of the picture altogether." I felt the sinking plunge of inadequacy. With all the love and affection we showered on him, I wondered if it was enough to replace a boy's longing for a mother.

"Who wants ice cream?" said Ruben.

His suggestion was met with silence from me and a lackluster "Okay" from Colton.

I had declined to be in the delivery room for Colton's birth. There would be blood, I kept thinking. All our friends and family pressured me to be present at that wondrous moment when my son entered the world. The decision was excruciating, but the fear of passing out and embarrassing everyone vanquished the other considerations. I knew I wouldn't love my son any less by not watching him emerge from the birth canal, and I hoped my son wouldn't resent me for not being there.

Ruben, on the other hand, couldn't wait to participate. He had gone to birthing classes with Joy and had a hundred books on the subject. They had been friends since college and had that singular connection of having played in a band together. He played bass, and she was the singer. He wouldn't miss the chance of this new composition, holding her hand and telling her to push.

I paced the waiting room, thinking I was a fool. Why couldn't I have just tamped down my fears and been present at my son's birth? Could it be worse than this waiting, not knowing? The seconds ticked on the large wall clock. The TV high on the wall was tuned to CNN, a constant loop of the doom and gloom of the housing crisis, banks failing, people losing everything. Though I didn't think we personally had anything to worry about, it seemed a completely inappropriate background for this extraordinary event.

"Isn't there a nature program or something?" I mumbled.

The two slack-jawed men glued to the set showed no reaction.

"Does anyone have the remote?" I said in a loud voice. They both shrugged.

I started down the hall to look for an aide who might be able to change the channel. Halfway to the nurses' station I ran into Ruben on his way to get me. By the beatific expression on his face, I could tell things had gone well.

"All good," said Ruben. "They're resting." Everyone had agreed the baby would be placed on Joy's chest and given time to bond with her. We also felt it was important to limit that time so the bonding process could begin with us.

Now that the messy part was over, I was hell-bent on getting to the room. I took Ruben by the arm. "Come on. Let's go in."

"I think we should give them a moment."

"He's been inside her for the last nine months. If that didn't bond them, what difference are a few more minutes going to make now?"

"That's what they recommended," said Ruben. "Something about having a chance to confirm the smells he's become used to over the months."

"You're so good," I said. I didn't tell him that enough. I grabbed him and pulled him into an embrace. Ruben drove me crazy at times, but in the events of life that really mattered, Ruben could soothe my frayed nerves and steer me in the right direction. His heart beat against mine, a syncopated drumming, the blood surging through us both. We stood in the middle of the hallway oblivious to the people hurrying by, holding on to each other, strengthening each other for the moment we would meet our son as a team. It was hard to believe two years of endless waiting was now coming to an end.

Ruben and I entered the room. The lights were soft, and the smell of new life hung in the air. And there he was. Our son. I had no idea how I was going to feel, but I hadn't quite imagined the complexity of it—intense, daunting love, yes, but mixed with it was the overpowering responsibility of keeping this helpless creature safe. And then, when the everyday tasks of feeding and clothing were achieved, we would have the gargantuan task of showing him the ins and outs of navigating the labyrinth of life. The thought of it all weighed on me. But mostly what I felt was an earthshaking, stultifying love.

Joy gazed at the baby, barely seeming to notice the other people in the room. Mother and child were a single being. A thing of striking beauty. After the amount of time agreed upon plus a few minutes, the delivery nurse stepped forward to take the baby and make the transition. The moment had arrived when all the players held our collective breaths. Despite all the contracts and agreements, nobody knew what would happen when the time came for Joy to give him up. I watched my husband, whose fists were clenched, ready to lurch forward and grab our son. I desperately wanted to feel that same willingness to fight, but I was mesmerized by the Madonna tableau. Perhaps I was just afraid.

In the frozen moment Ruben started to move, and I reached out to hold him back, Joy released her grip and the nurse took the baby. Joy lay back and closed her eyes. The nurse motioned for us to follow her.

As we left the room, Ruben whispered, "Thank you, Joy."

With eyes still closed, she raised her hand only slightly off the blanket as if to say, "Don't mention it. Now get the fuck out. I need to be alone. Love you guys."

In an adjoining room, the nurse said, "We're going to do a little cleanup and examination. You can watch." She lay the baby down on the warming table and opened up the blanket. He punched and kicked with his tiny arms and legs. His skin was purplish, especially his hands and feet. The nurse began to clean him with a large warm towel. He had pooped. It looked dark and sticky, the color of dried blood.

"Ew," said Ruben.

"That's a good sign," the nurse said.

"His skin is so light," I said.

"It will darken in the next couple weeks. It was the surrogate mom's egg, right?" We had used Joy's eggs, making her the biological mom. Most gay couples were opting for gestational surrogacy using an anonymous donor's egg to avoid a surrogate having a closer emotional and legal bond to the baby. But Joy had told us a thousand times she really didn't want her own child at this point in her life.

The nurse moved her hands over the baby's skin, behind the ears, the throat, the chest, the abdomen. She turned him over and ran her fingers down his spine. When she gently rolled him so he was again on his back, they noticed a rather swollen penis and testicles.

When I'm nervous and giddy I tend to say stupid things. "Heh-heh," I said. "Does he have a hard-on?"

"August!" said Ruben.

"Just a little fluid collecting around the genitals. Completely normal," said the nurse.

"Are you sure everything is okay?"

"Stop breathing down her neck, Augie," said Ruben.

"He's perfect," she said. She weighed him, took his vitals, and made prints of his adorable little hands and feet. Then she wrapped him in a blanket. She turned to the fathers. "It's time. Take off your shirts."

We had been told about the process, but it still felt odd. That morning we had scrubbed each other's bodies in the shower. We had been told not to use deodorant. We stretched out on the two side-by-side lounge chairs that had been brought into the room. I felt self-conscious about my hairy chest. How would the baby react? I caught a whiff of my nervous sweat. Would my child be ever imprinted with the notion of a stinky, hairy dad?

"Who's first?" said the nurse.

I looked at Ruben. "You go."

"No, you."

"I insist."

Ruben looked at me with his deep and tender brown eyes. "No, Augie, it has to be you."

Tears were already clouding my vision as the nurse put the bundle on my chest, opening up the blanket so we would have skin-on-skin contact. I was at that moment and forever, a father. I thought my heart might burst.

"Look at all that hair," said Ruben, touching our son's head, choking on his words, half-laughing, half-crying. "He looks just like you, Augie."

My body shook with weeping. Now my son's first impression of me would be a hairy, stinky, hysterical dad. "I'm afraid I might scare him," I said. I passed the bundle to my husband. "Here, Colton, meet your Papi." It was the first time I used our son's name, the two syllables that would become a song in my mouth for years to come—a love song, a sad country song, a hectic heavy metal song, a back-and-forth rap song, a silly pop song, but always a song.

4: AJ

A black Nissan SUV pulled up alongside Lio and me. A man with sparkling eyes and a scruffy beard leaned out the window and said to me, "Are you a movie star? I think I see you in movies."

At first I was startled, but the combination of alcohol and flattery smoothed my initial defenses. I'm not a big drinker, the dinner honoring Mom being an exception. By the end of the night, so much weirdness was flying around the table I was glad I was tipsy.

I stared at the man leaning out the window. "Now why would you say that?"

"Come on," said Lio. "Augie and M are way ahead."

The car had stopped on the narrow street, and the man seemed to hesitate as if flirting didn't come naturally to him. The driver said something to him in Spanish and he forced a smile. "Well, you know, I think at first you are Natalie Portman. She come to Mexico a lot."

"What did he say?" asked Lio, keeping a distance from the car.

"He said I look like Natalie Portman." I did share the high cheekbones, the brown wavy hair, but I was taller than Portman, not that it mattered.

"Jeez, AJ. You gonna fall for that?"

Despite the handsome Mexican's come-on, I saw a hint of shyness in his face, a vulnerability that touched me. The vehicle pulled over in front of a closed bakery. I took a step closer to the car window and bent down to see who was driving. "I'm Chato," said the man hanging out the window. He pointed to the driver. "And that's my brother Flaco. That means skinny."

"Hello," said Flaco, hugging the steering wheel. "Sorry if my brother scare you. He's really a nice guy. We just think you need be careful. It's late."

"He didn't scare me," I said. "Anyway, everybody told us it's not dangerous here."

I glanced over and saw Lio light a cigarette. He had bought a pack earlier, and I told him he was an idiot. He had worked so hard to break the habit. He claimed being in a foreign country where smoking was less of a taboo weakened him. He leaned up against the doorjamb of the bakery for support, and his whole body seemed to shudder as he stared at the sugary pastries in the window. I hadn't seen him this drunk in years.

"Oh, no, is not dangerous," said Chato. "Only we think maybe we can help you get to your hotel."

I leaned forward a little, fully aware I was showing cleavage. I had, for the moment, erased from my consciousness that I was a wife and mother of two boys. I was a woman on vacation, and a fine-looking man was talking to me. "That's so kind, but we don't mind walking." The sexy tone of my voice seemed to suggest quite the opposite. I didn't know why I was doing that, the husky voice men seemed to like.

A car full of teenagers with blaring *banda* music passed and honked at the SUV, still partially blocking the street. "*Güera linda!*" one of the youths shouted, leaning half out the window.

"See what I mean," said Chato. "Sometimes Saturday night people get a little crazy."

"What did that guy say?" I asked.

Chato laughed. "He just say you are pretty."

Lio took a last nervous puff on his cigarette and threw it to the ground. "AJ, come on. We should go."

"Is that your boyfriend?"

"He's my brother."

"Okay. See," said Flaco. "We are all family here."

Chato's perfectly formed hand dangled out the passenger window. I thought of the hand model we once had in drawing class. Like that day in class, I felt the urge to take the hand and rub it against my cheek. But the mention of family brought me back to who I was. "Look, you guys are very nice, but we don't mind walking. Really."

"What hotel are you?"

"The San Marino," I said, but I regretted it as soon as the words were out of my mouth. I wasn't thinking clearly.

"No problem. That's right on our way home."

Out of the corner of my eye I watched Lio lean over and convulse a couple of times. And then an avalanche of vomit hit the sidewalk.

I ran over to him. "Lio, are you okay?"

"Shit. I drank too much. The cigarette made me dizzy." We looked down at the expensive dinner painting the sidewalk.

Chato jumped out of the car. "Man, you don't look so good. Let's help him to the car."

"Wait," said Lio, still hunched over. He retched again.

I had my hand on Lio's back, rubbing it lightly. "Maybe we should take a ride from these guys."

Chato already had his arm under one of Lio's. "Take it easy, man. Don't worry. We get you home."

"I'm okay. Just give me a minute."

"You're not okay," I said. "Don't be silly. We need to get you back to the hotel." I took his other arm and we led him to the SUV. As soon as we had Lio inside the car, his head slumped against the door. I went around to the other side and let Chato hold the door for me. He touched my arm lightly as I eased into the back seat, sending a pleasant rush through my body.

Flaco started the car, rolled up the tinted windows, and turned on the air conditioning. A blast of cool air hit me, but this time the shiver that went up my spine felt raw and sinister. I looked at my brother's pallid face. His eyes were closed. Chato and Flaco conversed in Spanish, and though they spoke in low voices, they seemed to disagree on something. Or perhaps it was the phenomenon that Spanish speakers in animated conversation often sounded like they were arguing. I wished Augie were with us so he could translate. He had achieved the fluency in Spanish our mother never had.

Flaco looked at her intensely in the rear-view mirror. "*Oye, guapa, hablas español?*"

"No," I said with a smile. That much I understood. I tried to put my window down to let in some warm air, but the child lock was on. "Could you turn the air conditioning down a bit?"

"Oh, sorry," said Chato. "We think is good for your brother." He turned the fan to a lower setting.

Chato fell sullen and quiet in the front seat, his flirtatious behavior of before having disappeared. Flaco, on the other hand, wouldn't stop talking, long rambling sentences punctuated with his sinister laugh. Chato nodded, only coming to life after Lio moaned. "Oh, no," I said. It looked like Lio was about to hurl again.

Chato rummaged in the glove compartment, pulled out a plastic bag, and dangled it over the back seat. "Please," he said a bit apologetically, nodding toward Lio. "We just wash the car today."

At the next intersection, Flaco made a turn and started up a hill. Even in my drunkenness, I knew our hotel was straight and a little down the hill toward the beach. "Uh...you know where the hotel is, right?"

"Don't worry. We go up and around to avoid the traffic. So many people on the streets."

I accepted his explanation, but when we reached the top of the hill, Flaco took the highway that led out of town. Something was not right. It made the hairs on my arms rise up. I quietly took my phone out of my purse, keeping it low, trying to cover the light from the screen. All I could think to do was send a message to Augie and M, letting them know something strange was going on. Maybe they could contact the authorities, track my phone.

Chato glanced over the back seat and said something to Flaco, who jerked the car to the side of the road and stopped the car. The motion threw me forward, and I bumped against the front seat. Chato leaned over and grabbed my phone.

"What are you doing?" I screamed.

Lio woke up, wiped the drool from his mouth. "What the...?"

I tried to open the door. It was locked.

Chato pointed at Lio. "Give me your cell phone, too."

Lio was fully awake now. "No way, man. What the fuck is going on?"

Both Lio and I tried to open our doors again, pushing every button on the armrest. "Give it to me," Chato repeated. "Do what we say and nobody get hurt."

"Assholes! I can't believe you're doing this," I said. My anger was much stronger than any fear I felt. It still seemed unreal, like some kind of prank. I regretted my lapse in judgment, allowing my flirtation with Chato to lead us into the trap. It wasn't fair. As a wife and mother,

I never had the chance to be spontaneous, do something adventurous. But I had precious little time to lament my choices. Chato now had a revolver in his hand, pointed at us. He tossed two black cloth bags over the seat and told us to cover our heads.

"Seriously?" I said, staring into his eyes. "You really don't want to do this."

"Chill, AJ. Do what they say," said Lio. He held up his hands palms forward and dropped his phone over the front seat. He had sobered up quickly and shook with fear.

"We're not kidding. Put the bags on your heads," growled Flaco. He aimed his stare at me through the rear-view mirror. I wasn't sure which was more menacing, Flaco's eyes or the gun in Chato's hand.

"Look," I said, holding up my hand with my engagement and wedding rings. "You can have these. We'll give you all the cash we have. Take us to an ATM. We can each take out $300." I did my best to keep my tone disgusted rather than pleading.

Chato looked at Flaco as if he thought my offer fair. "That's not enough," said Flaco. "We need *mucho más.*"

"Christ! You think we're rich?" I fell back against the seat and crossed my arms. "Unbelievable."

"If it's just money..." said Lio with a shaky voice. "I'm sure we can get you money. How much do you want?"

Though Chato still held the gun, his face had taken on a worried expression.

"Shut up," said Flaco. "We don't talk money now. Put on the bags. *Rapido!*"

Cast in the darkness of the rough cloth, I now felt the fear I hadn't before. Flaco switched on the radio, and a ballad began to play. The heartrending male voice, though I couldn't understand the words, was no doubt singing of his lover's betrayal. My nails carved half-moons into my palms. I found Lio's clammy hand and held it. "I'm sorry," I whispered.

"No talking," said Flaco.

In the darkness of the hood, I saw my life—a short life, really, not yet forty years—quickly flash through my head. So many things I hadn't done. As long as I could see my kidnappers, I had hope. But this darkness sent me into a downward spiral. It was hard for me to hope we would get out of this unscathed. The notion that bad things happen in Mexico if you are unlucky enough to be in the wrong place at the wrong time has been burned into the brain of every American. I hoped Lio didn't blame me. More than ever, we needed each other. We had always been close growing up, defended each other in the face of M's badgering when we didn't do what she told us and Augie's ridicule when we did something he thought stupid.

Lio had even stood by me when I decided to marry Bart. He tried to be friends with him. Though he hated to admit it, a part of him admired Bart's service in Iraq, his knowledge of guns, his redneck swagger—all the things that drove Augie crazy. Augie had refused to go to the wedding at one point, but Lio convinced him he had to.

In the end, the election tore into Lio's friendship with Bart. As Bart spouted sound bites he had heard on Fox News, Lio at first tried to argue with him. Bart's opinions were emotional, not rational, so logic and fact provided no challenge to his ideas and, in fact, only made him more adamant. If Bart provided a challenge for my siblings, I had to put up with him on a daily basis. My marriage had always been problematic, but since we moved to Modesto, the situation had become exhausting. My consolation was my two boys.

After what seemed an interminable amount of time but was probably no more than fifteen minutes, the car stopped. Chato went to Lio's side and told him to get out. He put a plastic zip tie around Lio's wrists and pulled it tight. Flaco did the same for me. I cringed at the contact with Flaco's rough hand around my bare arms slightly sunburned from the beach. It felt so different from Chato's touch a little earlier. They walked us along a dirt road, the gravel popping under our steps like firecrackers in the quiet night. They led us up two steps, opened a door, and pushed us inside.

Lio and I stood close together, breathing heavily. "Can we take these off now?" I said.

"Sure, go ahead," said Flaco.

Our hands were still tied behind our backs. "And how are we supposed to do that?" I said.

"Oh, yeah," said Flaco. "Chato?" Chato removed the bags from our heads, and we both let out a sigh of relief. Aside from the hellish obscurity, the harsh cloth had been itchy and smelled musty. As my eyes slowly adjusted, I saw the Mexicans now wore ski masks.

Amateurs, I thought. We already had a good look at them. I wouldn't easily forget Chato's face, though in my head it had transformed from angel to devil. Still, these young men seemed to be playing at being tough rather than having the conviction to back it up, particularly Chato.

"Now what?" said Lio.

"You say something about other people in your group? Who you traveling with? Your parents is here?" said Flaco.

"Our parents are dead," said Lio with disgust. "Our mother just died."

Chato turned his head toward his brother, but I could only discern a slight reaction in Chato's eyes. Sympathy? His mouth opened as if to give condolences, but Flaco cut him off. "Then who is here?"

"Our older brother and sister," I said.

"Just them?" said Flaco

"You here with no families?" said Chato.

"We all left our families at home," I said. "In case you're interested, I have two little boys waiting for me." My voice quivered. I focused on Chato, or at least the eyeholes of his mask. Again, I detected a bit of sympathy, but he turned away.

Flaco again jumped in. "And husband?"

"Yes."

"Maybe he not like the way you look at my brother," said Flaco.

"This is absurd. Just tell us what you want," I said.

"*Mañana.* You sleep now."

The room was sparsely furnished—a broken down sofa, a table with two plastic chairs. The windows had been covered with dark film. Chato opened a door to a small room and turned on a light. The room had two cots.

"I need a bathroom," I said.

Chato opened a second door off the main room, bowed, and made a gallant gesture of welcome. "There's even some toilet paper," he said proudly.

But I stepped back, repelled by the smell. "You couldn't clean?"

"The maid's day off," Chato said with a scoff. Chato's hesitancy in the car had disappeared, and he was back to being contentious. Something was going on in his pretty little head.

"Can you release my hands at least?" I said.

Chato nodded and cut off first Lio's tie, and then mine. His fingers lingered on my wrists until I pulled my hands away.

"We talk in the morning," said Flaco. The brothers left by the main door and bolted it, sealing in the dank, hot air of what seemed to be a small cabin.

Lio and I lay on our cots and stared at the ceiling, sweat running down our cheeks. The dull bulb burned overhead. We had agreed on leaving the light on, afraid of what the dark might hold. Rats? Spiders? The ghosts of past captives? My head was filled with images of gruesome killings in Mexico I had read about or seen in movies: gang wars, retaliations against police, and the occasional murder of a foreigner who got in the way. And then there were all the kidnapping situations that had gone badly no matter what part of the world.

"Do these guys seem like killers to you?" said Lio in a shaky voice. He seemed to be coming to the same conclusion I had reached.

"I think this is their first rodeo," I said. "They don't know what they're doing."

"Does that mean they're going to panic if things don't go right and do something crazy? Or run away and leave us locked up here to die of suffocation?"

I rolled over and looked at my brother. For all its cuteness, my party dress was terribly uncomfortable in the current situation. I would demand more comfortable clothes in the morning. "I have a feeling about these guys," I said. "We have to work with them, get them on our side. I think they're in over their heads. They're doing this out of desperation."

Lio sat up and leaned against the wall. "Wait, wait, wait. These guys just kidnapped us, and you want to work with them. What does that mean anyway?"

"They are so *not* professionals."

"And you have a lot of experience in this?"

"Come on. You can see it in the younger one's eyes."

"Excuse me if I missed the tender orbs through the thug masks." Lio jerked away from the wall and swatted something on his neck. "Shit!" He moved to the edge of the cot.

"We have to find out what they need the money for."

"Really, AJ. What does it matter? We're screwed. Why did I agree to this trip?"

"Stop whining. We're here. We have to deal with it."

"I know." We fell silent and heard dogs barking in the distance.

"Do you think M is serious?" I said. "It's so hard to wrap my head around."

"Are you serious about leaving Bart?"

"I'm serious about wanting to. Reality is another thing. He'll fight me every step of the way. The other day I read one poll that said thirty percent of the respondents had ended a family relationship over differences in politics after the last election. Of course, that's not the heart of the problem with us."

"Why did you do it? You held him off for a long time."

"I think I knew he wasn't the one. But he was relentless, calling me day and night. There was no one else, at least no one that was interested in me." I sat up and tried to straighten my dress. "I can't bear the thought that my boys will end up like him."

"You wouldn't listen to anybody back then."

"Please don't give me the I-told-you-so. I can't take it right now. Anyway, it might be a moot point if we don't get out of this." A large insect fluttered its wings and bumped the light bulb loud enough to make a noise. Its shadow danced on the wall.

"Jesus, AJ, you're supposed to be the positive one."

"I'm going to do whatever I can to see my boys again. I'll kill those motherfuckers with my bare hands."

"I would suggest not trying that. They have a gun."

We were awakened by the sound of the bolt. Somehow we had managed to fall asleep in the early morning. The last thing I remembered was a rooster starting to crow, and Lio and I arguing over what time a rooster typically began its morning ritual.

"Rise and shine," said Flaco. "Time to go out and work the fields." Still wearing the mask, he gave a laugh so cruel it challenged the theory that they were basically decent guys who had fallen on hard times. He handed me my purse. "Get ready for your close-up. We make a video." He handed each of us a bottle of water.

My mouth felt like something had crawled in it and died. My head was pounding. "You got any aspirin?"

Flaco produced his insipid laugh again. "Let me call room service. Chato?"

"No aspirin. But I got coffee." He brought in paper cups from Starbucks and a bag of *pan dulce.*

"Starbucks?" said Lio. Though it seemed like it took forever for us to get to the hideout, we couldn't be that far from civilization. The coffee was still hot. I looked at my brother and raised my eyebrows as if to say, "See. They have some decency."

"Those ski masks must be hot," I said.

"Don't worry. Get ready for the video. We send to your brother."

Of course they wouldn't know M was really our leader, and all decisions had to go through her, but we didn't argue. "Let me splash some water on my face. You got any toothpaste."

"They're not gonna be looking at your teeth in the video," said Flaco, but I again noticed a kind of empathy in Chato's eyes. He worked his tongue around his teeth as if he just realized he had forgotten to brush them. He nodded at me almost imperceptibly.

5: Augie

M and I sat at an outdoor table at Salud Super Food, a café that made you feel guilty if you didn't order something healthy. I contemplated the granola, fruit, and yogurt dish they had just set in front of me. The sour smell of the yogurt mixed with acidity of the fruit made me feel ill. M sipped her black coffee and grimaced.

"This coffee tastes weird," she said. "It has some kind of spice in it."

"I think it's cinnamon." I took another sip. "You know cinnamon can lower blood sugar levels and reduce heart disease."

M gave me a look of disgust. "You're killing me," she said.

We had watched the video multiple times back at the hotel, still not believing what had happened. Going out to breakfast seemed a good idea to escape the confines of the room, as if we were the ones being held captive.

"When do we tell Bart?" said M.

"The last thing we need is him showing up with a bazooka or something. I can hear him saying, 'If only they had had a gun to protect themselves,'" I said in my best impression of a dumbed-down white male. "Did she tell you he gave her a little pistol to keep in the house? She promptly locked it in a high cabinet and hasn't touched it. Can you imagine having a gun in the house with small boys?"

"I know. The old self-defense argument. Add that to his great fondness for Mexicans, and he *will* go crazy. But we've got to tell him."

I had decided it was important to remain positive. I forced a smile. "Maybe we can negotiate our way out of this quickly, so he wouldn't even have to know."

M looked at me as if I was being hopelessly naïve. "Even if we agree on a ransom, how do we get the money? We need to tell someone back home, the logical person being Arnie. I think we could pull fifty to seventy-five thou from different accounts without drawing suspicion. What about you?"

"Uh, we just paid off the loan we took out for the surrogate mom. It's been tough, the house payments..." My roundabout answers sometimes frustrated her. It was all over her face.

"Anything?" she said.

"Five. Maybe ten." I really had no idea. Ruben dealt with the finances.

"I'm thinking we might have to talk to Mom's lawyer," said M. "There must be some of her money we can access. I want to keep a tight lid on this, though. I mean, the fewer people who know, the better, but I don't think we have a choice."

"Should we just go to the police?"

"I don't want to buy into the stereotype that all Mexican cops are corrupt, but for all we know they could be in on this."

My phone buzzed with a message. "This might be it," I said.

The kidnappers wanted one hundred and fifty thousand dollars. When we had the cash, we were supposed to contact them, and a drop-off site would be arranged. I answered the text, saying that we would need a few days. I also made it clear we wanted to speak to AJ and Lio directly as soon as possible. *Stay tuned* was the reply.

"I guess we should be relieved in a way. They didn't ask for a million."

"Even a hundred and fifty is a lot of money here."

I pushed away my untouched granola. The place had filled up, and a gay couple was eyeing our table.

"Their English seems pretty good, I mean, colloquial at times," said M.

"Who?" I said, distracted by the activity in the cafe. We seemed to be in the middle of a rush. At a nearby table, I saw the rude party boy I had bumped into on our walk home. He sat with a young Mexican guy. Ah, yes. Americans dabbling in a little local color.

"The kidnappers."

"Yeah. Right. But I keep thinking about AJ's attitude in the video. She sounded more angry than afraid, like she might be communicating something about the guys holding them hostage."

M sighed. "Not sure where you're going with this."

"You'd think she'd be petrified, begging us to get her out of there, but she wasn't."

"I gave up a long time ago trying to figure out how AJ thinks."

"And you're the psychiatrist."

"One thing they teach you at school is that analyzing your own family is a bad idea."

I again felt the evil eye from the couple waiting for a table. "Oh my God, that's Jess. I heard he was in town doing a show."

"Jess who?" M turned around to look.

"Jess Mathers. He's an internet personality, among other things. Huge queen. Very funny." I waved him over. "Hey, Jess. We were just leaving."

"We were?"

"Oh, we don't want to hurry you," Jess said as he pulled out the empty third chair and leaned on it. His companion stayed at a distance, looking embarrassed. Jess turned to me with narrowed eyes. "Do I know you? Did we date?" He gave a high-pitched laugh. But after looking me up and down, he added, "I think not." He softened the blow by slipping me a card. "Come see my show tonight."

M and I were both standing now. Jess hadn't even cast an eye in M's direction, though I'm sure she was used to being ignored in places where gay men congregated. "Tonight?" I said, not to be rude. "Well, thanks. We'll see if we can make it."

"It's a great show," said Jess emphatically. Just as quickly, he turned around and dismissed us.

M huffed outside the restaurant. "That guy insulted you, and you were gushing."

"I wasn't gushing. But he *is* kind of a star."

"Augie, please. We've got to focus. Let's go back to the hotel and call the lawyer. We have to tell him some reason we need money and need it quick."

"How about we found the perfect condo in PV and want to jump on it? A lot of Americans are buying places here."

"That could work. Then I'll call Arnie. I have to tell him everything. He'll worry. But it has to be done."

On the sidewalk in front of us was a gaggle of young men dressed in white yoga pants and T-shirts. Their combined waist sizes were equal to the girth of the tourist they had surrounded. But one of them spotted me and broke off from the group.

"You want massage?" The pretty boy with long lashes was a head shorter than me. Though he looked about sixteen, his intense coal-black eyes had him going on thirty.

"*No, gracias,*" I said.

"Oh come on. You look stress." The boy ignored my Spanish and continued in English.

"*No, en serio. No tengo tiempo.*" It was the little tug of war tourists often had to play with locals who dealt with foreigners. I wanted to show I spoke the language, and he wanted to impress me by showing he could speak mine. It even happened in situations where I was pretty sure my Spanish was much better than his or her English.

"What about you friend?" And then in a low voice, "Is he trannie?"

I nearly choked. "Oh, God! No."

"What did he say?" asked M, coming up beside me.

"Nothing." I gave the boy a strained smile and continued walking. M stood right in front of the boy and stared at him, but he didn't flinch. "Come on, M," I said.

The boy looked around M and shouted at me. "Maybe later."

Colton answered the phone. "Hi, Dad. Guess what? Papi got me this real cool thing. It's a fidget spinner. It's better than the one Jared's got."

I had no idea what he was talking about. "And why is yours better?"

"Because it spins longer. Duh!"

"Great! Cool. Where's Papi?"

"He's driving. I'll put you on speaker."

"Wait. I mean, yeah, okay."

"Hi, honey," said Ruben. "How's everything going down there?"

"Fine. Um...will you be someplace soon where you can talk?"

Ruben's voice shifted into worry mode. "What's going on?"

"Just wanted to talk about something."

"Uh-oh. Daddy's got a secret," said Colton.

"No, Colie, I just need to talk to Papi about some adult stuff."

When Ruben called back later, his voice was playful. "Let me guess, you fell in love down there, and you're divorcing me. Someone who will support you while you write."

"That's not funny." I said. I proceeded to tell him what had happened.

"That's insane. I told you not to go down there. You can't trust Mexicans."

"I trusted *you* from the moment I first saw you."

"Ha, ha, ha. Are you sure that was trust, not lust?"

I had to admit a good bit of lust had been in the air the night we met at a party. Ruben had the exotic look and outgoing personality of a boyfriend I had dreamed about but never thought I could have.

The other part of my fantasy—someone I could practice my Spanish with—had to be dumped in the can't-have-it-all bin. Ruben had been born and raised in the U.S. by parents who discouraged the speaking of Spanish at home. When it came to gangs or lowriders or saggy-panted youth, he cringed from a Mexican identity. But when it came to his mom's cooking, he was a hundred percent South of the Border. When the president railed against Mexicans, he identified with the pain of his stereotyped people. He was also fully aware that because of his looks, he could be a target of an anti-immigrant hate crime and it wouldn't matter if he spoke perfect English or held a U.S passport.

"Of course they want money," I said. "Is there anything we can access quickly?"

Ruben was very meticulous about the household finances. "Well, we've got ten thousand in Colton's college fund, which we promised to never, ever touch."

"I know, and I will replace every penny of it as soon as the estate is settled."

"Sure, baby. It's your brother and sister. We've got to do everything possible." Ruben hesitated. "And please, Augie, be safe. We miss you so much."

I missed them, too, more than I imagined I would. Tears were forming in my eyes. "You know I love you and Colie a lot." I took a deep breath and sobered myself. "Talk to Arnie. I think he's going to come down here with the cash."

"You've got me really worried. Are you sure about not contacting the police? This is not something you and M should be handling."

"M says—"

"M says? It's always what M says. What do *you* say?"

"I don't know. We have no idea who we're dealing with."

" I just think it's naïve to believe we give them the money and get back the hostages."

"What do you propose?'

"I have an uncle outside Guadalajara. He's kind of a badass rancher type. I don't know him well, but I was shocked he sent us a wedding gift."

"I seem to remember it was his wife."

"They both signed the card. Anyway, it wouldn't hurt to call him."

"I'm just afraid to get someone else involved, someone who thinks they're going to be a hero, and then screws things up."

"First, he's family even if the connection to your family is a bit...shall we say non-traditional."

"Hey, they had same-sex marriage in Mexico City before we did in San Francisco."

"And second, he and my mom are close. If she trusts him, I trust him." The closeness of family was another part of Mexican culture Ruben was proud of.

A freak rainstorm during the night left debris on the road. Leaves scattered as I rounded a curve and a small branch snapped as I drove over it. It had been months since I'd driven to Lio's house above Montclair, and I swore they had added more curves to the seemingly endless winding road. A wrong turn had already sent me a mile in the opposite direction.

The sun was out, making the wet road glisten, but the wind still swayed the tall pine and eucalyptus trees. I looked up at the treetops and wondered how large a gust it would take to topple a tree onto the car.

I had spent the night with my mother, and Lio was supposed to relieve me so I could get back over the bridge in time to take Colton to Capoeira class. Lio hadn't shown up or answered his phone. Though Gloria was stable, we tried to make sure someone was with her at all times. M filled in while I raced up the hill to find Lio.

I banged on the door, and then tried turning the knob. It was open. I heard the TV from the living room tuned to a Sunday morning talk show. As I rounded the corner, I came upon what looked like the remnants of a frat party—wine and beer bottles littered the coffee table along with half-eaten bags of chips, bowls of dried-up guacamole, and a container of salsa that had tipped over. A sour odor of warm hops mixed with pot hung in the air. Sprawled on the living room floor were the three roommates under one large blanket, sound asleep with their heads on sofa cushions. Lio was in the middle with his head half on Liam's shoulder while Brandon was pressed against Lio's back, his arm thrown across the other two.

I had an ain't-that-sweet moment, remembering our childhood when Lio used to crawl in bed with me. Lio always loved to cuddle. I was not a natural cuddler, and already aware of my attraction for boys, Lio's visits made me uncomfortable, especially when I wondered if Lio had the same kinds of feelings. I was relieved when Lio expressed interest in the girls who were constantly after him, but I also resented that it was easy for Lio to be Lio while every day I struggled with the inclinations that made me different from other boys.

There were things about Lio I would never understand, but now was not the time to dwell on it. I remembered why I was there and how furious I was with my brother. I leaned over him and said, "Lio, wake up."

Lio's eyes popped open. "What? Is Mom all right?"

"She's fine. No thanks to you."

Lio untangled himself and stood up. He wore gym shorts and a T-shirt. "Oh, shit! What time is it?"

"Late enough that I drove the whole fucking way up here to see if a tree had fallen on the house and squashed the three bears since you don't answer your goddamn phone."

Lio gave me his sweetest, most disarming smile. "We're not bears."

Liam snorted and rolled over.

"Lio, grow up!"

"If you're going to yell, let's go out on the deck." Lio opened the sliding door, and we went out. The deck was strewn with leaves and small branches. A couple of the plastic chairs had their feet in the air, blown over by the wind.

"So are you gay now?" I said in a huff.

"No, Augie, if we were gay, we'd all be naked and have crusty cum on our bellies. It's just bromance, bro. Look, I'm sorry I missed the turnover with Mom. You have every right to be mad at me for that. But you can't be freaked out because I like to have a little cuddle with my mates." Ever since he came back from his trip to Australia, he loved to call everybody mate. I did not find it amusing.

I groaned and looked at him as if he were an alien, or least from another generation even though we were only four years apart. How did he get to have some of the best parts of being gay and still have the comfort of being straight?

"Look at you, forty years old and you live like a college student. And this bromance thing? I don't get it. One of your buddies could be in love with you and you wouldn't even know it."

Lio hugged himself and shivered. "Augie, you are the most uptight gay person I know."

"Let's go back inside. You're freezing."

"I'll get dressed and get down to Mom's in a sec." He put a hand on my shoulder and looked me in the eye. "I wish you were happier."

"What are you talking about? I'm happy."

"I really am sorry I screwed up." He opened the door and waved me to go on in.

"I've got to go. M's with Mom, and I have to take Colton to Capoeira."

"Do you know how lucky you are...I mean with Ruben and Colton? You got love, man."

For all his faults, Lio had a way of cutting through the bullshit and getting to the essence.

"I know. And I'm happy, okay?"

When Gloria finally lost her battle with cancer, her four children were in pain. People in pain were M's territory and finding solutions her business. Hurting wants escape, leading M to suggest we take the trip to Mexico. No one was more anxious than me to get away from the emptiness I felt at my mother's death. In the many forms of mother-son love, ours was a quiet variety—sitting in a room with our books in hand, in separate worlds but connected in the simultaneous activity of eyes embracing words on a page. It was our shy way of loving.

It was quite opposite from Lio's way of lavishing affection on our mom, always telling her she looked beautiful, flirting as if she were his bride. When we were growing up, he was known to invade the Gloria-Augie sanctuary of letters, breaking the spell, demanding her attention. I would raise an eyebrow and watch how she was going to react. So deep was she into the labyrinth of phrases that her resistance would last for several long minutes. But in the end, she was a mother whose son wanted her. "Yes, dear. What is it?"

In the months when Gloria was on a slow, painful journey to leave the earth, I would sit at her bedside and read her the newspaper, a new best seller, or a biography. Occasionally, I slipped in one of my own stories. As I pulled up a chair beside her bed, her face would relax a tiny bit, her body forgetting for a moment its pain. She always asked, "So what are we reading today?" And when I said, "It's just a little story I wrote," a smile would bloom on her dry lips. "Your father would be so proud." All those years Ira was ensconced in his study pursuing what we assumed was academic work, he was actually writing poetry. After his death, we found a stack of composition notebooks filled with his thoughts in verse. It made us sad he never shared them with us.

Her words meant more than I could express. I balked at the idea that I needed my mother's approval in my forties, and yet I found myself craving it.

At the funeral, Lio and AJ wept openly, while M and I remained relatively quiet. M told me she felt like a vital part of her had departed, leaving her strength diminished. She cut her hair short and wore black. My reaction was internal, a sensation of being on a raft cast adrift at sea. There would be no more reading sessions or discussions of books or lamenting the latest atrocities in Washington. She would no longer be there to tell me how courageous she thought I was for the life I had created with Ruben and Colton.

I knew I would find my way back to shore in time, the pain of losing my mother diminishing year by year. I was less sure about what my mother had called my courageous life, particularly lately when something felt amiss at home. Ruben, Colton, and I had settled into the habit of each of us living in a pod surrounded by our technical devices.

After dinner the day M had called about the trip to Puerto Vallarta, Colton went to his room saying he had homework. Ruben announced he was going to watch *North by Northwest* on the living room TV, which he had commandeered in the last few years to feed his obsession for old movies.

"Haven't you seen it like five times?" I said. Ruben shrugged and slunk to the other room. After I cleaned up the kitchen, I retired to the bedroom TV where I searched for anything British on Netflix, settling on an old *Masterpiece Theater* mystery. When my show ended, I took a trip to the living room where I found Ruben snoring on the sofa as I frequently did. I then passed by Colton's room to find him asleep with his laptop resting on his chest. This is what we had come to. It hadn't been so very long ago we watched movies together and played board games.

As I gazed down at my son, I suffered one of my frequent moments of panic mixed with love. Were we doing right by him? Would he grow up to be a decent and happy human being? Was growing up with two dads enough? Ruben and I used to constantly discuss how we were raising him, obsess over ways to give him a richer life experience, try to make every moment the best. And then by tiny increments we had arrived at where we were that evening, each one in his pod. I took the laptop from Colton's chest, closed it, and put it on the side table. "Colton, get up and brush your teeth. Then go wake up Papi. He hates it when I do it."

Colton must have sensed my frustration. "Okay, Daddy." And then as if he might have done something wrong, he added, "I love you." The words always melted my heart even when I knew I was being manipulated.

6: AJ

Since my move to Modesto, Lio and I hadn't gotten together as much as when we lived just a couple miles from each other in Oakland. If the kidnapping had a positive aspect, we had plenty of time to reminisce about our lives and talk about a future if there was to be one.

"Remember that house in the hills Bart and I bought?" I said. "It seems like a dream. Especially if I'm going to end my days in this dump."

"Don't even say that!"

"We were living high back then."

Bart had teamed up with a buddy from the military to flip houses. They were so successful that shortly after I agreed to marry him, he bought an architectural wonder on Grizzly Peak Boulevard in the Berkeley Hills. It had views of the Bay Bridge and the San Francisco skyline, and when the fog was out, you could look through the Golden Gate Bridge and see forever. The four-bedroom house with three fireplaces and redwood paneling was classy in every detail. There was a chef's kitchen I had no idea what to do with, and a master bathroom of green marble laced with iridescent patches that looked like butterfly wings. A Jacuzzi sat on the back deck with the starry sky above and a bay view in three directions.

We moved from a small, thin-walled townhouse to our dream house just after Jason was born. It felt superficial, but all my misgivings about marrying Bart began to melt away after getting that house. He worked hard to give us a good life. The housewarming party was a coming out of sorts. My parents and siblings had no choice but to acknowledge I had reached a certain level of success despite all their trepidations. I loved watching M's eyes go wide, realizing she no longer had the nicest house of the siblings. Even Augie and Bart got along that night.

I knew my parents didn't enjoy the party much, but I refused to let that dampen my spirits. Dad never enjoyed parties. They mostly sat quietly in the corner. Mom had that look on her face that what she was seeing wasn't quite real. She must have been prescient.

Reminiscing about the house left me with a hollow place in my stomach. I had to watch my husband go from king of the mountain to a supplicant at his father's table. "Boy, did we crash!" I said.

"So did a lot of people," said Lio.

I stood up and went to the door of the cabin. I pounded on it, screaming, "Let us out of here!"

"They can't hear you," Lio said.

I turned around and leaned against the door. I slid to the floor and looked up at the skylight and a patch of sky bisected by a tree branch. Everything about the cabin was cheap and dismal. Strange that whoever built it had thought to put in a skylight.

"Soon after I became pregnant with Elijah, we lost everything. Bart had put all our money into fixing up the several properties he owned at the time. They were suddenly worth less than when he bought them. His partner split and left him holding the bag."

"That was a bad time for me, too. Kathy and I were having problems. At least we didn't have to worry about losing property. Bart had said he was going to give us one of the houses at a good price. Glad that didn't happen."

"Can you imagine what it was like, living the dream, and then having to wake up in his parents' house in Modesto? We had bought the house for the boys and only Jason got to live there briefly."

"I'm sorry I wasn't more supportive at the time."

"You were high all the time, trying to deal with your shit."

"It must have been awful living with Bart's parents."

"His mom was okay, kind of sweet, but a real stand-by-your-man woman. His father is a son of a bitch, but he did take Bart into his construction business even though things weren't going that well for him either. Bart and his dad used to sit around and talk smack about what a disaster Obama was, that everything was his fault."

"He wasn't even the president when the collapse happened."

"Didn't matter. They were so angry, egging each other on. That's when I went to Mom and Dad and asked them for a loan for a down payment on a house. They agreed to cosign. Bart was totally against it, said he wouldn't live in a house he didn't pay for, said he was perfectly capable of providing for his own family. I know everybody thinks I always bow to him, but that time I put my foot down. I told him I was moving to the new house with the boys whether he liked it or not. If he wanted to move with us, that was fine, but I wasn't going to raise two kids under the critical eyes of his parents. He agreed, but made me promise I wouldn't tell any of our friends I bought the house. Of course his father knew, and that nearly killed him."

We heard the crunching gravel of someone walking up the path.

"I hope it's Chato," I said. I had done the best I could with the too-short sweatpants and the faded T-shirt they had brought me. Must have been cast-offs from one of their sisters. I rolled the pants up to my knees and tied the T-shirt at my midriff. I pulled my thick hair back in a ponytail and put on some makeup.

Lio watched me, shaking his head. "Just be cool, AJ. Try not to piss him off."

I said very little when Flaco was around, but when Chato was alone with us, I couldn't shut up. I gave him the hard time he deserved.

For the evening meal Chato showed up with carne asada, rice and beans, and sautéed vegetables on paper plates. He set the food on the table and peeled off his mask. He winked at us saying, "Don't tell my brother.

This thing is so itchy and hot." He had shaved and smelled of cologne. His beautiful curly hair had been ruffled by the mask. I had the urge to smooth it like I did with my boys.

I jerked my eyes toward the food and lifted the foil off the plates. "I'm a vegetarian," I groaned. Lio glanced at me like I'd lost my mind. It was the first time he'd heard of it.

"*Ay, muchacha!* Just eat the rice and beans then," said Chato.

"Vegetables shacking up with meat are no longer vegetables. Anyway, they're probably cooked with meat products. I won't eat it. There's nothing fresh and green here."

Lio grimaced. He had seen me put up with all kinds of shit with my husband and probably wondered why I decided to speak my mind now that our lives were in danger.

Chato paced the room, mumbling something in Spanish. "Next time I bring you grass, okay?"

"And by the way," I said. "You really have to do something about that bathroom. It's disgusting. Would you want your wife using it?"

"I don't got a wife."

"Don't *have*. I don't have a wife."

"You no? I mean, of course, you have husband. You say before…"

"Yes, I have a husband," I said in an exasperated tone. "Where did you learn English?"

"Glendale." He slumped down into one of the plastic chairs as if the memory tired him.

"California?"

"Yep."

"So you lived in the States?"

"My brother and me went to work."

"My brother and *I*. I can't believe you didn't learn better English over there." I eased myself into the chair opposite him. I picked up a piece of sautéed zucchini, smelled it, and then popped it in my mouth.

"It might kill you," Chato joked.

"That would save you the trouble."

"Do you enjoy to make me angry?"

"Maybe."

I looked over at Lio. He sat on the grungy sofa with the food in his lap, devouring it like a caged animal. "This is so good," he said with a full mouth. Despite his feeding frenzy, I knew he was listening to every word. Back in high school, he used to tell me my aggressive way of flirting was off-putting. Taunting boys and acting uninterested had always been my game. It confused guys. They never knew if I liked them or not. And then I began to wonder if I was attracted to this idiot in front of me. At our dinner in Puerto Vallarta, I had made it very clear I was unhappy in my marriage and wanted out. No surprise there. But being hot for my kidnapper seemed a step too far.

Chato rested his hands on the table and looked down at them. I stared at his entwined fingers, both masculine and delicate at the same time. The hands were what I had noticed the first time I saw him. It seemed so long ago.

"We work always," said Chato. "Then we can come home to make a restaurant in our town. Mama she always want a restaurant. She cook really good even you don't like it."

"Does your mother know who you're serving her food to?" I said in a raised voice. Lio stopped chewing.

"We have problem because we save only little money before they make us leave States. We are picked up by the *migra* and they send us back. Everybody expect that we come back rich. We go to local guy who make loan for the restaurant. We don't tell our mom until later, and she very angry with us. You don't make business with this people, she say."

We heard someone approach and just before the door opened, Chato jumped up and pulled the ski mask over his face. "So, don't eat. I don't care," he said loudly.

Flaco surveyed the room and narrowed his eyes. "*Vámonos!*"

The brothers walked out and bolted the door.

Lio put his plastic spoon down. "AJ, what are you doing?"

"We have to try something. So, I use what I've got." I felt a smile trying to bloom, but I held it in check.

"Provoking him is using what you've got?"

I shrugged. "You'll see."

The next time we had a chance to talk to Chato alone, I asked if he had other brothers and sisters. "Of course," he chuckled. "I'm Mexican. I got five besides Flaco. Well, one brother die crossing the desert to USA."

"I'm sorry," I said. Empathy never hurt when trying to get someone on your side. Lio looked up from his magazine, an old issue of *People en Español* Chato had brought. He had told me he couldn't read it, but by using his high school Spanish and looking at the pictures, he could pretty much figure out what the stories were about. When Chato was in the room, Lio tried to fade into the background, letting me work my magic. He was still skeptical. He kept pointing out that even if I got Chato to fall for me, we still had the other one to contend with.

Chato's face showed lines and dark shadows under his eyes. "Was a long time ago. He first one try to cross over. Then I got two sisters near L.A. married to evangelicals. *Pendejos!* Republicans. We fight all the time. We ask for help, they say no. They no like how Flaco and me live, no go to church. Then I got one sister at home. She help my mom. Oh, and then other brother in Mexico City." He let his hand dangle with a limp wrist. "He, you know, *joto.*"

"You mean he's gay?" Not a lot of issues got me riled, at least they didn't use to. But homophobia is one I had never been able to understand. And it wasn't just because of Augie or being raised in a liberal household. Every homophobic man I had ever met had obvious issues about his own sexuality, including my dear husband.

"Yeah, whatever." His smirk revealed his feelings about gay people.

"And big macho man that you are, you don't like that. He's your brother!" I yelled. I got up from the table and stomped into the other room.

As I walked by Lio, he looked terrified I was going to go too far. Chato stood up as if to follow me, but then walked around the room mumbling in Spanish. Before leaving he said to Lio, "You sister is crazy!"

When I heard the door slam, I came back into the main room. "God, they're homophobic in addition to being criminals."

Lio shook his head. "You're going to get us both killed."

"Or free," I said.

The millennium was coming to a close, boy bands were all the rage, and garage dance parties were a thing in Hayward. I was in my junior year at Cal State, and my roommate had convinced me to come to the party. Some of our friends had rented a suburban house near campus and lined the walls of the garage with couches they had found on the street, now covered with bedspreads to hide the stains of past debauchery. A keg was in the corner next to a makeshift bar: a plank of wood on top of stacked milk crates.

I stood alone by the door to the yard. Every time a group of people entered, they would float in on a cloud of weed smoke. Through the haze, I kept tabs on my roommate who was deep in flirtatious conversation with a guy she'd had her eyes on for weeks. I tried to get her attention to remind her of the pointers I had given her: don't give it all away, don't be too easy, slow down. I couldn't remember how many times I had tried to counsel her when a guy she had jumped into bed with on the first date didn't call back. The way things were going, it looked like she wasn't heeding my advice and most likely she wouldn't be coming home that night. I could make an exit without feeling any guilt for abandoning her.

The DJ cued up a song that almost made me want to stay and dance even though dancing wasn't really my forte. Friends always teased me, saying I looked like a Barbie doll having some kind of fit. I would need a lot more to drink if I was going to take to the dance floor. From my wall perch I watched a bunch of white people gettin' jiggy wit it to the Will Smith song. The contingent of black people at the party, which amounted to two basketball players, were *not* dancing and had only been invited because one of them was dating the girl throwing the party.

A guy stared at me from the other side of the garage. My peripheral vision had logged his recent stumble in from the yard, handsome face, chin dimple. My first impression was that he was gay. He wore a tank top, and had his muscular arm draped over the shoulders of an equally muscular friend. The friend leaned into the guy in a way that suggested he never wanted to leave his side. They both had buzz cuts, the fashion territory of guys either trying to present a hyper-masculine image or were in the military. Neither interested me. But I had to admit he was cute.

The young man's face changed from a stare to a boundless smile that did not go unnoticed by the buddy who tried to break the spell and steer him toward the bar in the corner. But he weaved over to me, the smile intact even though I hadn't returned it. "I saw you on campus the other day," he shouted over the music. "You're a friend of Jeannie's, right?"

In his enthusiasm, he had neglected to stop at a socially acceptable distance. I could smell the beer and smoke on his breath. Though I took a step back, I did not walk away. "She's in my drawing class," I said, trying to act as bored as possible, glancing over his shoulder to see how things progressed with my roommate.

He rose on his tiptoes to block my view. My eyes met his, and I returned his stare, not because I was interested, but because I was fascinated how hard he was trying to focus in his inebriated state. As the designated driver, I had had very little to drink. I didn't care much for drinking really, and the fool in front of me reminded me why, his behavior a combination of silliness and desperation.

"Drawing class, huh? You an *artiste*?" He pronounced the word in *faux* French.

Instead of heeding the red flags lined up in front of me, I continued the conversation. "My major is actually Psychology. The drawing class is just an elective."

The man shook out his shoulders and puffed up his chest. "My buddy said I should be a model for art classes." He winked at me. "What if I had modeled in your class? Glad I didn't now. I'm kinda shy."

"Yeah, I bet," I deadpanned. "You short on cash or something?"

"What?" He acted insulted.

"I mean most people who take off their clothes in front of a class do it for money."

"Don't worry. When we go out on a date, I'll pay for everything."

I almost laughed out loud. "Not going to happen."

"Ah, come on. Don't be mean." He teetered slightly to the right and then stabilized himself." My name's Bart, by the way."

If I had known Bart was beginning his five-year plan, a gradual painstaking assault on my resistance, I might have treated him with more disdain. In looking back, I was quite sure I hadn't encouraged him, particularly since my heart had been captured by another who was, in fact, a model in the drawing class, but only a hand model. And those hands were all I needed to see. The day I sketched his hands, my mind trotted off to fantasyland. By the end of class we were married and had two beautiful children. I still had the sketch of his hands tucked in my old drawing folder, gathering dust in the attic. But the hand model never showed the slightest bit of interest while Bart's determination was limitless.

The night of the party, I used the bathroom excuse and slipped out the front door, nearly running to my car. But as fate would have it, I started bumping into him everywhere on campus. I agreed to go out with him in a moment of weakness. He took me to The Olive Garden. He was on his best behavior and didn't press for more when I deflected his kiss and allowed him to peck me on the cheek at the end of the date.

I was flattered by his attention, but I constantly came up with excuses why I couldn't continue seeing him. My roommate told me I'd end up an old maid if I persisted with my ice princess routine. We had a second and a third date. I learned that he was in the Army Reserves, but having caught wind of my left-of-center background, Bart insisted his service was only because the military was paying for his education.

We dated off and on for the next couple of years. I graduated and had no idea what to do with my life. My quirky family didn't exert any overt pressure to achieve. Rather, it was furtive glances at family gatherings, the way my mother said, "Ohhh," and M's nod as if listening to one of her patients when I gave less than substantial answers to what I planned to do with my life. I took a job at a hotel in Hawaii to avoid both the familial expectations and Bart's tiresome overtures. Just before I left, Bart got called up to go to Afghanistan. I breathed a sigh of relief and felt sorry for him at the same time. I assumed it would be the end of our relationship.

The letters started arriving within a week after starting my front desk job on Maui. At first I didn't read them. But one lonely night, my curiosity got the better of me. I sat down and read them all. I was impressed by his ability to express his feelings on paper. As soon as his tour was over, he was at the doorstep of the little cottage I shared with another girl who worked at the hotel. His experience in a war zone had both matured and traumatized him. As we sat on my lanai one evening, he recounted how his buddy, the one from the party where we met, had been killed by an IED. I hated to see someone cry, so I was soon in tears as well. I turned and looked at his profile. It was really quite lovely, especially striped with the rivulets of true feeling. As shallow as it sounded, I knew we could make beautiful children together.

7: Lio

AJ gently snored on the other cot while multi-screened, fast-paced loops coursed through my brain. In my pocket I had found an edible, a gummy. My sibs would have thrown a fit if they had known I brought some with me. I popped it in my mouth because, well, it couldn't make things any worse. I didn't remember if it was indica or sativa, but when my noodle switched into hyperdrive, I knew which it was.

I thought of a hundred and fifty ways I might get a message to my daughter and my ex-wife to tell them how much I loved them and how sorry I was for screwing up. In one loop, Kathy and I were working things out and getting back together, and in the next...oh, wait...she already remarried. But my beautiful daughter, Belle, was still mine, still called me dad. Earlier in the evening AJ had talked about fighting for her boys. She asked me what I would fight for, what I wanted when we got back home. That was after we started imagining a variety of best-case scenarios where we returned home with our tickers intact.

"I want a better relationship with Belle. I want her to stay with me sometimes," I told AJ. After Kathy and I split, I buried my head at raves and warehouse parties. I moved into a one-bedroom apartment where Belle could spend the weekends with me, though I felt lost with a small child. Kathy called every hour to check on me as if she were afraid I had gone out clubbing and left a four-year-old alone.

Aside from feeling inadequate, I enjoyed my one weekend a month with Belle. But the rest of the time, I hated the loneliness of single living, spending a fortune going out to eat with friends every night and rarely staying home in the evenings. Once when Kathy dropped Belle off, she went straight to my refrigerator. "Is that what you're going to feed her, stale pizza and beer?"

"Kathy, look. I haven't had a chance to go shopping? I'll take her to the supermarket this evening, and she can pick out the things she likes to eat."

"You're going to let a child run loose in the market and choose her own food? Let me know how that works out for you. Really, Lio? Grow up. Be an adult. Next time, if there is one, I'm going to give you a shopping list and you better have all those items in the fridge or I'm taking her straight home."

"Don't say that. I'm trying." I felt horrible Belle was listening to our conversation. It killed me she would grow up thinking I was inept, a dad who didn't know how to be a dad.

When two friends from college who also had failed marriages asked me to move in with them, I jumped at the chance. Kathy deemed my new living arrangement inappropriate for Belle to spend the night, and I had to agree. When she was a little older, it would be different. I continued to see Belle on Sunday afternoons, taking her to the Oakland Zoo and giggling as we rode the gondola over the animal pens. Sometimes we would ride the ferry from Jack London Square to San Francisco, huddling together as the cool breeze whipped across the bay.

Another loop spun off the years I started working the front desk at a dentist's office. I gradually took over more responsibilities until I became the general manager of a growing practice. If I managed my personal finances the way I did the office, I could have bought a condo or a small house in the Bay Area even with its inflated prices, though I continued living with my roommates in a three-bedroom perched on a hill above Montclair. The year I hit forty—Belle was thirteen—the regrets suffocated me. It had been too many years since I lost overnight privileges with Belle. I was still restricted to weekend and holiday afternoons. My career, such as it was, was solid, while my personal life remained that of an adolescent.

And my brain hit rewind to a conversation AJ and I had earlier. "Was Kathy the first girl you kissed?" she asked me. For some reason, she had started talking about a summer day when she, Kathy, and I had gone to Lake Temescal. AJ and Kathy had been best friends in high school.

"Yeah, I guess, my first real kiss. You never forget your first kiss."

I remembered AJ leaving the brackish water of the lake and going back to the small, sandy beach near the

Temescal Boat House. I knew she was keeping an eye on Kathy and me as we paddled out as far as the swimming ropes allowed us to go. The sun had gone behind the tall trees of the hills around the lake, and the light took on a golden glow.

"I'm cold," said Kathy. She moved a little closer to me.

I didn't want to go back to shore. The air and sky and trees and water and AJ's eyes all closed in on me. I took her in my arms. I knew we would have our first kiss, and at the same time, I was tripping on the fact that there could only be one first kiss, be it magic or messy. That would be it. I hesitated. In another second, she would break free and head toward the beach. I leaned in and we joined lips. It wasn't magic; it was electrifying. It was the beginning of a slow, percolating something that kept getting interrupted by the restlessness of youth. Our hopes and dreams veered off in separate ways, but we remained in contact. We went to different colleges. There were other girlfriends for me and boyfriends for her. I ended up going to Australia for a year, Kathy to Europe. When we found ourselves in the same place, we would have sex. I carried that first kiss with me like a good luck charm.

One summer, we were both at home. I was staying at my parents' house. We sat on a bench at a Grizzly Peak lookout with the sun setting beyond the Golden Gate Bridge and the sky ribboned with rose and purple hues. I lit up a joint and passed it to Kathy. She declined.

"I'm pregnant," she said.

I let out a full rip of smoke and started coughing like I was dying. I finally recovered enough to ask in a wheezy voice, "Is it mine?"

"Yep."

"Oh. Are you going to keep it?"

"Are you ready to be a daddy?"

"Yes!" I said as definitively as I could. I had just started working as a bartender. "Yes, a bartender," I had told my mother. She made me repeat it several times, as if the word meant nothing to her. She didn't say anything more, but her painful expression revealed her thoughts on the matter. It was just a temporary job while I took acting classes, I told her. Even though I wasn't ready to be father and a husband, I didn't want to miss the chance to be with Kathy.

We had a simple wedding a few months before our daughter, Belle, was born. I held the newborn girl in my arms with a love so deep I thought I might burst into tears. I pretended I knew what I was doing. I heard Augie's voice in my head saying, "Don't drop her like you did AJ," followed by an evil witch cackle.

I constantly questioned AJ's approach to our kidnappers, Chato especially. In the end, I had to trust her. I had no ideas. "Whatever you have in mind, just be careful," I said. "But I'm with you all the way. We've got to get out of here. I've made such a mess of my life. I need to make it right."

"I hate to say it, but we both screwed up in the relationship department," AJ said. "But we've got other things going for us. I've got my boys, and you've done great at the dental office, helping build up the practice and all that."

I looked away. "Uh, well..."

"What? Did something happen?"

"I haven't told anyone, but I kind of had to leave." It had happened just a week before we left for the trip to Mexico.

"She fired you?"

"No. We agreed it was probably not a good idea that I work there anymore."

"Did you fuck her?"

I tried to act ashamed, but a sheepish grin broke through.

"You know, you've got the thing," said AJ. "And I'm not sure the thing is a good thing."

"What's that supposed to mean?"

"People want you. People want to have sex with you."

"Is that my fault?"

"It ruined your marriage and now your job."

Mrs. Roth came in for her ten thirty cleaning. Despite a headache that made the entry alert chime sound like Big Ben, I greeted her with the usual mix of friendliness and casual banter. I had gone out the night before with some of the classmates from my Berkeley

Rep acting class to a bar offering two-for-one cocktails. And then just before last call, someone dragged me into the men's room to do a couple of lines. But I got up that morning and put on the face of star receptionist and office manager at Dr. Nazari's dental office.

"Mrs. Roth, you're looking lovely this morning."

"You're looking rather lovely yourself." She leaned over the counter, allowing me a view down her low-cut blouse. She changed to a throaty whisper. "Oh, Lio, I get so nervous. Maybe you could hold my hand," she said with a giggle. She was a widow in her sixties, but she dressed like she was going on a date rather than to a dental appointment—smart suit, heels, jewelry, and a dash of perfume. The dentist had asked me several times to put up a sign asking people not to wear perfume, but I hadn't gotten around to it. I didn't think it would be good for business.

"It's just a cleaning, right? You'll be out of here in a jiffy." I rolled back and collected some papers from the printer, wondering if I needed to tone it down a little. Flirting with the ladies, and not a few of the men, was, I thought, part of my job to make the experience of going to the dentist less traumatic. The dentist and hygienists often told me how much they appreciated my ability to make the patients more relaxed.

"Have a seat, Mrs. Roth, and Susan will be right with you." I put her papers in a file.

"Oh, well, if I must."

"I'll be right here."

I looked up to see the dentist motioning to me from behind a partition out of sight of Mrs. Roth. She was fanning her hand in front of her nose and mouthing, "Is she wearing perfume?" Dr. Nazari's doll-like features, Betty Boop eyes, and pouty expression made her look like a teenage girl but she was seven years out of dental school. I had been with her from the beginning, helping her build the practice.

I let my face fall to show my sympathy. "Sorry," I mouthed.

She stuck out her hand and made a vertical sweeping motion toward me, her way of beckoning me closer. I got up and walked to the other side of the partition. "I need to talk to you later," she whispered.

She didn't sound like she was upset with me. Maybe she wanted to share something about a patient or get my opinion about a business decision, which she frequently did.

The busy day passed without having a chance to speak until the last patient and the hygienists had left. She was straightening up one of the examining rooms when I walked in to ask if she still wanted to talk. She had her back to me, the video screen above her showing nature scenes. Chill music played. She nodded but didn't turn around. Her shoulders bowed under an unseen weight.

"Leila, are you okay?" When we were alone, she wanted me to call her by her first name.

"Not really." She faced me with tears running down her cheeks.

How I wished I had ducked out while I had the chance. Now that I didn't have to perform for the patients, I was suddenly exhausted and desperately needed to be home on the couch. The last thing I wanted was to deal with whatever crisis the boss was having. "What is it?"

"My lawyer called this morning. I lost my case." She had gotten a bad review on Yelp for a crown she had done. Several other patients had chimed in with less than stellar reviews. When Yelp refused to take down the one-star review, she went to a lawyer. I had started a campaign to get some of the regular patients to write positive reviews and recommend new patients, but the damage had been done. Leila had taken the review very hard and constantly complained about how unfair it was. Even an expensive lawyer couldn't fix it.

"Hey, you have patients that really love you. That guy was a jerk. I bet he's some kind of sociopath that goes around destroying dentists careers."

"My career is destroyed?" she wailed.

"No, I didn't mean that."

"I spent all that money on a lawyer. I'm not getting new patients. I know you're trying to help, but this is a disaster." It was true. My campaign wasn't working. The appointment book was barely half-full and deposits the last few months were much lower than normal.

Just talking about it seemed to increase her distress. Her body shook. I had never seen her so upset. She wrapped her arms around me. "What are we going to do?"

We? I thought. We were a business team, but being an emotional team seemed to be crossing a line. I let her hug me, but I didn't really hug her back. It felt as intimate as the time I got stuck behind the refrigerator when I tried to get it away from the wall. The only time we had any physical contact was when we shook hands at our original meeting. Not only was she my boss, but an Iranian woman. I wasn't sure if she was a Muslim, but it certainly seemed like we were breaking taboos.

She buried her face in my chest and sniffled. "Do you have a joint?"

"What?" I did not see that coming.

"Oh, come on. Do you think those breath mints cover up the smell when you come back from lunch?"

This was getting extremely awkward. Though we had steered away from discussing personal life and habits, I knew she wasn't married. At least I didn't have to worry about a jealous husband bursting in to perform an honor killing. And I now knew her olfactory sensitivities were much more realized than I had imagined.

Against my better judgment, I extracted myself from her grasp and went to my jacket hanging in the hall. I fished a doobie out of my pocket. I couldn't resist getting high with someone I never would have imagined smoking with. Soon we were laughing and talking. I sat on the edge of the dental chair and she on the stool rolled up close to me. She said it wasn't her first time. Pot had helped her get through dental school when the pressure was too much.

I felt the urge to put my feet up and leaned back in the chair. She hit the pedal, sending the chair into a prone position. "Oops!" she said.

I closed my eyes. If I can just rest a minute, I thought. The chill music from the speakers, "Sometimes" by B-Tribe, gently rocked me. I had chosen the playlist myself, one of the many playlists I had created for the office. I opened my eyes and she was looking down at me. Her features were delicate, and her skin was golden in the late afternoon light. We both giggled.

"Who's your dentist?" she asked. "I've wondered why you didn't come to me."

"I go to the same family dentist I've been going to since I was a kid."

"You have a beautiful smile," she said. "I don't think I ever told you that."

I blinked in the spotlight of her stare. I was going to get up in a minute. As soon as the song was over, I would walk out the front door, get in my car, drive home, and pretend it had been a normal day. And then she kissed me. Her lips were soft and tasted of the mango lip balm she wore. Had she prepared for this? Happy, innocent clown fish paraded across the video screen above her head. She snuck her hand inside my shirt and plucked the hairs on my chest. If she didn't touch my nipples, I would be free to go. Oh, wait. Shit. Too late. I had an instant erection.

I had looked at the dental chairs a thousand times and imagined having sex on one, but I never imagined it would be with my boss. In addition to being awkward, it was physically uncomfortable to the point of comedy. She bumped her head on the instrument tray as she went down on me. I couldn't stop thinking about the sharp utensils nearby. I was afraid one of us might accidentally hit the overhead examination light, and I would be forced to confess how uncomfortable I felt as if in an interrogation.

She pulled up her skirt and straddled me still wearing her white lab coat. I couldn't decide if the coat was sexy or not. Maybe if she had been naked under it.

The sun set and darkness crept in, providing a comforting veil as we uncoupled. She sighed, rearranged her clothes, and left the room.

The next day I called in sick. I spoke to her personally. "I really am sick," I said. "I think I have the flu."

"Oh, I'm so sorry, Lio. Take care of yourself. I'll call my sister." Her sister sometimes filled in when I was on vacation or needed time off. I returned to work the following week. I still had a cough, which allowed me to hide behind a surgical mask. Even with the mask as a sort of shield, I avoided being in the same room with her. She occasionally gave me conspiratorial smiles. She seemed to have gotten over her funk about the Yelp review. When I left that day, she suggested we go out for a drink when I felt better. I realized she wanted to continue. An affair with my boss? I couldn't.

I eventually agreed to the drink. I ordered a vodka tonic and she a ginger beer. As soon as the drinks arrived, I announced I would have to leave the office. She insisted it wasn't necessary. She said she needed me. We were a team. I insisted it wouldn't work. She started to cry and excused herself to go to the bathroom. I ordered another drink, but she was gone so long I had finished it by the time she came back. Her face looked fresh, and she had reapplied her makeup.

"I've been thinking about closing my practice and moving back to Los Angeles. The weather is better down there," she said without emotion. "I'll give you excellent recommendations, of course." She lowered her eyes and grinned. "I mean about your office work."

Despite the stab, I forced a smile. A woman scorned and all that.

8: AJ

It was our third morning of captivity. No one brought us breakfast and our bottled water supply was running low.

"What if they don't come back?" I said. "What if something happened to them, and no one knows we're here?"

"We might have to chew our way through the walls like that Labrador puppy Kathy and I had when we first got married."

"Interesting solution for someone who works, oops, worked in a dental office."

We discussed different escape scenarios. Busting out the windows wouldn't work because they had bars on the outside. The door was solid and had a metal gate in front of it. We wondered if we could make a hole in the floor and crawl out under the house.

"I can't even imagine what might be under there," I said.

Around two in the afternoon, Flaco arrived with a takeout bag, which he dropped on the table with a thud. "Burritos. One carne asada and one veggie. But first, you call your brother." He pulled a pay-as-you-go phone out of his pocket.

"Where's my phone?" I said.

"Use this one," said Flaco

"I don't have the number in my head. I need *my* phone."

Flaco pulled a scrap of paper from his pocket and put it on the table. "Here is number. You say you're fine. No long conversation."

Augie didn't answer. I left a message and Lio tacked on a couple words at the end to show he was okay. "Can we try again later today?" I said.

"Maybe."

"Where's Chato?" I tried to ask as nonchalantly as I could.

"Ha, ha, ha. You miss my brother."

"It's only that he brings better food."

Flaco grabbed the bag. "If you don't want it…"

"No, wait," said Lio. "We're good." We hadn't eaten since the evening before, and Lio was a firm believer in three meals a day.

Flaco held the food in the air as if he wanted us to beg for it. He gave me a creepy stare. "See, you complain too much, you take food from your brother's mouth."

"Sorry, really. Please. We're hungry." I didn't want to show my frustration, but involuntary tears welled in my eyes. I was afraid Chato had been banished from our quarters, or he had complained to his brother about my behavior and didn't want to see me anymore. That would foil my plan. And then the notion I might actually miss Chato slithered through my brain. I dismissed the idea as absurd.

"Good girl," said Flaco. He dropped the bag again and left the room.

Lio greedily unwrapped his burrito. "At least we won't starve to death."

"I don't feel hungry," I said. My stomach growled.

Lio raised his eyebrows. "Whatever," he said with a full mouth. "You better eat, though."

I unwrapped the foil and found a folded piece of paper. "Damn!"

"What's that?" said Lio. "A receipt or something?"

I unfolded it and the message read, *You mad at me?*

Lio stopped chewing. "AJ…"

"This is good news! He's thinking about me." I know I sounded like a giddy teenager, but it put my fears to rest.

"Maybe it's a prank by the older brother. I don't trust him."

"I don't think Flaco is that clever."

I went into the bathroom, now reeking of sickly floral air freshener Chato had bought at the local supermarket. I surveyed my appearance in the mottled mirror and grimaced. My T-shirt had food stains on it. I ran my fingers under the faucet and dabbed at the stains. From my purse I found lip gloss and coated my lips. Then I fluffed up my hair. From the other room I heard, "Come here and eat your burrito or I will." When I didn't answer, Lio added, "AJ, you've got to eat."

I emerged from the bathroom. "He's probably waiting for his brother to get a distance away so he can come over."

Lio looked at me like I had lost my mind. "Come over?" he said. "You sound like a girl jazzed about a visit from a neighbor boy. Have you forgotten that we're prisoners in this hellhole? This is not a game."

Lio didn't usually express anger. I took notice.

We had no idea where we were or where the brothers lived in relation to the shack. We could see nothing out the windows, though the skylight did allow us a small patch of blue and the view of a branch hanging over the house. The path we had walked up when we were blindfolded was a fair distance from the road, yet not so far we couldn't hear the muffled rush of traffic. Each time a car arrived, we could hear it pull off the highway and stop. Chato sometimes used a small motorbike when he came alone. We would listen for the crunching gravel of someone's approach, hoping it was a rescuer. We had learned to distinguish the footsteps of the two brothers—one fast and heavy, the other hesitant and expectant. We would know immediately if it was someone other than the two brothers.

I heard the high-pitched drone of a motorbike. "See?" I said at the sound of his steps. Then I went in the bedroom and closed the door, leaving it slightly ajar. "Tell him I'm sick."

Through the crack in the door, I watched Chato lean in the room and look behind the door as if he expected an ambush. He had dispensed with the ski mask as he always did when Flaco wasn't around. He carried a cheap travel bag over his shoulder, depositing it on the table next to my uneaten burrito while he looked around the room. "*Hola,*" he said to Lio.

"Did you bring that Spanish phrase book?" said Lio. "Might as well put my time to good use. You know I studied Spanish in high school and I used to listen to my mom speak with the maid. Some words sound familiar, but I have no idea how to put a whole phrase together."

"The maid? And you say you have no money."

Lio shrugged.

"Anyway, is really a book for to study English with translation in Spanish. You can use like in reverse."

"Thanks."

I relished in my position as voyeur, watching Lio walk over to the table and pull packages of what looked like dollar store underwear out of the bag. He held up a package of men's briefs and let out a mildly disappointed "Oh." He wore boxers. At least they would be clean.

"Where is your sister?" The words came out as if they had been on his tongue since the moment he entered the room. "Why she not eating?"

"Probably bathroom. She's not feeling so great."

"What?" A expression of alarm crossed his face. He looked at the bathroom door. "I need talk to her."

"Let me go check on her," said Lio.

I opened the bedroom door and marched out. "Oh!" I said, as if Chato being there was a complete surprise.

"You okay?" said Chato.

"You know, there's no air in here. It's stuffy. No wonder I'm sick."

"You don't look sick."

"Hah!" I glanced at the things on the table. A smile spread across my face. "You got me panties. How sweet! With little flowers on them."

Chato looked mortified. Lio faded into his corner with the phrasebook.

"What did you want to talk to me about?"

"Please sit down," said Chato. "You should eat."

"That's it? You're worried that I'm not eating?" I held the underwear package in my hands, turning it over, fondling it.

"Please," Chato said again, indicating the chair. We both sat down.

"You got my note?"

"Oh, that was from you?"

"My brother, it's not what you think."

"You mean Flaco?"

"No, the other one. In Mexico City. It's his life. I love my brother, but he chose…"

"He chose?"

"Let me finish! I mean…you are impossible to talk to. He chose to move to the city, tell no one where he is. This hurt my mother."

"Maybe he didn't feel welcome here."

"This is not your business."

"You brought it up."

I continued to play with the package of underwear, even holding it against my cheek. Chato reached across the table and grabbed it out of my hands. He put it in the bag and dropped it on the floor. Our eyes met, and mine flashed anger.

"How is this going to end?" I said in a more serious tone.

"What do you mean?"

"This!" I indicted the space around us.

"We don't want hurt nobody."

"What a joke! We are prisoners in this stinky little house. You have already hurt us. You ruined our vacation and are holding us against our will in inhumane conditions."

Chato snorted. "Inhumane? You live here better than most people in Mexico. Look, is very simple. Your family pay the money, you go home. No problem."

"No problem? You've kidnapped us and are extorting money! You're criminals."

A dark cloud of Mexican fatality seemed to form above Chato's head. The muscles in his neck tightened, and he pounded his fist on the table. "They threaten my mom."

"Who?"

"If you have business in my town, you must pay. Every time they ask more. We don't have."

I found myself sucked into his black mood, overwhelmed by the futility of it all. "If you don't pay, they hurt you. If we don't pay, then you hurt us. This is crazy," I said.

"No. Your family gonna pay. I know it."

"Well, if we don't keep trying to call our brother and sister, how are we going to know if they're getting the money together?"

"Flaco has the phone."

"So he calls the shots, huh? If you don't get the money, and your brother tells you to get rid of us, are you going to do it?"

Chato turned his head and grunted, a sound like he was gargling air. "You'll find the money. Is gonna be okay."

"But what if we don't? Are you going to use the gun? Like this?" I put two fingers to the side of my head. "Look at me!" I yelled.

"Shut up!" He stood and walked toward Lio who sat gaping at me stirring the pot, raising the heat. "Tell her to be quiet," he said to Lio.

I stood up, too. "I bet you didn't think about the consequences, what you might have to do. I could tell from the beginning you never wanted to do this."

Chato turned back to me. My anger was no longer a source of amusement to him. "Stop worrying about something that's not gonna happen." He stopped a few feet in front of me, holding out pleading hands. "I couldn't hurt you, okay?" he shouted. "I don't want hurt nobody."

I saw him as more of a caged animal than we were and was moved to stop my assault. We stood facing each other as two people desperate to fall into each other's arms. His unassuming beauty made me furious and slightly ill at the same time. I felt my blood pounding in my temples.

Lio was up out of his seat as well, hunched forward, hands in front of him. I saw the odd look on his face as if he had visions of tackling Chato, wrestling the keys from his pocket to open the door Chato had locked from the inside. He stared at me with doubt, unsure if I would help him or try to stop him.

Chato started to back to the door. We heard the sound of a vehicle outside. "My brother," said Chato. He pulled out the ski mask he'd tucked in his belt and put it on. "Let me handle this."

I did my best to hold Chato's eyes. They looked inhuman, without a center, but I would not let him look away. "It's in your hands."

Lio returned to the sofa and collapsed on it. I went back to the table. I grabbed the bag of things Chato had brought and took them into the bedroom.

Flaco opened the door. "*Que pasó*, Chato?"

"*Nada.*"

The brothers exchanged a series of tense comments before Flaco turned to Lio. "Where your sister? We call now."

Lio came into the bedroom to fetch me. He whispered, "God, if there were just some way we could secretly communicate where we are."

"I know, but how? All we know is that we're in the radius of a Starbucks where the coffee is still hot when it arrives."

It was almost hilarious how unthuggish the brothers looked when we came out of the bedroom. Chato had sat back down at the table and was staring at my unfinished burrito. Flaco paced the room. Chato clearly had little determination to carry this through, and even Flaco's resolve seemed to be waning.

Augie answered the phone on the second ring. "Thank God you called," he said. "We were worried. You okay?"

"Yeah," I said, staring at Chato staring at the food on the table. "Feeling a little sick. I think it's the food."

Augie and M were on speaker. "How's Lio?" said M.

AJ passed the phone to Lio. "I'm good," he said. "Making any progress?"

"Arnie is flying down tomorrow with all the cash we could put together," said M.

"Put on speaker," Flaco demanded.

"Someone is flying down with cash tomorrow," said Lio. He put the phone in speaker mode.

"How much?" said Flaco.

M hesitated. "Uh, a hundred thousand is all we can get right now."

"Shit," said Flaco. "This is not the deal."

"I know," said Augie. "More is coming. We can give you this money, but you have to do something for us. An exchange. Let one of them go."

"No way."

They lapsed into silence. I caught Chato's eye. Chato spoke to his brother in Spanish. He was angry. They argued. "Hang up," said Flaco, reaching for the phone.

"No, wait," said Augie. "Just give us a little time and we'll give you *more* than you asked for."

An idea popped in my head, something I had been thinking about. "Give my love to my boys and the O'Hara brothers," I said.

"This conversation too long," said Flaco. He tapped the phone to end the call.

"What are you doing?" I said. "You have to talk to them to get the money!"

As soon as the conversation ended, Flaco headed for the door. "*Vámonos,*" he said.

I sensed Chato was afraid of his brother's temper. When Flaco's back was turned, Chato made a slow downward gesture with his hands to me before following him out the door.

"What was that all about?" asked Lio. "The O'Hara brothers?"

"Last night while I was trying to go to sleep, I remembered a short story Augie published online years ago. The O'Hara brothers were the two brothers in the story. I think it was called 'Brotherly Love.' He sent us all a link. Didn't you read it?"

"I guess not. It was probably during the time I was pretty much checked out of everything. What was it about?"

"Somewhere in the Midwest these two brothers, I think they were around eighteen and sixteen, kidnapped a teenage girl from down the street and held her for ransom in a tool shed in the back of their property."

"You're kidding. This is a story Augie wrote a long time ago?"

"Yep. The boys' father had abandoned the family some years before, and their mother was sick. The older brother, definitely a boy born under a bad sign, convinced his more naïve brother they had to do the kidnapping to pay for their mom's cancer medicine. That turned out to be untrue. The older boy had a reputation for mischief, but this time he had delved into a true crime. And the younger brother idolized the older one so much, he got dragged into it even though he had never been in trouble a day in his life. The girl's family delayed paying the ransom, saying they needed more time."

"This is too weird," said Lio.

"I know. But the police were a tad bit sharper than the brothers and showed up at the O'Hara's door. The older brother delayed answering the door while little bro went out the back door to get the girl out of the shed. But she had to put on the blindfold. When she came out, he dragged her into the woods behind the house. Truth is he had a crush on her, and when they got deep in the woods, she asked if she could take off her blindfold to see his face. Was she playing along or did she really like him, too? It was growing dark. She kissed him and said she needed to go to the bathroom. She told him to turn his back, and she went into the bushes.

"She took off running as fast as she could toward where she thought the road was. It was fully dark now. She ran into the middle of the road and was hit by a car, killed instantly. Little bro took all the blame, said he and the girl had been in love and planned the kidnapping together to get money to run away. He was trying to protect his older brother, and the older brother let him do it. No one believed the younger brother did it alone, but they couldn't link the older brother to the crime. He even had an alibi for the evening the girl went missing."

"Oh my God! That's terrible. Glad I didn't read it. It's creepy."

"I know. But that's not the point. I was trying to send a message our kidnappers had some similarities to the brothers in the story."

"But how does that help us?"

"At least they could tell the police they should be looking for two brothers. Maybe the older one had been in trouble, the younger not."

"And the part about the younger brother being in love with the girl and the girl possibly reciprocating?"

"Augie wrote it, not me," I said with a smirk. "It's fiction."

9: Augie

The black Ram pickup took up two spaces in front of the hotel. Its trim and hubcaps were polished like silver for a state dinner. A dark man in a cowboy hat unfolded his long body from the front seat and let his tooled nose pickers hit the pavement with authority. People on the street stopped to look at him and cowered slightly. He smiled and tipped his hat to a young woman walking by.

M and I stood in front of the hotel both amused and stupefied by the stranger's arrival. Ruben had given us few details, but this had to be the uncle we were supposed to meet. Ruben only had to mention to his mother that my siblings and I needed help in Mexico. She immediately called her brother and gave the phone to Ruben. Ruben went into the other room and told his uncle what had happened. He didn't know the family in Mexico well and had no idea what to expect from them. But Tio Tomas didn't hesitate a moment, saying he would drive right over to Puerto Vallarta and do whatever he could.

"You Augie?" the man said, sticking out his hand.

Tomas nearly crushed my hand with his large and somewhat rough grip.

"And you must be Tomas. This is my sister M."

"Very good. Okay, sorry my English..."

"Don't worry about it," said M. "Augie's Spanish is pretty good."

"Yes, Ruben tell me this."

A man from the front desk came out and looked disparagingly at the truck, but he hesitated to say anything when he saw Tomas. Tomas smiled and tossed the keys to the young man. He snatched them out of the air and looked delighted as he slipped into the driver's seat, promising to park it in a safe place in the garage. He started the truck, and it roared.

"Let's go into the bar," said M.

The three of us raised our beers and clinked glasses. "It is pleasure to meet you," said Tomas. "How is the young one?"

It took me a minute to realize he meant Colton. "Oh, he's fine. Growing up fast." It felt odd my little family would be a topic of conversation even on the other side of the border.

"Why you don't bring Ruben and your son?"

"Just the brothers and sisters on this trip, the four of us. Our mother died recently, and we needed some time to sort things out," I said.

"My sympathies," said Tomas. He put a hand on my shoulder, squeezing it gently. Then he turned to M. "You have children, *señora*?"

M was obviously not pleased with the question, but it was innocent enough. I suppose she was used to it. When you travel the world, people always want to know about children. M knew as well as anyone it was a way of sharing in something universal, children being perhaps the easiest topic of conversation. "No," she answered simply.

We simultaneously took sips of beer and fell silent. I wondered how much Ruben had told him.

"We have big problem, no? You know anything who this people is who…how you say take your brother and sister?"

"Kidnap," I said. *"Secuestrar."*

"First I ask, you are not businessmen, right? Not DEA agents, right?" His eyes had the same twinkle as Ruben's. The crow's feet distinguished his handsome face, and I imagined how Ruben might age.

"We're just plain old tourists," I said with a chuckle.

"Yes, so tell me what you know."

"We had dinner in an expensive restaurant that night and were all dressed up. We walked back to the hotel, but M and I got separated from AJ and Lio. The next day, we get the video message. From certain things AJ said in the video and later a phone call, we think they might be two brothers and not professionals."

"Cartel *jefes* tell their people leave tourists alone. For this, I think we have some *pendejos* who know nothing."

"They could still hurt our brother and sister, so we can't take any chances," said M.

"How much they ask for?"

"A hundred and fifty thousand," said M. "We have only collected a hundred. My husband is arriving this evening with that."

"When we have the money, we're supposed to contact them," I said.

"I want hear this conversation. I get a room here...that is if you want me help."

M and I looked at each other with doubt. We knew each new person we brought into the negotiation complicated things. And yet a relative of Ruben's had driven all the way from Guadalajara to help, never having met any of us. Ruben had insisted we should at least have some support if we weren't going to the police. "Do you think we should contact the police?" I asked Tomas.

"To be honest, no. They are often useless. I see you are afraid about me, that I do something no good for your brother and sister. Don't worry. I know to deal with this people. I think we can save your brother and sister...and your money."

"We don't want to put you in danger," I said.

He laughed as if the word danger meant little to him. "Just let me listen to conversation. Then I know how I can help. I need get some feeling who they are."

Not knowing when the kidnappers would contact us, we would have to spend time together for the next few days. I was already feeling awkward and strained for topics Tomas could handle in English. If I spoke in Spanish, M would be left out of the conversation. After exhausting the conversational possibilities of Tomas's family, I wondered if I should ask about work, unless Tomas was involved in something we shouldn't know about. And then I felt ridiculous, drawing conclusions based on the truck he drove and the way he dressed. But my suspicions were given some credence when Ruben told me in a phone call that night he honestly didn't know what his uncle did except that he had a ranch with several men working for him.

Tomas got an adjoining room in the hotel. As soon as the phone rang, one of us was supposed to rap on his door.

I lay awake worrying not about my brother and sister, but Colton. Had AJ and Lio not been kidnapped, I would be going home the next day, back to my husband and my son. Instead, tickets would have to be changed, people back home informed, and Bart would have to be handled with believable lies. A number of worrisome issues lined up to march through my brain, but the one leading the parade was being away from Colton during a time he was going through difficulties.

This was the longest I had been separated from Ruben and Colton since Colton was born. I had been there for Colton's first steps, his first words, his first day at school, his tummy aches, and one broken bone. Just a week before I bowed to M's wishes and agreed to make the trip alone, Ruben and I had sat in the principal's office with our heads down. I felt slightly feverish. She delicately asked if something was going on at home to cause Colton's aggressive behavior. My leg started twitching at the suggestion we were somehow at fault for Colton's inexplicable actions. Ruben put his hand on my leg. I let Ruben answer, knowing he would be far more diplomatic.

For Colton, pushing boundaries had become a full-time commando operation, and threats of punishment no longer worked their magic. He seemed to be obsessed with asserting himself, manifested in the disruption of the immediate environment—rearranging products in the shower, leaving drawers open, switching lights on that Ruben and I had just turned off. It was a direct assault on my admittedly absurd preoccupation with order, particularly when I was the parent of a nine-year-old.

We had to repeat even the simplest directive multiple times before getting his attention, only to have the inevitable "why?" form on his lips. Why did he have to put his shoes in the closet when he would have to turn around and take them out again later in the day? Why did he have to go to bed when he wasn't tired? Why did he have to eat the peas when Papi wasn't eating them?

The most disturbing was Colton's occasional lashing out. His eyes would go all Damien the Antichrist, and some awful declaration would escape his lips. I fell into the parental trap of wondering if we had done something wrong. Ruben and I had read books and articles warning us gay parents had to work twice as hard in the face of society's expectation we would fail. Despite our best efforts, a crisis with Colton would reach a boiling point. The monster would return to its cave an hour later, leaving the sweet, affectionate boy we knew cuddling up with us on the sofa, making astute comments about the nature program we were watching.

Ruben kept reminding me shaping another human being was a daunting task no matter what the parental configuration. And still the enormity of the venture would occasionally invade my brain. I would attempt to tamp down a feeling of helplessness, realizing I could go crazy if I didn't stop thinking about it. I reminded myself about genetic issues that couldn't be altered, the random factors of environment and experience—all the things over which I had either limited or no control.

Ruben and I could do everything in our power to love and protect and enrich the life of our child and still he could turn on us and say, "I hate you." At the beginning of my endeavor into parenthood, I truly believed all you needed was love. But each day Colton edged toward being his own person, I realized how hopelessly naïve that was.

A few days after Colton had posed questions about his mother, he had become inexplicably obsessed with the garage door opener on the wall just outside the kitchen door into the garage. He stood on the top step leading down to the garage, opening and closing the door.

"Do not push that button again," I said. "Do not push…I said do not…" The long grind of the descending door began, causing a contrasting rise in my brain temperature. The thump of the door on the pavement made me jump.

With a finger still on the button and a devil's grin, Colton said, "Oh, you want the door open?" Click. And the door began its grumbling ascension.

"No!" I screamed.

"Oh." The door halted halfway up, shook, and then started down.

"Take your finger away from that button now!" I spoke in my rarely used sergeant voice, indicating, if it hadn't been crystal clear before, that it was not a game. "If you touch that button one more time today, you forfeit your iPad time for the rest of the week."

If Colton loved one possession, it was his iPad. It was the only thing that held his attention for long periods of time. Ruben and I were frightened by its power over him. We would sometimes demand he put it down, and then thrust a book into his empty hands. He would stare at the book as if it was an amusing relic, scanning and deciphering the words for a good five to ten minutes before looking up and plying one of us with a question he had thought up and catalogued for just such an occasion.

"If the stars are already burned out, how can we see the light?"

"Is that related to what you're reading?"

"No. I just wondered."

"If you read five more minutes, I'll tell you the answer." That would give me time to google it on my smart phone.

But the day of the garage opener, the drunkenness of defiance trumped Colton's love of his iPad, leading him to push the button again.

"Go to your room and bring me your iPad now!"

"Nooo," Colton began in a mournful whine. "I was just playing."

"I told you it was not a game. Bring me your iPad this minute or it will be two weeks."

I was awakened from a dream about bees in the backyard triggering the alarm system. Judy, my girlfriend from the third grade who I hadn't heard from in almost forty years, was staying in the guest room and started shouting. I was afraid she'd wake up Colton, who was just a baby in the dream. I came to realize it was not an alarm but my phone ringing, and the person shouting was M. She had insisted on sleeping in my room on the couch while we were waiting for the call from the kidnappers. "Augie, wake up. I looked at the caller ID. It's a blocked number. I'll get Tomas."

Tomas answered immediately when M banged on the adjoining door. He walked into the room fully dressed, the smell of coffee wafting from his room.

"I think it's them," M said.

I held the ringing phone and waited for everyone to get settled.

"Try make them talk," said Tomas.

I answered and put it on speaker. "*Buenos días*," I said. I heard the person hesitate on the other end, and I silently cursed myself for letting on I might speak Spanish.

"You got the money?"

"Yes. I mean we will very soon. The flight was delayed, but the person who's bringing it, he arrives this morning."

"This is bullshit," said Flaco.

M motioned for me to keep talking.

"No, really. You can check the flight, Alaska from San Francisco. Engine trouble."

"How much he bring?"

"We told you. We can only get a hundred thousand right now. We're working hard to get the rest."

We heard another voice in the background speaking Spanish. Tomas moved closer to the phone. "*Callate güey*," Flaco said, telling the other person to shut up.

"So we agreed you'd let one of them go when we give you this money," I said.

Flaco laughed. "I no agree. You dreaming."

"Please, be reasonable. I told you if you work with us, we'll give you extra."

"How much?"

Tomas held up ten fingers. "Ten thousand," I said.

"Make it twenty, and we think about it," said Flaco. "I give you answer soon."

Just before Flaco hung up, we heard Lio say, "Say hi to Joey Sims back home." The line disconnected.

M and I looked at each other. "Joey Sims?" we said at the same time.

M shrugged. "And what was the other guy saying in Spanish?"

"He wants to take the money we have and let them go," I said.

"Is good they don't know you speak Spanish," said Tomas. "I think you right the other guy is younger brother. He have no stomach for this."

"It's like your story," said M.

I nodded and gave Tomas a brief explanation of the story we were referring to. But we had no idea how much of AJ's hidden message applied to her situation. At the very least, they were dealing with an older brother, possibly the mastermind, and the younger one more reticent.

"In your story, you say the boy fall in love with the girl and maybe the girl like him too. You think?"

"Oh, no." said M. "AJ? She's not...we call her the Ice Princess. I mean..." I stared at M intensely. "Augie, why are you looking at me like that?"

"There's something going on with AJ that is not normal, I mean besides the not normal of the whole situation. Why did Lio mention Joey Sims?"

"The guy back on Forest Street?" said M.

"Do you know another Joey Sims?"

She seemed to resist the thought, but after a brief sigh, she turned to Tomas to explain. "Joey was a boy who lived down the street and he was crazy about AJ. Everybody teased him about it. We later found out the attraction was mutual, though AJ kept her feelings hidden."

"They were kids. And that was a long time ago. I can't believe AJ..." I stopped and rubbed my forehead. "...but then we *are* talking about AJ."

"Even if there is some kind of flirtation going on, which still seems a stretch, how does that help us?" said M.

"I don't know, but Lio wanted to tell us something."

"So their English pretty good, no?" said Tomas.

"We think they might have lived in the States."

"I think too," said Tomas. "Now, two boys who need money. We must imagine why."

"Some trouble?" I said. "They owe money?"

"Yes. I think to do something so crazy mean they in danger. Like from gangs. They maybe owe money to local *jefe*. Okay. Good. I have many questions. I get to work." He started for the door back to his room.

"Tomas," said M. "We appreciate your help, but if it involves cartels, maybe..."

"Don't worry. I know many people in this area. I just ask a few questions."

10: M

Arnie arrived at the airport wearing a travel vest with multiple pockets, rolling a new model bag that matched the backpack slung over his shoulder. He also wore an expression of worry, a habitual look not necessarily related to what he had just smuggled into the country.

"Smile," I said to Augie. "Don't act like you're greeting someone carrying a great quantity of cash in the false bottom of his bag."

I embraced my husband. I was genuinely happy to see him. "You're so brave," I whispered in his ear. I gave no indication my reality had been changed ever so slightly now that the words had been spoken that night in the restaurant. The kidnapping had given me a crisis to focus on rather than the notion that I could transition to the person I harbored inside. I knew Augie was watching how I acted with Arnie, ready to pounce on the slightest sign I might treat him differently. I tucked my arm in Arnie's and held him close.

The words I had spoken could not be taken back. There were witnesses. My feelings, once locked inside my head, now floated on the air around the siblings, even though none of them had had the chance, thanks to circumstances, to process the concept of transitioning.

Burdening my siblings with that knowledge was one thing, but I had no idea how I might share those feelings with Arnie. Having him next to me made me feel more confused than ever. Yes, the man inside me was strong, though I had always known my certainty wasn't as strong as Sid's, the child who had come to my office so many years before. Yet that didn't lessen the conviction I just wasn't comfortable being a woman, a woman with large breasts and a womb I never planned to use.

"Let's get the hell out of here," said Augie.

"I'll second that," said Arnie. "Thank God I got the green light."

"You always know you're in Mexico when you have to confront the red light/green light button at customs," said Augie. The red light, which caused one's bags to be searched manually, was supposedly random, but Augie had tried to convince me a wizard behind a curtain controlled the lights, on the lookout for people who appeared nervous.

A tall dark man in a cowboy hat stood by the sliding glass doors of the airport and stared at us intently. Then he started walking toward us.

Arnie tensed up. "Do we make a run for it?" he said in a shaky voice.

"Don't worry, Arnie," I said with a chuckle. "He's our escort. Ruben's uncle."

An orange-breasted robin took off from its branch about five feet from the floor-to-ceiling windows along the dining room and banged into the glass with a dull thud. With its wings still outstretched, it fluttered to a position flat against the window a pair of seconds before somehow reversing its trajectory and returning to the branch. After a brief rest, the bird took off again and repeated the exact same action. Several lines of bird excrement ran down the glass.

I stood watching the antics of the bird through the sliding glass door of the living room perpendicular to the dining windows, in fact had been drawn there from my office by the repeated thud against the glass. The bird continued its seemingly self-destructive display time after time. It was clearly a male. I realized his beak took the brunt of the impact. If it had been the head, it surely would have been the equivalent of someone banging his head against a wall until he was brain dead. I also realized I had been hearing the thud for a few weeks and had never been able to identify its source. Just the day before I had heard it and thought the neighbors were doing some work on their house.

My first guess was the bird was trying to reach someplace beyond the glass, and it didn't realize it couldn't fly through a hard surface. But even the dumbest of birds wouldn't repeat the same action with such a sense of purpose hour after hour, day after day. Perhaps it saw the reflection as a male encroaching on his territory and was attacking it in a genetically programmed response. Or, I mused, it was like Narcissus who fell in love with his own reflection and was trying to mate with himself. It was just one of the mysteries of the garden, Arnie's domain.

For years I had sat at my desk in my home office overlooking the backyard and watched Arnie transform the bare space into a jungle of plants, shrubs, flowers, fruit trees, and vegetables. He would devote every weekend to scouring nurseries for something new, loading up the back of his SUV with soil, lending his gentle hand to creating a paradise. The multi-layered fountain in the middle of the yard attracted birds of all varieties, and the bright red and white flowers of the salvia bushes were a magnet for a particular variety of iridescent green hummingbirds. It was an oasis for birds, bees, and butterflies. In addition to flowers, he had managed to grow luscious tomatoes, a particular favorite of Gloria's, along with beans, broccoli, zucchini, and lettuce.

He would walk the yard with his morning coffee, pinch off a wilting flower, make mental notes of what needed water, and listen to the buzzing of bees going from one bush to another. Sometimes he would come inside and announce the first flower on the gardenia bush had arrived or a bird had robbed them of a strawberry.

I contemplated the brown grass of the backyard in the third year of a drought. At the beginning of the summer, Arnie had tried so hard to maintain the green that the winter rains had brought—watering, seeding, and staring at the lawn as if he could will it to grow. But as the hot summer wore on without a drop of rain, Arnie declared he was giving up. "It's not right to be using so much water when we're in a drought. Maybe we should consider artificial grass. A lot of people are doing it these days." The look I gave him made him add, "I guess not." I knew he would not be happy with a fake lawn.

Though we were coming to the end of the dry season, we weren't quite there yet. The sky had turned gray over the weekend, the air heavy with moisture. The heavens opened and spit enough to make us gather up the lawn chair cushions and hurry them to the garage. A few minutes later, it was over. The ground wasn't even wet. We could hear the garden screaming its disappointment. As the sun came out, the leaves on the plants drooped immediately, even the drought-tolerant ones Arnie had focused on in recent years. The birds, too, seemed to have all gone away for greener pastures. Arnie worried about the bees.

I stepped back from the window and caught my reflection, my breasts appearing huge as if magnified by the glass. I reached up and cupped my hands over them, confirming they were as large as they looked. No, they had not diminished as so often had happened in a reccurring dream. What an encumbrance! They interfered with my golf stroke, my tennis game. I had developed early, and from the moment I saw the mounds begin to grow, I felt betrayed, my body doing something against my will.

While all my friends desperately wanted boobs, I had hoped and prayed to be flat-chested. I had gotten very excited reading about Amazon women who sacrificed their right breasts to be better archers, though Mom told me it was just a myth. By the time I was sixteen, my breasts were huge, and I was disgusted. I tried to wear clothes that hid them, but still boys stared and acted like fools around me. Now in my mid-forties, I had to worry about them sagging.

Earlier that morning, I had gotten a surprise email from Sid, now a teenager. I hadn't heard anything from or about him since the day Sid's mother had called to cancel his therapy. I had often wondered what had happened to him, if he was lucky enough to be flat like my neighbor Bette who I golfed with, or if he had gone through the operation.

Sid reminded me who he was and apologized for being such a difficult patient. He had been devastated when his mother switched to a therapist who told him what the mother wanted to hear. It made him realize how sympathetic I had been in comparison. He was happy to say the therapist and the one after that, and the one after that had failed at changing his mind.

His father had eventually overruled his mother and allowed him to go to a sexual reassignment therapist who recommended he begin hormone replacement therapy. He had been on hormone therapy for almost two years, and he was looking forward to surgery to finish the process. The most important thing was that he couldn't be happier. He said he completely understood if I didn't want to respond to his email, but he wanted to let me know how things had turned out.

I was torn. A part of me wanted to know every detail of the procedure from a psychological perspective. I thought about setting up a casual meeting, coffee perhaps. I wanted to see the result first hand. But I also remembered how Sid had challenged me and seemed to see through me, falling just short of saying I should consider transitioning. I opted for sending a brief note, congratulating Sid and wishing him all the best. With my mother's failing health, I couldn't even think of facing the demon that had long dwelled within me.

The motorcycle cruised through bands of color along a perfectly flat gray ribbon of road. On either side, fields of tulips were in full bloom, first swaths of red, then yellow, then white, then pink. I came upon a field of flowers that looked black at first. Ah, the elusive black tulip, I thought. I pulled over and stopped the bike. On closer examination, they were a velvety deep maroon.

I pulled out my map. I was near the Dutch town of Lisse, halfway between The Hague and Amsterdam. Though the sun was starting to go down, flooding the fields with gilded light, I didn't think I would have any problem making Amsterdam by dark.

I started my bike and roared onto the road with "Born to be Wild" playing in my head. I had ceased being M. Burd, recent graduate Magna Cum Laude from U.C.

Berkeley, headed to Stanford Medical School in the fall. I was a bad boy on a hog blazing through the back roads of Europe with no particular goal except to lose track of who I was.

Always an overachiever, I'd graduated early in January. I had six months before I would dive into med school and spend the next seven years swimming upstream against long hours, absorbing tons of information. Hard work and physical exertion had never frightened me, but I also relished the chance to take up a challenge of a different sort—being a man on the road, free and independent.

I cut my dark hair short, but still long enough where I could slick it back behind my ears. I told my hairdresser I didn't care if I looked like a man because I was going to be traveling by myself through Europe and it would be safer. I hadn't told anyone my plan of doing it by motorcycle, not even Augie. Augie and I had tried to get together several times before I left, but something always got in the way. He was going to school at the University of San Francisco on the other side of the Bay and living in the Haight where he was discovering gay sex—safely I prayed.

Through a catalogue, I ordered a binding garment that claimed it would flatten my breasts. I slipped the spandex tank top over my head and tugged the tail down around my hips. The instructions said to reach inside the garment and push my breasts down and to the side. I stood sideways in front of a mirror and couldn't believe my eyes.

I was a stocky man with a developed chest rather than a "big-boned" woman with large breasts. I pulled a black T-shirt over the undergarment and slipped into a pair of jeans. I worried about my hips looking too wide, but the long top helped in slimming my thighs. My gym routine had kept my tummy flat and my arms strong.

The day I tried on my new binding top was unseasonably warm, making me glad I had chosen early spring as a time to travel in Northern Europe where it was still cool. I could comfortably wear the black motorcycle jacket I bought at a South of Market leather shop in San Francisco. The final touch was a pair of aviator sunglasses.

I stood in front of the mirror trembling. I was inhabiting a body that was not mine but the one I had always wanted. The effect was far beyond any of the feeble attempts I'd made doing male drag for Halloween. One year, a guy I was dating dressed as Bonnie and I was Clyde. We were the hit of the party. But on my trip through Europe, no one would know me. It would not be a joke. I gazed with excitement at my reflection, knowing I could pass. I had even been practicing speaking in a lower register.

After landing in London, I caught a taxi to a shop on the outskirts of the city where they sold used motorcycles. As soon as I saw the maroon Honda ST1100, I knew it was for me. It was masculine without being macho. The seller talked about reliability, comfort, and performance for the long haul. Not ready to tackle London on a bike I wasn't familiar with, I toured southern England along the coast for a few days until I got to Dover. From there, I took the ferry to France.

A light rain began to fall as I rode along a canal on the outskirts of Amsterdam. A group of cyclists had stopped to watch several swans paddling near the water's edge. I pulled over as well, took my helmet off, and slicked back my hair. A few of the cyclists turned to look at me with alarm in their eyes. It confused me at first, and then remembering my new image, it pleased me to think I might look like someone to reckon with.

"Hi," I said in a deep voice. "Do you speak English?" It was the last time I had to ask that question. Everybody I met during my time in Holland spoke nearly perfect English.

"Can we help you?" said a pretty blonde woman in her tight hi-tech fabric jersey unzipped as far as it would go. She appeared more daring than the others.

"Just wondering what is the best way into the old district."

Another girl came over. "What is he looking for?"

My heart leapt. People I had interacted with so far were mildly curious, but gave no indication whether they thought I was a man or a woman. The desk clerk that first night in England at the inn outside Portsmouth looked at my name on the passport, May Burd. His eyes flashed briefly as if it solved a mystery.

"I'm staying at a hotel on Kerkstraat," I said to the girls. "It faces a canal." I pulled out my map.

The blonde girl traced the directions on my map and gave me a few pointers about avoiding traffic.

"Thank you so much," I said.

"Pleasure," the girl said, sticking out her hand. "I'm Anna."

"Nice to meet you. I'm M...Marlon."

I spent the first day in Amsterdam visiting the Van Gogh Museum and the Rijksmuseum. My ancestors handed down the tradition of culture before fun as if the blood of my people mandated it. And yet every experience, every room in every museum, was fun in my new persona. I was the star of my own work of theater. At the end of the day, I would record my impressions: how I felt in my new body; how people who perceived me as a man reacted differently from those who weren't sure; how having a person of questionable gender in any setting changed the dynamic.

Though my plan for the fall was to specialize in child psychiatry, all human behavior fascinated me. And being in Amsterdam, one of the most progressive cities in the world, meant I could push the limits of gender and sexuality with the added benefit that I was a stranger here. Many of the characters I saw would, at the end of the day, find a place in my notebook. I wondered if and how I would be portrayed in the notebooks of others.

On the second and third days, I continued being a tourist, taking a canal cruise, walking around the Red Light District, and trying not to get knocked down by the thousands of bicycles careening through the streets. On the way out of the charming boutique hotel on the third night, I stopped to talk to the young woman behind the desk. With her spiky hair, nose ring, and stars tattooed up her arm, she seemed like a person I could ask where to find the marijuana places without anyone feeling uncomfortable.

"First thing," she said, "you need to find a coffeeshop, written as one word, not a coffee shop or café or coffee house. I can recommend a couple."

"Do they have space cake?" I asked. I had tried smoking marijuana a couple of times but found it problematic. I hated smoke and was not fond of anything that slowed my mind. The times I had tried it, I felt stupid for an hour and then fell asleep. But a good friend at school had raved about the space cake he had tried in Amsterdam, so I was willing to give edibles a try.

As I stepped out into the cool, drizzly street, I reaffirmed my plan for the evening, the biggest challenge of my trip. I was going to Argos, a men-only leather bar, a place my friend had also talked about. "Too bad you can't go there," he had said. I reached into my jacket pocket and touched the accessory I would add to my outfit of leather jacket, T-shirt, jeans, and boots, but was embarrassed to put on before I left the hotel. At a theatrical makeup shop, I had purchased a glue-on mustache that was called "the crime doctor." I loved the name. It allowed me to do anything.

Two hours after I had eaten the space cake, I proclaimed it a dud. If I felt the slightest bit different, it was because of the glass of wine I had with dinner. I took a deep breath and walked in the door of Argos. It felt more like accidentally walking into a men's room with a distinct odor of urine, beer, and man sweat than crossing a forbidden portal. It was nearly empty, and people ignored me. I took a seat at the bar and ordered a beer in a bottle. With a dark bottle, no one would notice I was just taking sips and not really drinking something I found disgusting. The other patrons were clearly leather aficionados, all of them wearing some combination of leather jackets, leather pants, biker caps, and chaps. One skinny, white-haired man was shirtless and wore a harness. I would have a lot to write about in my journal later.

The music was at first some popular songs of the day. I recognized Madonna's "Justify My Love," and then George Michael's "Freedom." I had never paid much attention to the lyrics of "Freedom," but, at that moment, the words spoke to me. The message of freedom pulled my emotions into a dance, telling me there was something I should know, something deep inside of me, something I forgot to be. I shuddered and looked around, wondering if other people were impacted by the words.

The "Freedom" chorus sounded as if a choir of celestial voices had joined Michael, surrounding me with voices from on high, causing a tingling on my skin. My binding made me sweat, and I wanted to take off my jacket. But I didn't. I almost felt something at dinner had disagreed with me, causing this strange sensation. I had completely forgotten about the space cake.

The bar began to fill up, and the music changed to a more synthesized sound with heavy bass and driving percussion. The pounding went directly to my chest. Men were all around me now, some of them staring at me. I began to fear the mustache I applied in the restaurant bathroom was coming loose. They knew I was not a man. I had no beard, no Adam's apple. I was sweating a lot, and it didn't smell like a man. I was a moment from being discovered and thrown out.

The white-haired man in the harness stood behind me and whispered in my ear. "Do you want to go downstairs?" My friend had told me about the playroom on the lower level and given graphic details of what went on there.

"Got to finish my beer," I growled. "Maybe later." I was relieved he didn't see me as a woman. Or did he? He turned to his companion and said something in German. They laughed.

Voices swirled around me, lights and shadows constantly changing, the music distorted. My brain kept losing track of where I was, a different country, continent, dimension maybe? I was suffering space cake paranoia. The effects had crept up on me as it was now hours since I'd eaten it. It was powerful, and I didn't like it. I needed fresh air and to get back to the hotel. I stood up and made my way through the crowd.

Outside the door of the bar, I was disoriented and couldn't remember if I was supposed to go left or right, confirming what I disliked about being high, the loss of control. I could have asked plenty of people on the street, but I didn't, afraid if I opened my mouth I would sound stupid or the words wouldn't come out. I chose one direction and started walking rapidly, regretting I had left my map in the hotel.

I pulled up the collar of my jacket against the cool, damp air. Nothing looked familiar. The streets were soon dark and empty. I heard loud singing in the direction I was walking. As I got closer, I recognized it was English, some kind of rowdy sport song sung by five men in buzz cuts with scarves in team colors and aggressive manners. I crossed the street, hoping they wouldn't see me.

They stopped singing and looked at me. "Hey, macho man!" one of them yelled. They were drunk British soccer fans, a bad combination. In this case, I wondered if it was more dangerous to be a woman or perceived as a gay man. I picked up my pace, but they started in my direction. "Hey, we're talking to you."

"Where you going, faggot?" another said.

"Want to suck my willy, you fucking poofter?" said the one who seemed to be the ringleader.

Ignore them, I kept telling myself. I heard voices down one street and turned at the corner. They followed.

"Come on, I need a blowie." They were right behind me now.

Though I knew I needed to keep quiet, my anger was about to explode. I turned around. "I probably wouldn't be able to find it," I said. Then I started to run toward the other voices I had heard.

I was a good runner, but no match for them. I no longer heard other people, only the senseless shouting of the gang, their words no longer simple profanity but the garbled grunts and growls of animals. They grabbed me and threw me up against the wall.

The leader snarled in my face while the others held me. "We're going to mess you up, fag."

"I'm not a fag," I said in my normal voice.

"Bloody hell," said one of them. "She's a girl."

The leader focused on my mustache. "She's a fucking bull dyke." He tugged at the mustache, and when it gave, he ripped it off my face.

They pushed me into a narrow alleyway. I struggled, managed to elbow one of them. I yelled as loud as I could. They put a hand over my mouth. I felt their fists making contact with my face. I tasted blood. They pulled my jeans down. I kicked. And then a blow knocked me out.

I woke up in the hospital. One eye was swollen shut. My head throbbed. A woman stood over me. "You're safe now," she said. "How do you feel?"

"Like shit," I said. They had removed my clothes and put me in a hospital gown. "Did they...did they...?"

The doctor nodded her head with pursed lips. "I'm sorry. I've ordered a rape kit. Your clothes have been bagged for possible evidence. We believe it was only one of them. Luckily, some guys from a bar nearby arrived before it got any worse and the hoodlums scattered. I guess it was the place where you had been because they said they recognized you."

"Oh," I said. And then I began to sob uncontrollably.

"There is a policewoman outside the door who would like to talk to you."

The bruises and cuts were bad enough to need stitches and would take time to heal. The rape would stay with me for a lot longer. The policewoman came in and talked to me. I described the young men, but I told her I couldn't stay in town for identification and possible trial. More than anything, I needed to go home. I would not press charges. Though she was sorry about my decision, she said she understood. The young men had most likely already returned to England.

I left the hospital that afternoon. The woman at the hotel helped me sell the bike, though at a significant loss. Two days later, I was on a flight back to San Francisco. I went to the Berkeley apartment where I lived alone and told no one I was home. I stayed there until my wounds healed, only venturing out for food. And I never told anyone what had happened to me in Amsterdam.

I threw myself into med school in the fall. I got rid of the binding garment and with it any thoughts about trying to change or hide the body I was born with. But the feeling that my body wasn't right never left me.

11: Lio

My stomach churned, and a trail of sweat ran down from my temples to my cheeks. I couldn't agree to what AJ had proposed, but I wanted to be free, to see my daughter again, to sort out my life. In a surprise reversal, the brothers had consented to take the money and let one of us go. We had to choose who would get released, and the other would have to stay until they got the remainder of the cash.

I knew I wouldn't be able to live with myself if I was the one released and anything happened to AJ. And yet the force of survival coursed through me, seeping into every cell and teasing it with hope.

"I'm not being a hero, Lio," said AJ. "It's the only scenario that makes sense."

"We refuse the offer. It's that simple."

"You're no good at this. I know how to control Chato. How do you think Flaco agreed to this deal in the first place? I can handle Chato. Chato can handle his brother."

"You really believe Chato will protect you?"

"I know it."

Earlier that morning when I emerged from the bathroom, Chato and AJ had suddenly stopped their conversation. They had been sitting across from each other exactly where AJ and I were now. I might have seen someone's hand swiftly recoiling to its side of the table. Eyes fell to the tabletop.

Chato had come over to announce the deal, while Flaco finalized the rendezvous and timed the motorcycle ride to the location where the money would be dropped off and one of us could be picked up.

"Is there something going on between you two?" I asked.

AJ shrugged.

"You don't know?"

"I mean it started as a way to get Chato on our side. I could tell he had doubts, and it wasn't hard to see he was attracted to me."

"You guys were arguing all the time."

AJ gave me a sad look that summed up all she believed about my ability to understand women. "He's really quite handsome, you know, and there's another guy behind that macho façade."

"So you're saying that you do have feelings."

"It's probably just that Stockholm thing, you know the Patty Hearst syndrome."

"That usually happens when captives are abused. Has he threatened you?"

"No. Nothing like that. I just don't want to see him sent to prison or murdered in some SWAT team rescue."

"You're doing it again."

"What?"

"Going all soft on some guy who later turns out to be an asshole. Don't do this, AJ."

"My decision is final. You know I can take care of myself. I'll play along. They should have the rest of the money in a day or two. Then I'll be home."

I nodded my acceptance, but I didn't trust her decision. Chato was not a bad guy, and you could tell he wanted the situation safely concluded as much as anyone. But there were too many variables, too many chances for something to go wrong. Bad things can result from good intentions. Decent people can be forced to do terrible things.

My best friend Pete and I walked home from school together every day. We were in the same sixth grade class. We took different routes, sometimes stopping for ice cream on College Avenue or visiting a game store on Telegraph. Once we walked by a church and Pete said, "That's where we go. I'm a Catholic." He seemed very proud of it, making me feel a little embarrassed my family didn't go to church. I hoped he wouldn't ask, but he did.

"Do you go to church?"

"Well, if we went somewhere it would be temple. We're Jewish. But we don't, you know, participate."

"Oh," said Pete, like he felt sorry for me.

Pete told me he was an altar boy. He described in detail what he did to help the priest during mass. He knew a lot about the church, including the doctrine of transubstantiation. The word rolled out of his mouth like a shiny new Mercedes-Benz. I was impressed he knew a big word like that and could explain what it meant. Sometimes he assisted at funerals or weddings and got a tip of ten or twenty dollars. I was fascinated and asked a lot of questions. It all sounded pretty cool to me, and I wondered why we didn't observe any rituals.

When we weren't talking about his church, we talked about sex, another subject he seemed to know a lot about. I asked him how he knew so much, and he tried to change the subject. I kept after him until he finally admitted he had seen some videos. He wouldn't say anymore about it.

One day we were in front of the church rectory, and he said, "Let's go say hi to Father Dan."

"You call him Father?"

"That's the way we do it. He's like a spiritual father."

"We can't just go ring the doorbell, can we?"

"Sure. He told me to stop by anytime."

Father Dan answered the door with a big smile. "Ay, would you look at this! A sight for sore eyes." He had a funny accent. Pete later told me he was from Ireland.

Pete introduced me, and Father Dan put his hand on my shoulder and squeezed hard. "Come in. Come in." Right by the front door was a large bowl of miniature Snickers even though Halloween wasn't for at least a month. He must have seen me looking at the candy. "Go ahead. The Lord helps those that help themselves," he laughed.

"Lio wants to become a Catholic."

"I never..."

Father Dan immediately picked up on my discomfort and said, "Oh, we won't be worrying about that now, lads." He seemed to be around forty with prematurely gray hair. He had icy blue eyes and smiled a lot. We didn't stay long. He said he had to hear confessions. He served us some milk and cookies, and then we were on our way.

I was furious with Pete. "Why did you say that about me wanting to be a Catholic?"

"Well, don't you? We could go to church together."

"I can't. I told you I'm Jewish."

"Anybody can become Catholic. You just have to be baptized. You want to go to heaven, don't you?"

He had my thoughts all tied up in knots, and I felt inadequate talking about religion. "I have to get home."

A few days later, Pete wasn't at school. They said he was sick. I walked alone down College Avenue, and I stopped to look at some sneakers in a shoe store window.

I heard someone say, "Hey there, lad." In the reflection, I saw a black car had pulled to the curb and the passenger window was down. I turned around and saw Father Dan. He back-footed me with a wave, and yet I walked to the car.

"Hello, Father Dan."

"Would you be needing a ride?"

My parents had warned me against taking a ride from strangers, but Father Dan wasn't exactly a stranger. He was my best friend's spiritual father. "Okay."

I got in the car and told him my address.

"You're not in a hurry, are you? I have to stop by my house. There's something I want to show you."

"What is it?"

"It's a surprise."

The surprise turned out to be a new pool table. I sometimes played at a friend's house down the street and loved the crack of the balls hitting each other and the thrill of drilling the ball into the pocket. When I eyed the table with an excited expression on my face, Father Dan told me I could stop by any day after school and practice.

He racked up the balls and told me to break. After a few shots, he started giving me pointers. As I lined up a shot, he came up very close behind me. He leaned over and readjusted the position of my hands along the cue. I could smell onions on his breath. I missed the shot, but I was flattered he was taking an interest in me. My father was distant, and the only game we ever played together was horseshoes.

My next shot he pressed his body against my back. I could feel his erection, though I tried to convince myself that wasn't really what it was. My next shot went in. He hugged me and shouted, "That's my boy!"

After the game, we sat in leather chairs at the other end of the game room. He got me a soda and sat on the edge of his chair. His look leapt from jovial to grave in half a second. He told me part of his responsibility as a priest was to counsel boys going into their teen years.

Nice-looking young men like me would certainly get a lot of attention from girls, and I needed to be ready for it. He started asking me if I had erections and wet dreams and sexual thoughts about girls. Just that day in history class I had developed a relentless boner for no particular reason.

He informed me he had also studied medicine and could examine me to see if I was developing normally. No one had ever talked to me so frankly about sex. I appreciated he was treating me like an adult, and yet something didn't feel right. I was a bundle of emotions. I didn't want to insult him or act like I thought he was doing anything wrong. He gently prodded me to pull down my pants.

"Ah, you are circumcised. Are you Jewish?"

"Yes." My voice was shaking. I was afraid he was going to tell me I was going to the devil.

"No need to worry, my friend. I must show you, so you can have knowledge of what the good Lord intended men to be." He pulled down his pants and boxer shorts in a single gesture. "This is what uncircumcised looks like." He began to stroke it. The head slid out of the foreskin. I was mesmerized but now absolutely sure I needed to leave. He reached out and pulled me toward him.

"Please," I said. "I have to go home."

"Yes. Yes. But first I must give you my blessing." He got on his knees and took my penis in his mouth. Tears rolled down my cheeks at the same time my erection grew.

I pushed him away and ran to the front of the house, pulling up my pants as I went. I felt like I was in a horror film, and the front door would be locked or I wouldn't be able to find it or he would grab me just as I got there.

The door was unlocked, and I hurried down the front steps. I ran home and never told anyone what happened. Pete and I began to spend less and less time together. On our way home from school one day, he said he wanted to stop and see Father Dan. I told him I had a dentist appointment.

I sat on the orange plastic seat with my hands resting on the sun-mottled tabletop. I stared at a can of soda that was supposed to settle my stomach, but I was still on the verge of vomiting. A light rain began to fall. Moments earlier, Flaco had taken off on his motorcycle with the backpack full of cash. The exchange had gone off without a hitch. I was free.

I took another sip of the soda and wondered how long I would have to wait before someone picked me up. I was expecting Augie and M might come in a taxi. The rain cooled things off enough that I was ready to go inside. But before I could move, a black pickup pulled in front of the convenience store and screeched to a halt. The passenger door swung open.

"Come," said the driver. "Get in."

I wasn't about to jump into the truck of someone I didn't recognize. The image of Father Dan flashed in my head. How did I know this wasn't a friend of Flaco and Chato's?

"Hurry. I am the uncle of Ruben. We must go."

It started to rain harder. I got up and sauntered toward the truck. I stared at the driver. "Ruben's uncle?"

"Yes. Please get in."

As soon as I closed the door, Tomas stepped on the gas, scattering gravel in our wake. "Sorry. I am Tomas. You safe now. Your sister okay?"

"Yes. I think, at least for now."

Tomas got on the highway and stomped on the gas, throwing me back in my seat. I grabbed the seatbelt and put it on. Tomas hunched forward, his large body draped over the steering wheel, examining the road through the windshield wipers. A Chevy Suburban in front of us sprayed water from its tires and disappeared around a bend in the winding road. Tomas took the curve at high speed and came close behind the Suburban. He flashed his lights. The other vehicle increased its speed and Tomas followed close behind. I grasped the oh-shit handle above the door and held on for dear life.

Around the next bend, I could see the motorbike about a quarter mile ahead. "Are you going after him?" I said.

Tomas pointed to the Suburban. "They are my friends."

"I mean the guy on the motorcycle."

Tomas didn't answer.

As I was thrown from side to side, I put the missing pieces of the puzzle together. Ruben had gotten in touch with relatives in Mexico and asked them to help. I didn't want to believe the kind and gentle Ruben would have a vigilante type for a relative, but the way the two vehicles bore down on the motorcycle made me rethink that assessment, causing me further distress in my unsettled stomach.

I had no great love for Flaco, but I didn't want to see his guts splattered over the road. The Suburban was close behind the bike now. It pulled alongside and swerved toward the bike, forcing it off the road. The bike skidded and Flaco tumbled into a ravine out of sight. "Shit!" I said.

Tomas pulled over and got out. "Stay in the car," he told me.

The two men from the Suburban climbed down the ravine. A few minutes later, they dragged Flaco up and sat him on the side of the road. He was clearly in pain but alive. They took the pack off his back and handed it to Tomas. Tomas asked Flaco a question. Flaco shook his head, and one of the men slammed a fist across his face. I winced as if the pain were mine. I was afraid I was going to witness an execution. I had to stop it. I opened the door and got out.

Tomas walked over and told me to get back in the truck.

"Don't kill him," I pleaded.

Tomas looked at me in surprise. "You want mercy for these men who hurt you and your sister?"

"No, I mean yes. I don't want them to die for what they did."

"Don't worry. We need him to show us where is your sister." He gently pushed me back into the truck, handed me the backpack, and closed the door.

I rolled down the window and watched the men through a steady rain. One of the men put pressure on Flaco's shoulder. It must have been injured, as he screamed in pain. Flaco held up his other hand in a gesture of submission. A few minutes later, they put Flaco in the back of the Suburban and drove off. Tomas returned to the truck.

"All good," said Tomas. "You go home now."

"I hope you know what you're doing."

"Ruben is family. His family is my family. I only do what I can."

"What are you going to do with them when AJ is safe?"

Tomas looked at me with a smile. "Don't worry, my friend."

Tomas's pickup honked once as he pulled into the loading zone in front of the hotel. M, Augie, and Arnie rushed out from the lobby. I jumped out of the passenger seat with a big smile, though I tried to hold it in check out of respect for AJ. Augie embraced me. "I'm sorry for every fucking mean thing I ever did to you…or said…or…"

"Whoa, Augie. I'm back, but AJ isn't."

"I know. I know. We're getting the rest of the money in a day or two. Our lawyer is wiring it to Tomas."

Tomas got out of the truck, holding the backpack heavy with cash. It was caked with reddish-brown mud. Or was it blood? He handed it to M.

Augie and M both looked at Tomas in shock.

"Or maybe not," said Augie.

M refused to touch the backpack. She stood in front of Tomas, and despite him being a head taller, her fists were clenched as if she was going to punch him in the face.

"What have you done? We agreed no one would be hurt. You put our sister in danger," she screamed. People walking by on the street gave them a wide berth.

Tomas was relaxed and straightforward. "Well, we need some information, so we punish the guy a little bit. Don't hurt him too much. And we take his phone so he no contact his brother."

I stepped forward. "He's alive. I saw them put him in a van. He was the mean one. AJ is with the other brother, Chato. He's not a bad guy."

M whirled toward me. "And you! You left your little sister alone with the 'not bad guy'?"

"We argued about it and she insisted. She feels safe with him. He's the one who convinced his brother to make the exchange deal in the first place. And the deal? That was *not* our idea."

Everyone looked at Augie.

"It seemed like a good idea at the time. Negotiations. Isn't that what you do? Get them to agree to something?"

"Don't worry," said Tomas. "My men get your sister right now."

M huffed. "Your men? What? You have an army?"

Tomas shrugged. "Only few guys. You're not happy to have your money back?"

"It means nothing," yelled M, "as long as our sister is not safe."

12: AJ

Flaco had taken Lio on the motorcycle to the rendezvous, leaving Chato and me alone at the cabin. Flaco was supposed to text as soon as the exchange was made. Chato had brought some food with lots of vegetables, but it sat untouched in front of me. Our alone moment had arrived and, like a first date, we didn't know what to do with it. Chato stood and walked around the room.

I smiled at his awkwardness. "Chato isn't your real name?"

He stopped pacing, but didn't look right at me. "Nobody in my family uses given names. Sounds too formal. Plus my parents chose old names."

"Old names? So, what is it? Can I at least know your real name?"

"You'll laugh."

"No, I won't."

"Gabino."

I chuckled, more from the tension than any humor in his name.

"See? Damn it!"

"Sorry. It's not that bad. Really."

He pulled out one of the chairs and sat on it backward. "Why everyone calls you AJ? I like April."

"How did you know that?"

"Your driver's license."

"You went through my purse?" I acted offended, but was at the same time flattered that he was curious about me. He would know my age, too. I guessed I was at least five years older. "That is not cool."

"What? That you are older than me?"

"Shut up. You can't just go through people's things."

"Sorry, April."

"Nobody calls me that...except my husband. He calls me April June."

Chato winced as if an injury he had forgotten suddenly flared up. "You are missing him?"

We had avoided talking about my other life. He didn't know my marriage was in trouble and had been for a long time. How should I answer his question? If I told the truth, it could give him false hope. "I miss my boys."

"Yes, they look very nice."

"You looked at the pictures in my wallet, too?"

"You don't tell me nothing, so..."

Chato stopped talking, and his ears pricked up. A car had stopped out on the road. Cars doors opened and closed. It obviously wasn't Flaco. Chato put a finger to his lips. We both stared at the door, expecting it to burst open. Chato grabbed his backpack and motioned for me to get my purse.

He opened the door a crack and peered outside. He couldn't see down to the road because of the trees, which meant they couldn't see him. We had a chance.

Chato took my hand, and we slipped out the door, running toward the back of a nearby shed. Around the corner of the shed, we saw shadows on the path moving toward the cabin.

"This is not good," Chato whispered.

I could scream. They could be my rescuers. But what would they do to Chato? I touched his arm, and he turned toward me. I looked him in the eye. I saw fear and sorrow and tender regret. I felt like a tragic character in one of Augie's stories.

"I'm sorry," he whispered.

I nodded at the woods. "I'm a good runner."

"*Vámonos.*"

We stepped lightly at first, trying not to snap branches underfoot. Chato pointed in one direction as if he knew where to go. We started to jog. The sound of the cabin door being kicked open echoed through the woods. We ran faster. After about ten minutes, we came upon a group of houses. Chato pointed at one of them.

"What?" I said.

"Is where we live, me and Flaco."

"Where's your car?"

"What car?"

"The SUV. The one you picked us up in."

"Oh, that one," Chato said with a snigger. "It was a rental."

He led me along the side of the house to the back. Paint was peeling from the stucco walls, and I noticed a broken window. The yard was overgrown with weeds, and the fence to our left was made of old rusty bedsprings. I guessed the inside wasn't much better. This was where he lived. What was I thinking to tie my fate to his?

As we went around the back corner, Chato stopped short and motioned for me to squat down against the wall. The back door hung on its frame. He crept forward and looked inside. The place had been ransacked. We waited a moment, listening for any sounds coming from inside the house, but we could only hear clucking in the neighbor's yard. On the other side of the fence, a young girl threw grain to the chickens.

"We can't stay here. We have to go," said Chato. "They found us."

I felt a new fear. We were both in danger. "Who?"

"I don't know. Wait here," said Chato. He approached the fence to talk to the girl.

I sat on the back stoop and examined the scratches on my arms from the branches in the woods. When I looked up, the neighbor girl had gone inside the house and a few minutes later a man came out. The man pointed at Chato's house several times while they conversed in Spanish.

Chato came back to get me, and we hurried to the neighbor's truck.

"Where are we going?"

"Dropping you off at your hotel like we should do that night we pick you up." He checked his phone messages for the third time in the last half hour.

"What's the matter?"

"This whole thing is a disaster. Flaco never send me text. He promised. Something happen."

"What are you going to do?"

"You see I can't go back to our home. And those men who come to cabin, I fear for Flaco. I try to find out what happen. Then I have to leave town. Disappear."

His desperation caused a twitching inside my chest. He would drop me off, and I would never see him again. Emptiness shook me. Why wasn't I overjoyed to be reunited with my siblings? Then home to my boys? I imagined a scene on my front lawn, Elijah running to hide his tears in my hug, Jason standing back a moment, then giving in to embrace his mother. Over the top of their heads, I saw Bart, arms crossed in front of him, smug and angry.

I would walk by him and into the house. Food my mother-in-law bought would be in the refrigerator. I would fix breaded chicken, roasted potatoes, and broccoli. Only I would eat the broccoli. I would start drinking white wine while I prepared dinner and continue throughout the meal as my boys talked about things that had happened since I left. My husband would ask about my "vacation" in a sarcastic tone, and I would give him a cautionary look, and then smiling at my boys, would pretend the trip had been uneventful. I would send the boys to do their homework, and Bart would slink off to his converted garage space to do whatever he did there. Later, I would put the boys to bed, and they would tell me I was acting funny. Then I would crawl into bed and hope Bart wouldn't try to touch me when he came in at one or two in the morning.

I would wake up the next morning with the notion I couldn't do it anymore. And yet divorce seemed like a mountain I couldn't climb. If I stepped out of the vehicle at the hotel and said a final goodbye to Chato, it would be the first step in a trajectory back to the life I dreaded. My sibs would, of course, pledge to support me and then reality would force them back into their complicated lives, their crises, their insecurities. The trauma of the kidnapping would soon be overshadowed by the march of time.

I found Chato's hand on the seat between us. A pulse shot up my arm and then danced through my body. "Where exactly are you going?" I said.

"I think DF."

"Where?"

"Mexico City."

"To your brother's."

"Maybe."

"I want to go with you."

"No, no, no. You crazy!"

I squeezed his hand. "I'm serious."

"You can't. No way." He let me play with his fingers. "Why you don't hate me?"

"I should, huh?"

I sat in the corner of the bus station with my hair tucked into a Puerto Vallarta baseball cap and my eyes hidden by large sunglasses, both of which I had just bought at a kiosk outside the main entrance. Chato had left to see if he could find out any information about Flaco.

"I come back soon as I can," said Chato.

"Be careful."

He started to leave, and then turned around. "Are you sure about this?"

"Yes," I said, though I wasn't sure about anything at that moment.

He backed away, a sad look on his face. I guess he didn't expect to see me again. I was no longer a prisoner, neither physically nor psychologically. I could stand up, walk out the door, and never look back.

I took out the phone Chato had returned and opened my photo app to look at pictures of my boys. In a photo from our last trip to Tahoe, Elijah peered out from his hoodie, soft and vulnerable. Jason clowned for the camera. I had a silent conversation with them, telling them why I couldn't come home right now. Being away from Bart this past week, albeit most of it in captivity of a different kind, had made me realize I didn't miss him at all. How could I feel so little for someone I had known for almost twenty years and been married to for the last twelve? Running off with Chato was insane, but going back to the life I led before seemed crazier.

I went to the message app and sent a text to Lio, asking him if he could bring my bag to the bus station, but only if he could do it without anyone knowing. I could face Lio with my decision but not M or Augie. An hour later, he showed up.

"You're the best," I said when he rolled my pink carry-on into the station, drawing raised eyebrows from some of the other travelers.

We hugged. "My crazy sister," he said.

"I don't expect you to understand."

"Things are really that bad with Bart?"

"How bad is feeling every day that you have made a big mistake? I suppose I got used to his moping and whining during the Obama years. But his empowerment has become really unbearable after the last election."

"So, the answer is running off with a kidnapper?"

"I don't in my wildest dreams think it is *the* answer. I want to see if it is *an* answer, if anything real is in what I'm feeling. I just need some time. We're going to Mexico City for a few days. And please make sure everyone knows Chato's not coercing me in any way. Of course M will roll her eyes, but what can we do? By the way, who were those men that came to the cabin?"

"Ruben called his uncle here in Mexico and asked him to help. I guess he's sort of a big shot in these parts. We're still not sure exactly how big or how bad, but he does have men I wouldn't want to mess with working for him. They chased down Flaco and got our money back."

"What? We got the hundred thousand back?"

"Right after Flaco got the money, he left me at a convenience store. Ruben's uncle picked me up. Then he and his men followed Flaco and forced him off the road."

"Did they hurt him?"

"It wasn't gentle. He was still alive the last time I saw him."

"Should I tell Chato?"

"He might already know. You said he went off to figure out what happened to Flaco. But if he doesn't find out, I wouldn't tell him. It might delay your departure. If you're going to do this, you need to get as far away from here as possible."

"What the brothers did was fucked up, but those men need to be called off. We got our money back. We're both safe."

"What was that you said a while back about killing the motherfuckers who would keep you from your kids?"

"I guess they aren't the ones keeping me from my kids anymore. Believe me, this is not easy. It's tearing me apart. It sucks how kids always get caught in the struggle. I guess you know something about that. It's not fair."

"I screwed up with Belle. Don't want you to do the same."

"I won't. But I'm *not* going back to him." We both fell silent as my thoughts wandered through the emotional minefield of being a parent. I put a hand on his arm. "Could you do one thing for me? Visit my boys and tell them I love them? Give them these? Tell them I'll be home as soon as I can." I pulled a couple of souvenirs out of a bag: a *lucha libre* mask for Jason and a hand-carved flute for Elijah. "You're probably the only one Bart will let in the house."

"Lucky me. What do I tell him?"

"I'll call him."

"And say what?'

"I don't know yet."

I wasn't sitting in the same place when Chato returned. I had gone to the ATM across the street so we could pay for the tickets in cash. Upon my return to the terminal, someone had taken my seat, and I had to choose one on the other side of the waiting room. His face went through the complete repertoire of emotions that a Mexican male might allow himself to express in public. There was the controlled panic of his searching brown eyes, the gentle falling of his bruise-colored lips, the subtle collapse of his shoulders, and then a last-ditch desperate sweep of the room.

When his eyes met mine, the corners of his mouth lifted in surprise, his eyes blinking in case it might be an apparition. I smiled, and he started toward me, shifting his bag back to its position after it had begun to slide on his slumping shoulder.

I fought the inclination to jump up and run to him, remaining instead frozen on the seat, checking my emotions, telling myself to breathe. I had reached a milestone. When I had been a captive, I looked forward to seeing him because it broke the boredom. Now that I had my freedom, I anxiously awaited his return because I really wanted to see him.

He looked down at my bag and chuckled slightly.

"I know. It's god-awful ugly, isn't it? I had to pick something up at the last minute. M didn't give us much time. She just said we were going to Puerto Vallarta, and we had two days to get ready. I don't normally buy things in pink. I'm really not like that. I should've just gotten the black one, but everyone has black. I once almost walked off with the wrong bag, thinking it was mine." Nervous babbling. I felt a churning inside me I hadn't experienced in a long time.

"How did you get it?"

I realized he wasn't staring at the bag because of its color, but because of its presence. "Oh. Lio brought it to me."

"And you're still here. He don't convince you to leave with him?" This time, he let his smile expand to its full breadth.

"He thought it was strange, but he understands, sort of."

"If you was my sister, I think I—"

"Stop. Don't say it. I'm sure you wouldn't let your sister do something so crazy."

"But your crazy is good for me." He sat down next to me.

"I can't promise you anything. I'm just not ready to go home yet."

"So, I am like a distraction while you find where you are going."

"Meeting the way we did doesn't exactly give us much direction. Might make a good movie, though." I knew I had to be careful with sarcasm. It hadn't gone over well with him before. I put my hand on his knee. "I do like you."

"I said I'm sorry."

I tilted my head down and looked at him sideways. Clearly, sorry wasn't even close to being adequate. "Did you find out anything about Flaco?"

"He still don't answer his phone. Nobody see him. I'm worried."

"Sounds like he took the money and ran." I wanted to see how he would react. He could be lying to me. He could have met with Flaco. He might know their venture had all been for naught.

"You think I want some of this money? No. I don't want it. I'm done with this. I only want to go to Mexico City to find Abelino."

We spend a good part of our lives listening to people talk about small things and big things, trying to discern if they're lying or telling the truth. We look at eyes and facial expressions. We use our intuition and past history, trying not to let our feelings get in the way. Nothing about Chato led me to believe he was being untruthful with me. "I think it's good you're getting away from Flaco for a while."

"Maybe, but you see only one side of Flaco."

"When one side leads to me being kidnapped, I think that's all I need to see."

"He have much conflict with our father. I was still a little boy when my father die, but Flaco have it very hard with him. I think it make him a angry person. But for me and my mom, he do anything. When we go to States, he save my ass many times when I do something stupid. We have many bad things happen over there. Employers rob us. If we protest, we get beat up. So many things. Then they send us back. We are very angry with gringos."

"I get it. I was part of your revenge plot."

He grimaced and then smiled. "No, *mi güerita.* I know from first moment our plan is stupid. That night we pick you up, I argue with Flaco. He call me weak, *maricón.* I made him swear to me we never hurt you guys. Even we don't get any money. I told you I can never hurt you."

"You ruined my vacation, not to mention you made me afraid I'd never see my boys again."

"Maybe if you don't have problems with your, how you say, *esposo,* you don't flirt with me that night."

"It's my fault I got kidnapped? That's tremendous!"

"If there is something I can do to make it up to you, help you if I can."

"*You* want to help me?" I made it sound like a ridiculous notion. My core had begun to melt during his little speech about his struggles in the States. But then the voices revved up, questioning, doubting. If Bart had been a choice alien to the world of my upbringing, Chato was from a different universe.

Chato started to say something, but he was cut off by the announcement of our bus to Mexico City. "We must go," he said.

We fell into silence as the Primera Plus bus plunged into the darkness of what would be an almost twelve-hour ride to Mexico City. I stared out the window and shivered with the extreme air conditioning of the bus. Chato pulled a jacket out of his bag and draped it over me. It smelled of him, fresh-cut wood and soft-scented soap. I leaned my head against the window and fell asleep.

13: Augie

Tomas came to my hotel room with head lowered, portending bad news. He had gotten a text from his men. "Am very sorry," he said. "They find the cabin but no your sister or the guy holding her."

M and I looked at each other. "We know," I said.

"What?"

"We got a message from AJ just a few minutes ago," said M. "She *says* she's okay."

The despair on Tomas's face transformed into surprise. "Nothing more?"

M started to talk, but I jumped in with a more level voice. "She asks that we not look for her. She is with the brother, but not by force."

Tomas raised his bushy eyebrows. "*Hijole!*"

"She says not to worry," said M in a voice laced with betrayal. "Can you imagine? I think he still has some power over her. It doesn't make sense."

"Lio told us...well, we had suspected something was going on between them," I said.

"It's not real," M insisted. "Our sister is very confused right now, the captivity and everything. It's not uncommon."

"We know where the brothers live. Maybe they go there," said Tomas.

"We appreciate everything you've done, but we'll take it from here," I said.

"There is one more thing," said M. "Do you still have the brother? I hope you haven't done anything foolish."

"He is with my men."

M stood in take-charge mode. "We must speak with him. Please take us to him."

"Okay. We go."

"Shouldn't we wait for Lio and Arnie to get back?" I said to M. They had gone for a walk.

"No," M said. We both knew the longer we waited, the better chance we would have a murder on our hands. "Let's go."

It was a short drive to the cabin. M and I asked Tomas and his men to wait outside. Inside was a potpourri of musty wood, rank plumbing, and just a hint of AJ's perfume.

"This is the place all right," I said. "I can smell that Dolce & Gabbana shit AJ always keeps in her purse."

M shuddered. She claimed to have a perfume allergy, but it was really because she couldn't understand why anyone would want to smell like that.

Flaco sat hunched over in a chair with rays of sun from the skylight focused on him as if calling for the truth. His face was caked with mud and dried blood. He supported his left arm with his right as though he was afraid it might fall off.

My stomach turned when I saw Flaco. The sight of blood, dried or not, always made me queasy. I forgot for a moment this man kidnapped my brother and sister. He was a human being who had been beaten. I had a recurring nightmare Ruben was attacked by white thugs for being Latino or gay or both. Before Flaco raised his head to look at us, I had, for an instant, a flash it was Ruben sitting before us. I felt sorry for him.

M was not so ready to forgive and forget. She stood over him with the attitude that the kidnapping plot and AJ's disappearance with the brother was somehow against her personally. "Do realize what you have done?" she shouted. When he didn't respond, she put her face close to his. "You understand English, right?"

Flaco nodded.

I took a softer tone. "We just want to know where our sister is."

"I don't know."

"Have you checked your phone? Maybe there's a message from your brother," I said.

"I lose my phone when they force me off the road."

"Tomas says you live nearby. Do you think they are there?" said M.

"I don't think so. Probably he don't take her there. It is shithole. Maybe the house of my mother."

I gave him my cell to call his mother.

After he ended the call, he shook his head. "She no see Chato, not at home or the restaurant."

"Restaurant?" I said.

"*Mi mama* have restaurant. I mean *had*. She close it today. Can't make payment. They probably take it from her."

M and I looked at each other. "Is that what this was all about?" I said.

Flaco nodded. He paused, and a painful smile came to his face. "Don't worry. Chato won't hurt your sister. He like her too much." His voice changed to a whisper. "And please don't send these men after my brother. They maybe hurt him and then he look as bad as me. He have beautiful face."

"Come on," said M. "You must have some idea where your brother would go."

"No. Really, I don't."

"We won't share anything you tell me with Tomas and his men," I assured him. "We're finished working with them."

"I swear I don't know."

"Okay. We're done," said M.

M called Tomas to come inside. "We're taking him to the hospital."

Tomas shook his head. "Okay, *señora*, if that's what you want."

We took him to a clinic in town, and I offered to stay with him. I thought I might get more information speaking to him in Spanish without M looking over my shoulder and Tomas's men outside.

I sat doing my homework in the breakfast nook, a location central to the comings and goings of the house, between the kitchen and the dining room, near the back door, and with a view out the windows to the driveway. When I came home from school, I usually burrowed into my half of the room I shared with Lio and read, did homework, or simply polished my dreams. That was before Emilio, a foreign exchange student, arrived to spend his high school junior year with our family. I was a freshman at the time.

Gloria was in the kitchen preparing dinner, humming what was one of her current favorite songs, *"Piel Canela."* She had been listening to Trio Los Panchos a lot because her Spanish teacher told her the lyrics were easy to understand. She could do a mean impression of Eydie Gorme, who often sang with the group. Her Spanish phase had continued long after Lio had been born and she was still plodding down the long and winding road toward mastering the Spanish language. Agreeing to host Emilio was another stepping stone along that road.

"What does *piel canela* mean?" I asked.

"It means skin the color of cinnamon. Kind of like yours."

"I thought I was olive-skinned."

"Well, I guess, more like Emilio's then. The song also talks about *ojos negros*, black eyes, which is definitely Emilio." There was a heavy sigh in her voice.

I hadn't as yet dared to look at Emilio long enough to determine his eye color, but I planned to do so as soon as possible. "What are you making?"

"Oh, just a wild rice casserole and lemon chicken." Dinners had certainly improved since Emilio had arrived. Gloria was never one to fuss in the kitchen, and her cooking skills were mediocre. Lately, we would come home to find the kitchen counters lined with cookbooks she had brought home from the library.

The wall phone rang, and Gloria hurried to answer it. After her greeting, she changed to a halting Spanish, blushing slightly. She placed the receiver on the counter and shouted up the back stairs. "Emilio, *una llamada de Mexico.*" Then she came around the corner and winked at me. She stood over me, waiting for a comment on her Spanish.

"*Mucho bien,*" I said. My siblings and I constantly teased our mother about her Spanish obsession. I planned to study French, a cultured language I liked to say.

"No, darling, it's *muy bien.* Adverb," said Gloria. She went back to her cooking.

I stared at the receiver, thinking about the person, probably Emilio's mother, on the other end of the line in another country far away.

The back door opened, and M came in from tennis practice. "*Hola, madre,*" she said. "*Qué tal?*" If she had put her mind to it, she could have learned Spanish in a few months. But she wasn't interested except to torment

Gloria. She had chosen German at school, the most difficult elective.

M came into the breakfast nook sporting a warm-up suit and an Andre Agassi mullet. I noticed the beads of sweat sharing her upper lip with a light mustache.

"What are you doing?" she said.

"I'm studying. Stupid question."

"No. What are you *doing*?" Since Emilio had arrived, M hadn't been in a good mood. They had put Emilio in AJ's bedroom, forcing M to share her room with AJ. Since I was already sharing a room with Lio, it was the only arrangement that would work.

Emilio bounded down the stairs, plopped down on the stool next to the phone, scooped up the receiver, and put it to his lips as if he were going to kiss it.

"Oh, I get it," said M.

"Shut up, Andre!"

She sniggered. "I'll leave you two alone."

I had a chance to look at Emilio's eyes without being noticed. They were a mysterious black. With Emilio concentrating on his call, I could observe him, stare at the hairs on his chin. He would need to start shaving soon. His hair was wavy and thick, longish. He was wearing shorts, and I took in the cinnamon skin of his legs covered with curly dark hair. The hand not holding the receiver fell between his legs, and he very gently squeezed his crotch. I was mesmerized. I felt a chill run up my spine.

But the real magic happened when I listened to Emilio's voice, the flow of vowels and consonants that sounded like a glorious symphony to my ears. I had no idea what the words meant, but they surrounded me like a warm bath. This was what the language was supposed to sound like. I finally understood my mother's infatuation with Spanish. I could feel Emilio's joy at talking to his mother and see the stab of loneliness in his eyes. I broke my stare and looked down at my book. The words blurred. I wanted to listen to that voice, the melodious phonemes forever.

Lio came in the back door and broke my trance. He had been shooting baskets in the driveway. As he walked past Emilio, Emilio stuck out his arm for a fist pump without breaking the flow of his conversation. The fist pump segued into their special handshake.

Lio, nine years old, was at his most adorable. Everyone loved Lio. How was it that Lio and Emilio had a special handshake while Emilio hardly acknowledged my existence? I had a million questions I wanted to ask him about life in Mexico, his family, why he wanted to come to the States, what he thought about his experience so far. In the rare times we were alone together, my tongue dried up. My voice was changing, and I was always afraid my nervousness might make my voice crack.

Lio turned to me. "Hey, Augie, I just made six baskets in a row."

"I'm so happy," I said in a low voice. "Now, shut up. Emilio's trying to have a long distance conversation."

"You shut up!"

Gloria poked her head in from the kitchen. "Both of you be quiet! Can't you see that Emilio is talking on the phone? It's long distance!"

I had obliterated Lio's cheerful mood. "You're such a jerk," he whispered.

"Lio, come here a minute," said Gloria. "I want to tell you something."

I looked down at the blank page in my notebook. I was supposed to be writing an essay. I felt ridiculous. First M had called me out, and then Lio had his little moment with Emilio. I knew I should pack up my books and move, but I suffered from a profound inertia. I would look even more ridiculous if I left now.

Emilio's conversation seemed to be winding down. I heard the first *adios*. After he repeated *adios* at least five more times, he ended with a string of I love yous and hung up the phone. The emotion in Emilio's voice drew my head up.

Emilio turned to me and smiled with those sweet, black, slightly teary eyes. He sighed, and his shoulders drooped. I felt a powerful, troubling punch in my gut. Among the many lasting effects of that day of listening to and watching Emilio talk on the phone was an infatuation with Spanish. I never teased my mother again about wanting to speak the language, and the following semester I changed from French to Spanish for my foreign language requirement.

By the end of his year with us, we had become friends. He helped me with my Spanish homework. Having him sit next to me while he explained the lesson was both heavenly and torturous. Sometimes I would deliberately make mistakes just so he would correct me in his stern teacher voice.

We kept in contact with Emilio over the years, birthdays and holidays. I contacted him on one of my trips to Mexico before I met Ruben, and he invited me to visit. He picked me up at the airport in a limousine with a driver.

"You have grown up, *mi hermano*," he said.

I wanted to say, "And you've grown out." My first Latin crush had put on a lot of weight. He was only in his thirties and losing his hair. He looked much older, with crow's feet around his eyes and puffy cheeks.

"How's your family?" I asked. I knew he was married with three kids.

"Good. Good. I work too much, though." He patted his belly. "I have no time for exercise. How do you stay so thin?"

"I worry a lot."

He laughed. "How's your Spanish?"

I switched to Spanish, and he told me I spoke very well.

We arrived at his home, a compound, really, where his parents and a sister also lived with her family. The wall around the compound had razor wire on top, and an armed guard at the gate. I knew Emilio was rich, but I had no idea they had to live with such high security. He told me an armed driver took his kids to school because he knew a family whose son had been kidnapped. It ended badly.

His wife was lovely and the children were cute but spoiled. At that point in my life, I found children tiresome. We left the kids with the nanny while they took me to see the cathedral in the old part of town and the Government Palace Museum. But mostly we concentrated on the business and banking area of the city where they pointed out the headquarters of all the international companies. They kept telling me how Americanized the city was, as if that equaled progress. In the meantime, the driver with a bulge under his jacket kept a keen eye on the surroundings.

I only stayed a couple of days, though I had kept my schedule open to stay much longer. I told them I had obligations elsewhere. It was a sad visit. Emilio seemed stressed about work and the way he had to live. We drank a lot of whiskey one night after dinner, and he told me how wonderful the year he spent with us had been. He had never felt so free.

He talked a lot about the girlfriend he had dated when he lived with us. He said they were in love. He wished he had married her. They wrote regularly after he went back home until his family made him cut it off. I remembered her pert little nose and her blonde hair so straight it looked like she ironed it. Of course I hated her because he would insist on inviting her when we went swimming at Lake Temescal. While they made out, I would observe Emilio's technique, the way he slipped his tongue in her mouth. But my consolation for tolerating her presence was waiting for his hard-on, watching it grow as it pushed against his trunks.

Sometimes she would catch me looking. He would roll over on his stomach until it went away, and then get up and run into the water. She would look at me with a smirk, letting me know she was well aware of my crush. She probably resented me as much as I resented her. Emilio had the same charisma as Lio that drew people to him. It was bad enough that the girlfriend, nameless as I put no effort into remembering her name, had to fend off other girls who were after him, but she also had to put up with *mi hermanito*, his "little brother."

14: AJ

The bus pulled into the Terminal Central Del Norte at noon, squeezing into position in a long row of buses parked at an angle. We got off the bus and entered the building where we joined a sea of travelers rolling their bags over the polished stone floors. The halls were lined with the booths of various bus companies, each with several uniformed agents peering out expectantly for people needing tickets. Some of them shouted the destinations where their companies traveled.

We entered the pyramid-shaped central foyer, filled with light and the bustle of travel. I was comforted by the fact that Chato stayed close to me, leading me through the crowd, occasionally putting his hand on the small of my back. I felt overwhelmed by the number of people, the loudspeakers blaring announcements in a language I didn't understand, and the sheer absurdity of my decision to accompany Chato, knowing whatever road I ended up taking would lead to a complicated future.

"What now?" I said.

"Find my brother."

"You have his address, right?"

"Uh, no."

"A phone number?"

"No."

"So where are we going?"

"Zona Rosa. Is where we find the gay bars."

"What? We're going to bar hop until we find him? What's his name?"

"Abelino. I tell you we all have strange names." Chato held the door open for me. In front of the building, groups of taxi hawkers tried to steer us toward the line of the cabs snaking the length of the terminal. "We can take taxi or metro. I think is better taxi."

"Yes. And a decent hotel, please. Don't worry how much it costs. I need to take a five-hour shower."

We settled in the taxi, and Chato discussed the hotel with the driver.

"The plan?" I said when the hotel discussion seemed to have ended.

"Okay. Here is the thing. It's not totally looking for a needle in...how is it...dry grass?"

"A haystack."

"Yes." He exhaled. "This is difficult." He rubbed his palms on his knees. "Before Abelino go to Mexico City, he like go to Guadalajara on weekend. One time I am there, too. I am walking by a café, and he is sitting at an outdoor table with some friends. I stop where they cannot see me. One of them is dressed like woman, but is not woman. Abelino wear like a blouse and some eye makeup. They call my brother Lina. They talk and laugh very high like girls. They move their hands in the air."

"What's your point?" I said, amused and disgusted at the same time.

"Don't be mad. I'm just telling what I see. It hit me, you know, that he like to dress as woman. I feel awful."

"It's not about you. It's his life."

"I know. I'm trying to understand. But my idea is we go to bars where they have drag shows, and I think we find my brother."

The sincerity with which he came to this conclusion tickled me. "*You* are going to drag shows?"

"Why not? Is not contagious, I think."

"This might be fun."

"I think you maybe say that."

The taxi pulled up in front of Hotel PF on Avenida Florencia in Zona Rosa. It was midday, and the area was busy with lunch goers, many in business attire. Before walking into the lobby, Chato said, "Are we getting one room or two?"

"I'm assuming you might be short on cash."

"I have some money," he said without conviction.

"How about a room with two beds? I need nights of undisturbed sleep."

At the front desk, Chato negotiated the room with two double beds. The desk clerk asked, "*Cuantas noches?*"

Chato turned to me. "How many nights?"

The question caught me off guard. To answer a specific number would make it sound as if we had a plan for the future, which we most definitely did not. "Three," I answered definitively.

The discussion with the clerk continued. Chato again turned to me. "Dear, do you have our credit card?"

"Of course, honey." I gave him my ATM card connected to a personal account Bart didn't even know about.

The room was neither elegant nor shabby. The two double beds were made up with crisp white sheets and white spreads with gold brocade runners across the foot. Above each bed was a print with two swans under a golden sun in slightly different positions. To me it looked like heaven.

"Okay," I said. "I'm going to take a shower and then a bath. Maybe another shower. Then I'm going to crawl into those sheets for a nap. I'd like some privacy. You can do research, check out the neighborhood. Wake me up around six, and we'll go to dinner. I'll probably be bitchy when you wake me up, but don't take it personally."

He stood in the middle of the room slack-jawed.

I gave him the same smile I did with my boys after having given them a barrage of orders. "You can put your backpack down."

He dropped his backpack on a chair. "May I use the restroom?"

"Yes, but make it quick."

He started to walk past me in a snit. I grabbed his arm. "I'm kidding! Take all the time you need."

He looked down at my hand on his arm. He tried to pull me into a hug, but I resisted. "Not now. I feel grody."

He knitted his eyebrows. "What?"

"Dirty. I'm sure I probably stink."

He dropped his hand and sniffed the air. "I just smell the perfume...same since the first night I meet you."

"Go." I gave him a little push toward the bathroom.

I lay back in the bathtub surrounded by bubbles, all the little bottle of complimentary hotel body wash would produce. I tried not to deliberate for the hundredth time that day over the crazy thing I had done. I could, of course, back out at any time, hurry home, and resume my old life. I'd already had several opportunities to do that, and I hadn't. It was time to embrace the thrill of doing something completely against convention. I hadn't asked for the kidnapping that set me on this course, but perhaps it was an opportunity, a rope to climb out of the pit. What kind of mother could I be to my sons if the encroaching numbness I had suffered these last few years took over completely?

And then there was Chato. What did I pretend to do with him? Despite my unhappiness with Bart, I had never betrayed my marriage. I doubted Bart could say the same. Modesto was full of unhappy wives who would be more than happy to open their legs to him. It was so obvious at the parties I couldn't find an excuse to get out of, especially the backyard barbecues where I nearly drowned in the dual bogs of sweltering heat and tiresome conversation.

I thought of the time I spent in Hawaii. The front desk job was tedious and I was underpaid, but I loved making my own money and having free time all to myself. It was the complete opposite of being a stay-at-home mom. I knew I couldn't go back to those carefree days in Hawaii. I had to have my boys in my life. But I was determined to get back at least some of the independence I had back then.

I rose up out of the water, a new creature, clean and resolute. I had an hour before Chato came back. Most of my clothes I had brought to Mexico were still clean though wrinkled. I put on tight jeans and a blue top with a split neckline. I left my hair frizzy and wild. I didn't have time to do anything about it. I examined myself in the mirror and was happy with the results.

Chato knocked on the door. As soon as I opened it, he said, "You miss me?"

"I'm still here. That might mean something." I waved him in.

I sat on the edge of one of the beds while Chato stood awkwardly in the middle of the room as if he were visiting.

"Here I am very popular," he said. "Two ladies offer for to come to my hotel. I say I am with my wife." He chuckled.

"Oh, really."

"And one man on Amberes Street flirt with me."

"Did you beat him up?"

He still wasn't used to my acerbic humor. His eyes registered disappointment, and he clenched his fists in frustration.

"I'm kidding," I said.

"Hah! First I need informations from him. Then I beat him up."

I enjoyed teasing him, and even more when he recovered. "What did you find out?"

He reached in his pocket and pulled out a scrap of paper. "This guy write down for me where and when of drag shows. He work in place called Lollipoop or something like that."

I burst into laughter. "I think you mean Lollipop."

"Yeah, whatever." He leaned back against the desk and half sat on it. "They have show tomorrow night. Only one place tonight but is not in Zona Rosa. It is La Perla downtown."

"Do you want to go there?"

"I need eat first. You hungry? I saw this place near called La Casa de Toño. A lot of people waiting out front, so I guess is decent."

"I could eat something."

We stepped out in the street to the sound of honking cars, loud music from a bar up the block, bright lights, and crowds of people going in both directions. I balked at the overstimulation and had the urge to return to the peace and quiet of the room. I was not a city girl and never liked crowds much. Chato must have sensed it, because he put his arm around me and guided me in the direction of the restaurant.

The restaurant was almost as daunting as the streets of the Zona Rosa. Wait people in white polo shirts and black aprons navigated around full tables, carrying trays of pozole, tacos, burritos, and quesadillas. The air had the warm smell of fried corn. The animated crowd of mostly young people, many who appeared to be from the local LGBT community, spoke in loud voices to compete with the clattering plates, the shouting of orders, and the mariachi music coming from the speakers. The restaurant was a mini-fiesta of eating, friendship, and life. Tables emptied, bus people rapidly cleared piles of dishes, and new diners quickly descended upon the chairs.

"It seems like everyone in Mexico City comes here. Maybe if we sit here long enough, your brother will pass through."

"Yeah, maybe." He seemed preoccupied with the menu. "I think there is not so much vegetarian things."

I smiled. "That's okay. I'm not really a vegetarian. Anything with chicken is fine."

Chato's forehead wrinkled and his eyes narrowed. "*Híjole!* Why you like to molest me?"

I giggled. "Interesting choice of words. I don't think molest is the word you were looking for. We normally use it to talk about unwanted sexual advances."

"*And* you like make fun of my English!"

"Just a reminder. Less than a week ago, you pointed a gun in my face."

"It have no bullets."

"Oh, I'm so relieved."

The waiter came by to pick up the slip of paper where Chato had ticked off the items we wanted to order. "You want a *michelada*?" Chato asked me. "Is like a spicy beer cocktail."

"Sure. Why not?"

"*Dos micheladas*," Chato shouted to the waiter.

Chato intertwined his fingers and put them on the table. "Can we not talk about what happened? I say a million times 'I am sorry.'"

I stared at his hands. "Do you have a plan?"

"For what?"

"For the rest of your life."

"Do you?"

Good point, I thought. At least Chato had an immediate goal: find his gay brother and make amends for the way the family had treated him. I was tagging along because I had some as yet undetermined feelings for a man who had kidnapped me. Somehow that was preferable to going home to face the family I was about to tear apart.

While Chato was out of the room, I had called Bart. I told him I wanted to see a bit more of Mexico, but I would be filing for divorce when I got home. Bart immediately hung up, which frightened me more than if he had yelled obscenities at me. In addition to blaming all his troubles on others—the failure of his marriage was obviously Obama's fault—he had a vindictive streak and was probably at that moment trying to turn the boys against me. Within minutes, he would be at his parents' house whining to them.

I was awakened by the notification of a text message. My evolution to wakefulness followed a series of realizations: I didn't want to look at the text; I was naked; there was a warm body next to me; I was in a foreign country; I was hung over for the second time since I arrived in that country; I had acted on the disarming glow I felt when I first saw Chato's hands dangling out the car window; and I felt no shame though my actions made my life significantly more complex. Chato stirred, and I closed my eyes, feigning sleep.

"I know you not sleeping," said Chato. He rose up on one elbow.

"My head hurts."

"Let me kiss it." He leaned over and kissed my forehead.

"Please don't look at me."

"Why not? You are beautiful."

"I don't feel beautiful."

"Because of what we did?"

"No, not that. I don't normally even drink. But beer *and* tequila!"

"It was too nice see you relax and be funny."

"I have this vague notion that we danced."

"Oh, yeah."

"Another thing I never do."

"That was obvious."

"Shut up," I said, a little louder than I had intended. The words rattled around in my head like coins in a dryer. I held my head in my hands. "Ouch!"

"*Ay, mi vida.*" He kissed me lightly on the lips.

After dinner we had gone to La Perla. It was more of a nightclub than a bar, with small tables situated around an oblong stage that later turned into a dance floor. Above the stage in the same oblong shape was a skirt of crystal beads that surrounded the spotlights. The décor was kitschy cabaret, with red walls and globe wall sconces. The crowd was mixed in age and orientation, seemingly more straight than gay, making Chato seem more at ease.

Shortly after we arrived, a performer took to the stage. A couple at the next table told Chato we were in for a treat. Morgana Love was not a drag queen like a lot of the performers at La Perla. She was a transsexual. And she didn't lip sync, but rather sang with her own classically trained voice. She began her set with a haunting rendition of John Lennon's "Imagine."

Chato leaned across the table and said to me, "Is not possible this is a man." She was gorgeous, beautifully dressed in a pink satin ball gown, and she sang in a clear, natural soprano. Her hair was long and wavy, and appeared to be her own.

"You're right. She is totally a woman, and so comfortable in her skin that you've got to imagine that it's the way she was meant to be."

He called the waiter over to order shots of tequila and convinced me to drink mine in one gulp. I shivered with the burn from my throat down to my stomach. I was trying really hard to dampen my inhibitions and forget all the things playing on my mind. The rest of Morgana's set, we both sat as if in a trance.

Another performer came on next, a true drag queen dramatically dressed with orchids in her platinum wig, a cape with yards of tulle over a gold lamé prom dress, and a pound of makeup on her face. The next table again chimed in with how lucky we were to be there on that night. Now performing was Valentina, who had been on *Ru Paul's Drag Race*, to which Chato and I expressed awe though we had no idea what that was. The song she lip synced was "Asi Fue" by Isabel Pantoja, they told us. She was followed by La Perla's cabaret dancers, and then they opened up the dance floor.

Somehow I had managed to down three tequilas, each one getting easier. Chato had no problem dragging me out on the dance floor. Once when I was dancing free form, I looked up to see Chato had stopped moving and was staring at me in disbelief. "This you call dancing?"

"Don't laugh at me. I'm having fun for the first time in years."

He grabbed me around the waist and pulled me close. "Follow my lead," he said.

"I'm all yours."

"If you say so." He pulled me closer. I relaxed, and he magically had me dancing more or less to the beat.

The rest of the night was now just a blur, the flashing lights on the dance floor, the spinning, feeling Chato's body pressed up against me as if we were budding teens in a social dancing class. I barely remembered getting back to the hotel, a taxi speeding along the wide Paseo de la Reforma, skyscrapers all lit, fountains and sculptures and statues giving one the impression of being in the center of the universe.

In the room we kissed as if we had waited to do it for ages. There was nothing calculated or crafty about our next moves. We were drunk. We were adults. It was sloppy passionate. He kept whispering breathy, sexy things in Spanish that I didn't understand, didn't need to understand. His body was hairy and taut. He lavished in foreplay, something I had forgotten existed.

I remembered being impatient, that it was time to put to rest this thing that had been teasing us, taunting us for what seemed like years. I also remembered thinking the realization of fantasies looked so much better in the movies. Having him inside me felt more a fulfillment of a prophecy, a mandate by a playful God treating us as pawns. It lasted no more than ten minutes before we collapsed and then passed out.

I opened my eyes. Despite saying I didn't want him to look at me, my heart took a giant leap to see those treacherous eyes now as soft as brown velvet cushions staring down at me. They glistened slightly as if about to make tears. I ran my finger along his stubbly jaw.

"I'm sorry," he whispered

I quickly put my hand over his mouth.

"And not sorry," he mumbled through my fingers.

"I think we failed at our mission," I said.

"I think we succeed very good."

"Your brother, you idiot!"

"Oh, that."

In a break from dancing the previous evening, we had seen a toned-down Valentina in a sweater and jeans and a more subdued wig sitting at the bar.

"You talk to her," whispered Chato.

I saw in Chato's eyes how both terrified and fascinated he was. Accompanying him on this trip to find his brother gave me a sense of purpose. I could help him navigate this world of fluid genders, though I wasn't sure I should be making it easier for him. "How do you know she speaks English?"

"I hear her speaking to this gringo over there."

"*Hola, guapa,*" said Valentina when I approached her. She looked over my shoulder. "Your boyfriend is very cute."

My first reaction was to say he wasn't my boyfriend, but the way Valentina was ogling Chato, I felt the need to protect him. I smiled and got right to the point. "We just wondered if you might know a performer called Lina. We're trying to locate her."

Valentina twisted her lips and narrowed her eyes. She was not going to be told how wonderful her show was or flirted with. She had no time for questions about another, and no doubt lesser, drag queen. "Try some of the little dives in the Zona Rosa," she said coldly and turned her back.

15: M

On the flight home, I had the window, Lio the center, and Augie the aisle. Arnie had flown back the day before. With my husband gone and the cloud of the kidnapping lifted, nothing stood in the way of the discussion of my gender identity. I was sure Augie wasn't going to let it go.

The captain announced he was turning the seat belt light back on due to turbulence. Within seconds, the shaking started. I gripped the armrest as a sudden bump left my stomach at a higher altitude.

"Southwest has never had a major accident," said Augie.

"Does that mean they are due for one?" said Lio.

"Shut up, both of you. What we're *not* due for is more trauma on this trip!"

Lio turned to Augie with an eye roll as if they were kids with an unreasonable parent.

"I saw that," I said.

Lio giggled. "She woke."

The plane shuddered and dipped.

"*She* is here, boys," I said.

"Or is she?" Augie said. Perhaps his turbulence panic made him go out on a limb. "Are we all going to be boys anytime soon?"

Lio jabbed Augie in the ribs with his elbow.

"Was that supposed to be funny?" I said.

"No," said Augie. "I think we need to talk about it, I mean, now that things are back to normal."

"Normal?" said Lio. "AJ has run off with a Mexican kidnapper."

"There's that," said Augie.

"I do love Arnie," I began in a low voice. Augie leaned over Lio to hear me better. "I guess being away from him for a few days made me feel cocky. No pun intended. Delusional maybe. Our lives are so intertwined."

"Yeah, but what about one's own happiness?" said Augie. "We have to take care of ourselves. Ultimately we are individuals, each one looking for fulfillment."

I leaned forward and stared at Augie, wondering where this support had been when I needed it. Lio pushed back in his seat to allow us better crossfire. Another shudder and dip caused me to fall back in my seat. "Now you are advocating individualism? Does that mean you'll be abandoning Ruben and Colton to go off and write?"

Augie sighed. I could almost see his mind doing a file scan. "I don't want to be *como un latente relámpago.*"

"Uh...remember, Augie, we don't speak Spanish," said Lio, looking at me as if Augie was now being the unreasonable one.

"It's a poem. I can't stop thinking about it. The verses are embedded in the Puerto Vallarta Malecón with little pebbles, line by line. Hundreds of people walk over the words every day without paying any attention. When I realized the phrases were part of something, I tried to figure it out. And then I saw a little plaque on the side that said, 'Como un latente relámpago' was a poem by José Martin Orozco Almádez. I don't know what the title means to him, but I translate it like a latent lightening or an unrealized spark. I feel like my spark is getting snuffed out by domesticity."

Lio produced a snort of skepticism. "You couldn't live without your guys."

I nodded my approval of what Lio had said. But I also knew Lio was looking from the outside, a rosy view enhanced by his regrets at his own failed domestic life.

"We get just one shot at this life," said Augie.

"I think I missed my shot," I said.

Both brothers snapped their heads to me. "What's that supposed to mean?" said Augie.

"Arnie came along and saved me that first year in med school. Something really horrible happened on that trip to Europe. I came back weeks before I said I did. I barricaded myself in the apartment and talked to nobody. I needed to heal."

Augie got a sour look on his face. "Now you're telling me when you called and said you were back from Europe, you had already been back for some time? I thought something was off."

"But you never said anything," I said. "You left it up to me to bring up what was going on. I couldn't...couldn't talk about it. You always complain that I keep secrets while you spill your guts. Maybe you never give me a safe space to talk about me."

"I admit it. I'm a selfish bastard," said Augie. "You're not the first person to say that. I'm sorry. I failed. So, what happened?"

"I was raped. There's no other way to put it." I watch my brothers gulp simultaneously and cast their eyes down in shame.

"Do you want to talk about it?" asked Augie in a much softer tone of voice.

"It's still not easy, but there's enough distance now...what?...twenty-five years...that I can tell the story."

I told them everything from the binding garment to the motorcycle to the leather bar to the British hoodlums. By the time I finished my story, the plane was cruising smoothly. A calm had settled over the passengers, and the only sound was the purr of the engines. A man behind us coughed, and it startled us.

"I'm so sorry, M," said Lio. "Men are such pigs."

"That's exactly what I thought at the time. Why would I want to identify as a man when men do such horrible things? I say identify because back then transitioning didn't even enter my mind. Why is masculinity so often toxic? Though we have to admit women can be pretty awful as well."

"At least they don't rape. I mean...not normally," said Lio.

"And mass shootings," said Augie, "are almost always done by men, and usually white men. But back to the point, it's how you feel inside that should determine whether you transition or not, rather than how screwed up society is, that identifying with one gender is worse than the other."

I again noted Augie now seemed to be supportive of transitioning while I felt less convinced. "The thing is," I said, "society, screwed up or not, *is* a factor. Your desire to change has to be so compelling you are willing to put up with the pummeling you are going to suffer, I mean psychologically. But there is the very real possibility of physical assault as I learned."

"Don't forget they first attacked you because they thought you were a gay man," said Augie.

"But they raped me when they found out I was a woman."

"I've been called faggot a number of times when some noxious ringpiece thought I didn't quite meet up to his standards of masculinity," said Lio.

"I think we all agree being different puts you in the crosshairs of angry men," said Augie. "But, M, I really want to know how you felt back then. Did you just write off your experiment as a failure?"

"I barely left my apartment for a couple of months. The fear got mixed up in my head and transferred to a fear of exercising the difference I felt inside. Though starting med school forced me out of my apartment, it didn't allow me a lot of time to sit around and worry about who I was. And then I met Arnie. He was the complete opposite of those thugs in Amsterdam—kind, intelligent, and he seemed to like me for who I was. He liked my breasts!"

A woman from across the aisle looked askance at my overly excited outburst.

I chuckled and continued in a lower voice. "That was much later. It was a long time before I let him or anyone touch me. We began studying together, going for coffee, and I felt comfortable with him before long. I came to admire him and his gentle ways. He already knew he wanted to focus his practice on HIV patients. I thought that if Augie ever needed it, he would have a good doctor to go to."

"I was such a whore back then," said Augie. "Don't know how I dodged it."

"What made you start thinking about transitioning?" said Lio.

"Several years ago I had a patient, a boy born a girl, but really convinced of his boyness and able to convince me in about five minutes. At first, I was unsettled and didn't want to take the case. I had always referred gender identity cases to someone else. But something about the boy's determination and the way he saw right through me both terrified and intrigued me. I took him as a patient, though it didn't last long. The mother, of course, wanted me to make the boy 'normal,' and I couldn't do that. She found another therapist."

"I wonder what ever happened to him," said Augie.

"I actually got an email from him a couple of years ago. Turns out, his father—there you go, an enlightened straight white man—overruled the mother and took him to a gender reassignment expert. Even though he was only my patient for a brief time, I couldn't get him out of my mind. I started having dreams about him and a recurring dream about being flat-chested. I guess it was a combination of approaching fifty and reflecting upon my life. And then Mom dying made me wonder if she had been happy and fulfilled. I mean, all her life she wanted to speak Spanish and never really did."

"That's hardly the same," said Lio. "Anyway, Augie speaks perfect Spanish. Sometimes you achieve things through your kids."

Both Augie and I looked at Lio as if amazed by his astuteness.

"What?" said Lio.

Augie turned back to me. "You're not off the hook yet. I still want to know what you're feeling now."

"Numb." I had always been a person of action, never shied away from a challenge. I loved competition, sports, and achievement. But arriving at an acceptance of my own body, who I was inside, left me stymied.

"You'll have to do better than that."

"I will. I'll talk about it. But not right now. Telling the Amsterdam story left me empty." I pushed the call button. " I'm going to order another drink. Want one?"

Colton went off like a firecracker when he saw Augie come through the double doors of the arrival lobby at the airport, jumping up and down, screaming "Daddy," and then running into his arms. Watching a scene like that always made me regret for a moment not having kids. Ruben greeted Augie with the kind of hugs and kisses people normally reserve for someone coming home from the wars.

Though Colton was getting too big to pick up, Augie couldn't stop himself from lifting his son into his arms. "I saw you on TV," said Colton.

"What?" said Augie.

"He means the monitor," said Ruben. "He insisted on getting here early and he stood glued to the screen, watching several planeloads of people walk down the hall."

"You're too heavy," Augie groaned, letting Colton slide to the ground. Colton dashed over to hug me and his uncle Lio. "Where's Auntie AJ?"

Ruben shrugged. "I told him she was coming back later." Ruben enveloped his husband in another embrace. He sniffled and discreetly slid the sleeve of his jacket under his nose. "I wasn't going to do that. I was so fucking scared."

Colton was wrestling with Lio, but his radar was always up for bad words. "I heard that, Papi," he said.

"Sorry."

"But nothing happened to me," said Augie. "Aside from losing a few nights' sleep."

"I know. When it's close like that, though, it makes you think. Makes you appreciate what you have."

"What happened, Daddy?"

"Nothing," said Augie. And to Ruben he mumbled, "*Hablamos más tarde.*" They had been lazy about teaching Colton Spanish even though it was their original plan. Sometimes, however, Augie was glad he didn't understand.

"Your hair looks great, M," said Ruben. The day before we left, I had gone into a shop on a whim and had my hair cut and highlights added. After Arnie had gone back home, I had gazed in the mirror and thought I looked haggard.

"Thanks. Augie hardly seemed to notice," I said.

"Yes, I did," said Augie.

"And Lio, you look great for someone who…uh…just had a long flight," said Ruben.

Lio gave Ruben a big kiss on the mouth. He loved doing that in front of Augie, especially when it made Ruben blush.

"You'll have to fight me for him," Augie said to his brother.

"No fighting," said Colton.

Augie put his arm around Colton. "You're right, *mijo.*"

"I guess we should head over to BART," I said, pointing to the escalator.

"I can give you a ride," said Ruben. "I don't mind."

"Thanks, but the traffic is loco bloco crossing the bridge at this hour," said Lio.

"Arnie is picking us up at the BART station," I said. "And then I'll drive Lio home." I was also anxious to talk to Lio alone since he was the last one to see AJ. Augie and I had noticed AJ's bag was missing, so he hadn't managed to keep his trip to the bus station a secret.

When Lio and I sat down on the train, we had the strong sensation of being home, riding on the Bay Area's quintessential transit system with its spindly arms and legs spanning the Bay and connecting its two hearts—San Francisco and Oakland.

Lio and I sat across from each other in a section of four seats.

"I guess you're the only one that might have a clue what's going on with AJ," I said.

"I wish I could say I did, I mean, even watching the whole thing unfold I felt blind to what was going on inside her head. I thought at first she was playing the guy. You know how she does, flirting by dissing. She had him confuzzled, pacing the floor muttering in Spanish. It was kind of funny to watch except I was afraid she would go too far. When the other one, Flaco, was around, she was more or less cool. And then one day, near the end, I caught AJ and Chato holding hands. I started to wonder if she was still playing a part. You thought I was a shit for letting her stay while I got released, but I think it's what she wanted."

"Sorry about that," I said. "That was such a tense time."

"Dot nose."

"I was a little oblivious to the extent of her unhappiness with Bart until that dinner in Puerto Vallarta."

"Oh, yeah, she's been mis for a while, but, you know, the kids."

"Please tell me Chato is not like his brother. We had an encounter with Flaco, trying to get some idea where AJ and Chato had gone."

"Flaco's a bad hombre," said Lio, using air quotes. "Why Chato followed his lead is a mystery. AJ saw from the get go the younger brother had mixed feelings about what they were doing. Were you able to get anything out of Flaco?"

"Nada. Said he had no idea. He was scared. We told Tomas to rein in his men, but I had a feeling the local crime lords didn't like these young upstarts doing something on their own. The brothers could still be in danger."

"Flaco's lucky to be alive. If I hadn't been there when they found him, he might have ended up Osama bin Laden."

"Now I'm really worried about AJ. Could she be in danger just by being with Chato?"

"I tried calling her," said Lio. "She didn't pick up."

As we got into the downtown stations of San Francisco, the train filled up with tired commuters who gave us the stink eye for taking up two extra seats for our luggage. We moved to the two window seats and tried to balance the bags on our laps. Soon we would plunge into the underwater tunnel and pick up speed, really making conversation tough. We sat back and pulled out our phones, mimicking nearly everyone else on the train. I sent a message to Arnie that we were just going into the tunnel.

16: AJ

Flashing blue and pink lights rained down on Chato and me as we climbed to the second floor of the complex of three interconnected bars. Two boys wearing makeup, though otherwise dressed normally, emerged from the rosy glow at the top of the stairs and gave Chato the once-over as they descended. One of them tossed his head over his shoulder and said something to the companion just behind him, setting off a fit of giggling.

The poster had announced the Knock Down Drag Out—no translation into Spanish—contest in the upper bar. The winner would pocket about the equivalent of a hundred U.S. dollars. It was packed, and Chato insisted on staying in the back where he had more room to breathe in the crowd of mostly gay men. Now that we had been intimate, he had latched on to me as soon as we entered the downstairs level, broadcasting he was taken...by a woman.

"You're being kind of clingy," I said.

"Clingy?"

I sighed, thinking I should be getting paid as a private tutor. "It means you're hanging on me."

Chato removed his arm from my shoulders. I didn't have to look at him to know that he was pouting. "Don't be upset," I said.

"You are not feeling it?" he said in his deliberate, sporadically idiomatic English.

I was feeling it, perhaps a little too much. That was why I needed to slow things down. "Everything's fine," I shouted over the music. "I like being with you. But I have a lot going on right now."

"Do you want another drink?" Chato asked.

With a half-finished margarita in my hand, I put my other hand on Chato's shoulder and leaned close to his ear. "Clever boy. But I don't want a repeat of last night."

Chato's body edged toward the first step of disintegration. "Oh."

In order for him to not end up in pieces on the floor, I added, still close to his ear, "I mean the drunk part."

Chato's torso expanded slightly. "Okay," he said, drawing out the final syllable. "But I got to get another beer." He pulled his ear away from my mouth, and my hand dropped into the space he had left.

"Be careful," I said to his back.

When he returned with his beer, Chato stood a good two feet from me. I reached out, grabbed a handful of his T-shirt, and pulled him close. "People might think you're alone and cruising," I said with a laugh.

"Well, if you don't want me, there is many here who do. The bartender say to me things I can't repeat."

"Would you even know what to do?"

Chato wagged a finger in my face. "I know you, *mi amor,* you try to make me say something so you can make fun of me, tell me I am some dinosaur man."

"You know, I read an article recently that said you have to try everything to know what you like. I'm just saying."

"You want me say if I have sex with a boy or not? Okay. Where I grow up, you don't believe the games we play with all the country cousins in the woods all day with no parents. Older boys making young ones do things. Always seem very normal to me. Until I go to States. Every place I work over there, all the guys, Latinos, always talk *maricón* this and *maricón* that. They talk all the day about what men do in sex, always in bad way. So boring. Probably this guys do same as kids but try pretend no."

I decided against a witty comeback. I realized I had been imposing my expectations how he would react to gay issues, making assumptions, when in reality it was more complex. He wasn't Bart. I had a feeling Chato and Augie would get along, any attraction on Augie's part aside, once Augie got over his outrage that I had run off with my kidnapper.

The music faded just as the MC flounced onto the stage. Conversations quieted. Squeals and jeers rang out from the crowd. She wore a massive curly blond wig and a ruffly polka dot skirt puffed out like a bell, adding to her already considerable girth. She looked as if she had just walked on stage at a child's talent contest and was about to tap dance. That's just what she did two seconds later, but fortunately she knew to cut it off after a minute. The crowd cheered. She then launched into a series of jokes I didn't understand. By the way people were laughing, I gathered they were raunchy, getting even Chato to chuckle in a twitchy kind of way.

After a couple more jokes splashed with banter, fierce looks, and shade, they brought out the first contestant. From the opening moments of the act, I felt we had come down several levels since the previous night's experience. I guessed from the twisted grin on Chato's face that he was feeling the same. I tucked my arm in his.

When the second performer came on, Chato's body tensed up and he let out a *"Dios mío!"*

"What is it?" I said. But from the complete transformation of Chato's demeanor I knew. It had to be Abelino.

Chato stared at the stage, his mouth agape. The MC announced, *"Desde los rincones calientes del estado de Jalisco,* Lina LaTorre!"

I had not imagined she would be so tall, at least Chato's height, but with the five-inch heels, she would tower over him. Lina wore a *Traje de Percal,* a traditional dress of Jalisco in Mexican pink with ribbons of color, lace, and a wide skirt she swirled in a kaleidoscope of color. Her long black hair was in a single braid down the back and she wore large gold filigree teardrop earrings.

The mariachi music began and she launched into Azucena's "Sufriendo a Solas."

I watched Chato's face. The gaping had transitioned to a look of awe. His eyes glistened.

"This is my homeland. Music and dress of Jalisco," he said as if in a trance. He seemed to have forgotten it was his brother on stage, accepting the changeover without question.

"He's very good," I said. "Maybe he'll win."

At the end of the five performances, they brought all the contestants on stage and awarded the prize to the one who received the loudest applause. Chato cheered and whistled as loud as he could for his brother. I joined in. At first I thought he was so enthusiastic to impress me with his openness, but the expression on his face couldn't have been faked. Lina won the prize.

At the end of the night, we made our way to the dressing room behind the stage and knocked on the door. Abelino opened the door, now in sweat pants and a sequined T-shirt, the makeup half-removed. He screamed and slammed the door.

"*Espera, Lino! Quiero felicitarte.* Congratulations!" Chato knocked again. "Come on, *hermano.*"

Lino opened the door slightly. "What do you want?"

"To see you. Talk to you."

"Did mama send you? Is she okay?"

"She's fine. Nobody knows I'm here."

Lino looked over Chato's shoulder at me. "Who is she?"

218

"Uh, simple answer? A friend. American. Her name is April."

"April showers bring May flowers," said Lino. "Sorry. Something I learn in school."

I stuck my hand through the opening in the door. "Nice to meet you. I've heard a lot about you."

"I bet. Did he tell you how they used to torture me?"

"Torture, huh?" I said. "I guess I got off easy."

"Come on, Lino," said Chato. He brought his hands to prayer in front of his chest. "New beginning, okay? I apologize. And don't say torture. What is my new friend going to think of me?"

"What does she mean 'got off easy'?" said Lino.

"That is a long story, but I can't tell you through this little opening."

From inside the cramped room, someone screamed, "*Chingado, cierra la puerta!*"

"Wait for me in the hall. I'll be out in a few minutes."

We moved away from the door and Chato shrugged.

"What did you expect? Hugs and kisses?" I said.

When we turned around, a man gave us a hard stare. He looked to be in his fifties, trimmed silver hair, nicely dressed. Chato nodded at him as we walked past. "Are you one of the brothers?" the man said in English.

Chato stopped and turned around. "Yes, I'm Chato. And you are?"

"I hope you haven't come to harass him. He's been through enough." The man leaned against the wall and crossed his arms.

Chato's surprise was turning to anger. I walked over to the man. "Hi. I'm AJ—or April if you wish."

"Michael," the man mumbled.

"I only just met Lino, but I can assure you Chato is here to support his brother. We came to see the performance, and I think Chato's loud cheering might have had something to do with Lino winning. Right, honey?" I reached for Chato's arm and pulled him closer. "Now, let's begin again. Chato, this is Michael. Michael, Chato."

Chato put out his hand.

Michael uncrossed his arms reluctantly, as if he was bending steel. "We...uh...live together," he said after a pause. "Lino and I."

"You sound like an American," I said. "I mean your accent."

"I am. From Minnesota. I live here now most of the year."

"I'm from California. The Bay Area." It didn't even occur to me to say I lived in Modesto.

Lino emerged from the dressing room without makeup. He had on jeans and the same sequined T-shirt. In the dimly lit hallway, the four of us blinked as if to provide more clarity.

"I guess you all have met. Michael is my partner. We live together," said Lino, speaking as if he had waited all his life to say it. He moved close to Michael and stared triumphantly at Chato, daring him to say anything against it.

"Yes, he told us," said Chato.

"Well?"

We stood like statues next to a smelly men's room just around the corner from the blaring dance music. Flashing lights cast eerie shadows on the wall. People pushed by us without apologizing. If Bart were there, he would truly think he had descended into hell—his wife with a Mexican in a drag bar in a foreign capital, pumping dance music. Since no one else was going to say anything, I shouted, "Can we go outside?"

Lino took the lead. The rest of us followed single file through the bar, down the stairs, and out the door. Once out on the street, Lino turned to us. "I'm hungry. I never eat before a show." He sucked in his already flat stomach and rubbed his belly.

"We could go to Vips," said Michael. "We can get a booth and it's relatively quiet for a conversation."

Michael and Lino walked ahead, stepping into an animated discussion. I put a slight pressure on Chato's arm, indicating we should fall back a bit. "Are you going to tell them how we met?"

"I think maybe is not a good idea," said Chato, sucking in air through his teeth. "Is going to be difficult enough already."

I grinned. "We can just say we met on the street and it was love at first sight."

"Always so funny. Help me. I can't tell him the true. He already think I'm a criminal because they send me back from States. He say I'm stupid because I follow Flaco who always get in trouble."

"Sounds like good advice."

"You never forgive me, right?" He moved in front of me and fell to his knees in the middle of the sidewalk. He looked up into my eyes, producing what looked like tears. "I beg you."

I had a moment of confusion, thinking he was desperately serious. But then he had had a lot to drink in anticipation of seeing his brother. "Chato, get up. People are looking."

"I won't get up until you forgive me."

Lino and Michael stopped and looked back.

"You're being ridiculous."

Lino and Michael started walking back to us.

"You want me to tell them? I tell them. No problem."

"Tell us what?" said Lino.

"He's drunk," I said to Lino. "Okay, Chato, I forgive you. God, you're such a pain in the ass."

"Why you forgive him?" said Lino. "I'm sure he doesn't deserve it."

Still on his knees, Chato turned to Lino. "And you too. Forgive me."

"Hah! Not if you crawl on your knees all the way to Our Virgin of Guadalupe." He posed with his arms fanned out at his sides and an expanded rib cage, a diva who had just won a prize. And yet his frozen demeanor hinted of a thaw. Michael stood at a distance, bewildered. Some of the passersby had stopped to watch Chato's curious display.

"For the love of God, Chato! Will you stand up?" I said.

Chato rose to his feet and hugged me. "Thank you. One out of two isn't bad."

"Let's go," said Lino. "I'm starving." Lino put his arm through mine and pulled me along in front of the others. "I don't know you or what is happening. You seem like nice person, but you need be careful. When he get silly like this, trying to cover something bad he do, watch out. Sometimes he say terrible things to me and then pretend it was only a joke."

I looked back to see how Chato was doing with Michael. They were not talking. "Why is he so influenced by Flaco?" I said.

"You meet Flaco? He is *pendejo*. Asshole. He treat everyone bad except Chato. He make my life very difficult when we growing up. They say he is like my father. I don't know my father cause he die when I was baby. Chato tell me he is very mean to Flaco." Lino paused and turned to look me in the eye. "I think something strange in how you meet Chato."

"Why do you say that?"

"A few days ago I talk to Silvia, the sister at home. I call her from time to time. Nobody know about my calls, not even our mother. She say Flaco and Chato acting weird lately. Then Flaco disappear. Then Chato disappear. And now you are here." Lino took my hand and saw the ring. "You married?"

"Yes. But I'll probably be divorced soon."

Lino shook his head. "Because of Chato?" His voice rose up the scale in an absurd fashion.

"No, not at all. It's been a long time coming. I have only stayed with him because of our two boys." I realized how ridiculous it all sounded, and Lino only knew half the story. I questioned my sanity for the hundredth time in the last few days. "We should talk about Chato. My situation is way too complicated."

"But I think you have some relation to why he is here."

Lino's intuition reminded me of having a conversation with a girlfriend. I felt an immediate camaraderie. "My brother is gay. When Chato told me about you and how you left, it made me very angry."

"Then he is here to impress you."

"Part of it maybe. Still I think he wants to be a good person."

"I think this too, but sometimes I wonder. I know you don't tell me something, but I can wait. And he's crazy if he think I gonna forgive easily!"

We arrived at Vips on Hamburgo and were seated in a booth at Michael's request. The cheery hostess presented us with large, indestructible menus covered with glossy photos of selections that seemed to be a hybrid of American family dishes and denuded Mexican standards, Denny's meets Baja Fresh. Lino ordered

Milanesa con chilaquiles y huevo. Michael got a Vips Club. I ordered a mango juice and Chato a michelada.

"Don't you have to watch what you eat to fit in those dresses?" I asked.

"Honey, I eat one big meal a day. That's it. I work out three times a week, treadmill and elliptical," said Lino.

"Puts me to shame," said Michael. "All I do is walk, and then we ride bikes when they close off Reforma on Sundays."

Chato poured the beer into the tomato concoction, but he put too much and leaned down with a loud sucking sound to stop the foam from overflowing. He realized everyone was looking at him. "Sorry."

Lino produced a royal eye roll. "This is what you're leaving your husband for?"

"What did you tell him?" said Chato.

"Well, I certainly didn't tell him that!"

"Girl, I know you're on a mission to bring him into the modern world, but you don't know what you're getting into," said Lino.

"Go ahead and tear me down if it makes you feel better. But April is a grown woman who can make her own decisions. This is between you and me. Look, I am not proud how I treated you and I apologize. *Perdóname.*"

"Not so fast, *hermano.* Is not even one hour you waltz into my life, my...my...territory and start giving me this bullshit how you've changed and you're sorry, blah, blah, blah."

The server's timing was perfect. She arrived with the tray and distributed the food, giving all the players a chance to gather their thoughts. Everyone stared at the plates of food with exaggerated interest. The cool air from the vents above us gave me a chill. Lino grabbed his knife and fork and tore into the *milanesa*.

"I *have* changed," said Chato. "Before I don't understand how being different can be so painful, thinking if you just try to be like everybody else, then you are okay. When I go to States, for first time I am different one. People treat me like shit, call me all kinds of names. I can't change who I am. Then I think maybe is same with you."

Lino dropped his shoulders and put down his knife and fork. "You always make fun of me as kids when I stay in the house with *mami* while everybody go play in the woods. You know why, right?"

"I think you don't like snakes and spiders and shit."

"No, is because what happen."

"Chato told me," I said, "about the little sexual games with cousins."

"I am *not* talking about games! I'm talking about Flaco rape me."

Chato let out a guttural gasp. "No. Flaco? What you mean?"

"I think you know what rape is. He force me do something I don't want. Then he threaten me not to tell. I surprise he don't tell you like brag or something."

It was agonizing for me to listen to the murky revelations of siblings. My sibs were mean to me at times, but nothing like the trauma I hear about in other families. I couldn't imagine hating a brother the way Lino seemed to hate Flaco and, by association, Chato.

"I swear I didn't know. I'm sorry. Flaco do some messed up things." He looked at me with a wry smile.

I gazed through him as though he were a ghost. I had the sensation of drifting away, done with the conversation, the brothers, the screaming lights of the restaurant, the cheesy smell of the food.

"I really, really didn't know," said Chato, now seeming to speak to me rather than his brother. "April! Are you listening?"

Lino touched my arm. "Chato never hurt me physically. Maybe I am so mad at him for being too handsome," he said with a laugh as he turned to Michael. "How's your meal, *cariño?*"

"*Deliciosa.*"

I stared at the fluted glass, empty but flecked with particles of mango. I was desperate to get out of the booth, but I was wedged in between Chato and Lino. I wanted to call my brothers and sister to tell them I was coming home. These people had nothing to do with me. I had an overwhelming desire to hug my boys.

"Can you let me out?" I said to Chato in an edgy, desperate plea.

"Of course. What is it?" He took hold of my hand, but I pulled it away. I stood up, and the restaurant swam around me. I looked in every direction and then chose one, hoping I would find the restroom where none of the men could follow me.

I pulled my hair back in a ponytail and leaned over the sink, splashing water on my face. I patted my skin with a paper towel and reapplied lipstick. I didn't have to worry about streaming mascara as there had been no time to do full makeup with Chato pressuring me to leave so we could get to the club on time. The dizziness began to subside.

I wasn't quite sure what had hit me or why it had happened at that moment. Despite my dramatic exit from the table, it seemed to have had little to do with the discussion between the brothers. Perhaps the sibling issues reminded me I had abandoned my brothers and sister. The trip to Puerto Vallarta, conceived as a chance for the four of us to disconnect from our day-to-day lives and reconnect with each other, never had a chance to reach that goal.

After the big blowout dinner, we'd had no opportunity to assuage damaged egos, get clarifications. Thank Mr. Chato for that. Having gone through the most traumatic experience of my life, I chose to flee with my captor instead of reuniting and flying home together with the gang. What was wrong with me?

The door opened, and Chato barged in. I looked at him in the mirror without the slightest bit of surprise. My first thought was that men are such idiots. They never know when to give women the space we need. We stared at each other's reflections. I remembered Lino's amusing quip earlier: "This is what you're leaving your husband for?" No, I told myself. I was leaving my husband for me.

The standoff was broken by the loud click of a stall door unlocking. A woman stepped out and immediately began shouting at Chato in Spanish. A frustrated Chato responded. The woman then turned to me and started yelling. I grabbed my purse and walked out the door. Chato followed.

"What's going on?" said Chato in the hallway, papered and shellacked with old newsprint.

"I don't belong here."

"Where do you belong?"

"Home."

"What's stopping you?"

"Bastard."

"I'm the bastard? I didn't ask you to come with me. You like use me for distraction. You afraid to go home and face your husband. I am for your entertainment."

"It was a bad idea. I'm sorry. Go back to your brother. That's the important thing. I'll see you at the hotel." The last part was possibly a lie. I wasn't sure I would see him back at the hotel. I could pack my things and head to the airport before he got back.

The trenches of his forehead showed he read my thoughts. "I'm not giving up on you."

Sometimes absurd decisions need to play themselves out. I put my head down and followed the hideous geometric pattern of the carpet all the way to the front door.

17: Lio

I had just gotten on Highway 132 in the last leg of my trip to Modesto. Instead of dealing with my own issues, specifically my relationship with my daughter, I had embarked on a mission for AJ to see her sons. I was mulling over how I would approach Bart when I got a message from AJ saying she was on her way home. I pulled over at the next gas station and answered her text. *Halfway to Modestoland. Should I abort mission?*

AJ must have realized the conversation was too complicated for a text. My phone rang.

"Where are you?" I said.

"Mexico City airport. Trying to get on a flight."

"What happened?"

"Sometimes it takes me a little longer to see the light. We were in Mexico City. Things were actually going pretty well."

"And then?"

"I just left. Does someone who has held you against your will deserve an explanation why you have come to your senses? "

"I want to know everything, every juicy detail."

"Too much to talk about on the phone. To answer your question, no, don't abandon the mission. I don't know when I'll get there. I want to talk to you and M and Augie before I do anything."

"Damn, girl. I feel like I'm on a suicide mission. You told him, right? He was bizzaro on the phone."

"He hung up on me. What did he say to you?"

"He said I better set you right, and that M and Augie put you up to this. That's why we had to take this trip without him. And a bunch of other shit I won't bother to mention."

"I assume you didn't tell him what happened to us."

"No way. He'd go off on Mexicans until he popped a vein. He thinks all we did down there was sit around, drink margaritas, and plan his demise."

"Of course. All about him. Are you going to spend the night there?"

"We'll see how it goes. Probably drive back late."

"The good thing is the boys love you, so just focus on them. Drive safe. Hopefully, I'll be home tonight. I'm going to ask M if I can stay with her."

"She'll be geeked to hear your story and of course, offer her advice, do her Oprah thing."

I stopped my MINI Cooper in front of AJ and Bart's 1950's ranch style two-bedroom house. It was losing its pale blue paint in large, curling chips. Bart was out the screen door within seconds, marching across the front lawn. He had let his hair grow long and wore a white tank top stretched over his paunch. His eyes were hidden behind mirrored sunglasses, but I could tell he had been drinking from the way he moved.

He had gone from a fit veteran I had secretly admired in his youth to a caricature of the white male sidelined in self-imposed exile, aggressive yet whiny, privileged yet paranoid. Jason and Elijah followed him out the door, but Bart ordered them back into the house. Perhaps this wasn't a good idea. Was the plan to deny me access to my nephews? I got out and joined Bart in the middle of the yard. It was worn bare in spots and overgrown in others.

"What the fuck is she doing?" said Bart. His expression was a mix of anger and desperation.

"Don't kill the messenger," I said.

"What's the message?"

"It's for the boys."

Bart looked back over his shoulder at his sons standing behind the screen door. "She needs to be here right now."

"Have you called her?"

"I have to talk to her face to face. Let's see if she'll say those things she said on the phone to my face."

"Do the boys know anything?"

"Naw, but they're asking a lot of questions. How could she do this? She can't just tear this apart. We took vows. Things haven't always been easy, but I have provided for my family." Bart stopped to slick back the hair that had fallen in his face with the excitement. "Oh, everything was fine when we were living high on the hog. But now that we're in a little dip, this is the thanks I get. She can't even fucking face me?"

I could have said a lot of things. The little dip had been going on for years, and I wondered how faithful Bart had been to those wedding vows. Despite his ranting, I felt a pang of sympathy. I was an inch away from telling him AJ was on her way home, though I didn't know what that would mean in terms of calming him down. And as much as I understood AJ needed to be done with this guy, a part of me wanted everything to be conflict-free, for my nephews to have a mom and dad, for families to stay together. I often berated myself for not fighting harder when my marriage was on the rocks.

The sun beat down on us, and my head began to bake, sending sweat running down my cheeks.

"Sorry, man. I didn't even offer you a beer," said Bart. He turned around and started walking to the house. "Come on."

"Wait. I have to get something out of the car."

I slung the backpack with the boys' gifts over my shoulder and walked into the house. Something was different. Particles of a treacherous perfume that was not AJ's floated in the air. Bart's mother, Wanda, sat in the living room reading the paper.

"Oh, Wanda, how are you?"

She didn't get up, though she smiled at me with the mistrust Central Valley people have for Coastal people. "Hey, Lio. Nice of you to come all the way out here to see us. I'm cooking dinner if you'd like to stay."

I wasn't sure how much she knew, but I was happy to play along with the uncle visiting his nephews gambit. "Thanks, Wanda. That would be nice if it's not too much trouble."

"Not at all. Always room for one more."

Bart came into the living room with a couple of beers in his hand. "The boys are back in their room if you want to say hi."

I took the beer, and we clinked bottles. Wanda sighed disapprovingly and snapped the paper to flatten it. Bart stared at me like he wanted to crawl into my head and excavate everything I knew. I nodded to the back of the house and headed that way.

The boys were playing a game on the computer when I walked in their room. I had to shout "Hey, guys" before they acknowledged me. Elijah got up and gave me a hug while Jason continued the game. I put the backpack on one of their beds and stood behind Jason. "Can you turn that off for a minute?"

"What's in that?" said Elijah, pointing at the bag.

"I brought you some gifts from your mom. From Mexico."

Jason turned around. "Why didn't she bring them?"

"She'll be home in a few days. Since I was coming here first, she asked me to bring them." I opened the bag and gave Jason the *lucha libre* mask and Elijah the flute.

"Cool," said Elijah.

"Thanks," said Jason. He had his mother's brown eyes, and she could never hide her unhappiness in them either. "When's she coming home?"

"Soon. She wanted me to tell you that she loves you guys."

I looked around the room to avoid Jason's skeptical stare, spotting a new bible on each nightstand. I picked one of them up. On the cover was a rocky sea and two sailboats in the background, gliding on smoother waters while sunlight graced the horizon behind them. "Where did you get these?" I was fairly certain of the answer.

"Nana gave them to us," said Elijah.

I smirked, imagining Wanda wouldn't be terribly upset if AJ and Bart got divorced. She was probably half moved in already. "And these are from me," I said. I pulled out a couple of T-shirts, one with a circular Aztec calendar on it and the other with the Huichol shaman figure. I hadn't thought about it when I bought them, but now I couldn't wait for Wanda to see them. She would go apeshit over the pagan symbolism.

At the dinner table, over a bland meal of Salisbury steak, corn, and mashed potatoes, Wanda asked us to join hands in a prayer of thanks for the food, something AJ and Bart never did as far as I knew. The bulky thick-legged table we sat around had come from our family home when Gloria decided to replace it with something a little more modern.

It had been party to countless discussions about art and politics, as well as the mundane incidents at school on a given day. Now the table was like a nonbeliever who suddenly gets religion as his life comes to an end, just in case. The only thing missing at the gathering was Bart's father talking about the godlessness of the Democrats and the witch hunt aimed at the president, who had been chosen by God. As if reading my thoughts, Wanda announced out of the blue it was her husband's card night.

"She means poker," said Bart to tease his mom.

"It's just a friendly game," said Wanda, and then quickly changed the subject. "You didn't none of you get Matahuma revenge or whatever it's called?"

"Montezuma. No, we were fine."

"That scares me, the contaminated water and all, not to mention all the other shenanigans going on down there." She cast her eyes at the kids as if she wanted to spare them the gory details.

I hadn't been the most positive about Mexico, particularly after our experience, but when I heard the comments coming from Wanda's mouth, delivered in her transplanted Oklahoma drawl, I felt compelled to defend the country. "It's a lot nicer than people think."

"I guess for some people," said Bart.

I assumed he was alluding to AJ's decision to stay in Mexico longer. I wanted so bad to tell Bart the real reason she had stayed that the words burned the insides of my mouth. But the kids. I wondered at the millions of times the presence of children had deterred adults from saying something horrible. When it got to the point

Kathy was no longer inhibited from saying terrible things in front of Belle, I knew my marriage was over.

After dinner, I helped carry dishes into the kitchen and offered to wash them. Bart didn't lift a finger and neither did the boys.

"Oh that's real nice," said Wanda. "But I got it." I had the feeling she would be happiest if I was on my way.

Bart walked me out to the car with about five more beers under his belt.

"When you talk to her, tell her she needs to come home," he said.

"Why did you hang up on her?"

"My mom came in the room, and I couldn't talk. Plus she sounded funny. Is she having an affair?"

Gulp. I'm not a good liar, but I refused to be the rat. In any case I didn't think running off with you kidnapper was technically having an affair. "AJ? Are you kidding me?"

"Oh man, I can't fucking believe this shit."

"You guys need to talk. I'm not getting in the middle." I regretted making the trip. I had accomplished nothing, and I had my own issues to deal with.

As soon as I got in the car, I called Belle.

"Hi, Dad. You back from Mexico?"

"Yeah. Just got back."

"Sounds like you're in the car. Where are you?"

I wasn't about to tell her that I had gone to see her cousins before I went to see her. "Running errands. On my way home. How about dinner tomorrow night?"

"Let me ask Mom. Mom, it's Dad. He wants to have dinner tomorrow night."

No response from Kathy at first. And then, "I was going to make veggie lasagna."

"It doesn't have to be tomorrow, does it?" Belle said to her mom.

Kathy responded in a disappointed voice. "No. It's up to you. It would be nice to have a little more warning."

"Did you hear that?" Belle said to me.

"Are you vegetarian now?"

"Mostly."

"What about your mom?"

"She's trying it. Rod says meat production is killing the planet." Rod was Belle's stepfather.

"Well, if Rod says..." The sarcasm just oozed out. I couldn't help myself.

"Don't be mean."

"We could go to Cha-Ya."

"Perfect!"

The last time I had seen Belle was at Mom's funeral. Not a good time to talk, but I couldn't believe how much of a young woman she had looked all dressed up. It was the first time I noticed she was wearing a bra. Sitting across from me at Cha-Ya restaurant, she looked younger and much more casual in a sleeveless T-shirt and jeans. She had just had her thick black hair cut short for summer. I couldn't believe she would be starting high school in the fall. She would probably start dating, and I wouldn't be the one answering the door to size up the young man taking her out.

"Dad, you've got that look," Belle said, narrowing her dark eyes until I could barely see her pupils.

"What look?"

"Like you're getting ready to apologize. Again."

"I was just thinking of all the things I missed."

"Don't, okay?"

"But I mean it. I really am sorry."

"Dad, please. I get it."

I had vowed after coming back from Mexico to follow new rules, but I was already falling into old patterns. "All right. Let's talk about something else. I want to take you on a trip."

"Where?"

"If you could go anywhere in the world, where would you like to go?"

"Are you serious?"

"I'm getting some money from your grandma, and I can't think of a better way to spend it than taking you on a trip. Before you start school in the fall."

"I don't know."

"You don't know *where* you want to go, or you don't know *if* you want to go."

"We've never done anything like that. And you know Mom." She began to open to the idea. Her smooth upper eyelids lifted so that the excitement in her eyes was visible. Her lips that tended toward poutiness showed her perfect white teeth. I was amazed by a flash of exotic beauty, imagining how stunning she would be when she reached full womanhood. Her features were gleaned from around the globe. From Kathy she had Japanese and Native Hawaiian, and from me Eastern European Jewish.

"How about Hawaii?" I had originally thought Australia. I hadn't been back there since I was in my early twenties. But as soon as she mentioned her mom, I got a reality check. Hawaii sounded much safer. Kathy's parents lived in Hawaii.

"I've been there like three times."

"But not with me. I know you usually go to Oahu where your grandparents are. Have you been to other islands?"

"We went to Maui once."

"Okay. The big island. There's a lot to do there."

18: M

I was aware of my blessings as I strolled downhill on Trestle Glen Road, a street of oversized storybook cottages nestled amongst tall trees and overwrought landscaping. It was the main artery that delivered me from my upscale neighborhood to the Grand Lake shopping area and the eastern end of Lake Merritt, from wealth and privilege to a hub of diversity. Though my address was Piedmont, an exclusive municipality surrounded by Oakland, I identified with the city where I had lived my whole life. After arriving home from Mexico, I was anxious to reconnect with my city.

I was proud of the drummers who gathered on Sunday afternoons near the lakeside Pergola and Colonnade, often provoking the ire of some of the neighbors who lived on the hill above the lake. I was also proud of the fifty-two-foot high Grand Lake Theater sign. It always warmed my heart when I drove by, especially at night with its nearly three thousand colored bulbs splashing across the sky. The marquee, in addition to announcing the current movies, had in recent years become a message board for liberal causes, proudly proclaiming the politics of Oakland while the rest of the country treaded water, unsure how to reconcile what was happening to democracy.

My goal was the Saturday Farmer's Market, which spread over Splash Pad Park at the foot of the theater. I loved to stroll among the food stalls and feel a part of one of the most diverse communities in the country. Once I crossed the busy Lake Park Avenue, I was enveloped by the crowd, my people: Asian women carrying bags overflowing with yardlong beans and bitter melon, black lesbian moms with babies in strollers, interracial straight couples holding hands, Ethiopians shopping for the mysterious products that will turn into *wat* and *tibs*, Latino growers lovingly arranging organic fruit and vegetables in displays of rainbow colors, and blond children with powdered sugar speckled faces, gleefully munching on Belgian waffles.

It was a sunny, warm day, and I felt the urge to weep with joy. Puerto Vallarta was behind us, and even with the road ahead still unclear, I could relish the fact that I was surrounded by the city and people I loved. Arnie attended a Bikram yoga class just across the street, and I imagined he might look out the window while doing the triangle pose and see me among the stalls. He loved this city too, even though for him it was an adopted one.

I plucked a yellow and red Rainier cherry from a sample tray and popped it in my mouth. At the same moment, I felt someone tap me from behind and say, "Dr. Burd?" It took me by surprise to have my professional life slice into my weekend reverie. I spun around to see a handsome young Asian man smiling at me. He had a moustache and a little goatee. He wore a tank top showing off muscular arms and a defined chest.

I said a garbled hello with the cherry pit still in my mouth. "Excuse me," I said and spit the pit into my hand. Not wanting to throw it on the ground, I held it, wet and slippery in my palm.

"You don't recognize me, do you?" The tone of his voice was calculated, not too loud. "I'm Sid."

It took me a minute, but I recovered enough to say, "Of course you are." I would have shaken his hand, but I still held the pit.

"Are you shocked?"

"Pleased," I said with a growing smile. All the emotion I had been feeling before came back, bringing tears to my eyes. In front of me, I had a male version of Botticelli's *Birth of Venus*, perfection growing up from the sea around us, the Farmers' Market of healthy eating, love, and diversity. I imagined he was everything that he wanted to be, physically at least. "My God, Sid, I'm so happy to see you."

"I wasn't sure at first."

I dropped the pit and wiped my hand on my jeans. "Let me give you a hug." I pulled him into my arms, noting our opposite bodies, his thin yet solid frame so different from my own voluptuousness. "I was glad and, I must admit, a little surprised to get your email a while back. I thought about reaching out to you. But this is perfect, meeting like this. Would you have time for a cup of coffee?"

I saw a slight hesitation on Sid's face as if my enthusiastic response was far beyond what he expected, as if it might be awkward to have a chat over coffee. He pulled his phone from his back pocket and looked at the time. "Uh, sure. I have some time."

"I'm waiting for someone to finish with yoga class across the street." I wasn't sure why I didn't say my husband. "We can go to Peet's."

At a table looking out on Lakeshore Avenue, Sid contemplated his chai latte while I smiled into my decaf cappuccino.

"How is your mother?" I asked.

"Not happy," said Sid with a chuckle. "My dad's cool, though. We go to Warriors games together. I moved out at sixteen. Went to live with my gay uncle."

"Do you talk to your mother?"

"Nope. I tried, but she won't have it."

"I guess I should say, though I hope it's obvious, I'm here as a friend, not a therapist," I said. "And part of my curiosity is for personal reasons." Sid nodded knowingly. "If I had had your conviction at a young age, I might have gone down the same path."

"There's no expiration date for it. One person in our group—I lead a group—is transitioning at fifty." Sid had grown from an androgynous boy into a masculine young man, and perhaps no longer found it necessary to mimic street talk, dropping the roguish edge he had adopted as a boy.

"More than the age factor, I think it's the certainty, or lack thereof. One thing that so impressed me about you was your unwavering conviction about being a boy. As you get older, you're more settled, things are more complicated. You have careers and financial ties and, in my case, a husband to consider."

"Sounds like you're looking for excuses."

We stared at each other for a moment. And then burst into laughter. "Role reversal!" said Sid. "Now it's my turn to say I'm here as a friend. But these are exactly the issues we deal with in group all the time."

"I do love my husband. We're a good team. It wouldn't be fair to him."

"You're afraid your husband doesn't love you enough to allow you to be the person you are on the inside. I could see it even as a nine-year-old."

"I understand intellectually what you're saying, of course. My brother, who's gay by the way, says pretty much the same. But Arnie and I have been married over twenty years. I've never talked to him about it."

"Then he must know you very well. He must have an idea how you feel. Oh, and you can tell me to shut up any time."

"Oh, Sid. I would never tell you to shut up even though I might want to. Everything you say makes sense." I took a sip of my now-cool cappuccino and looked out the window. I saw my husband crossing the street. Time had gotten away from me. He was coming to meet me at Peet's as we always did after his class. "Speak of the devil." And then I groaned. "Hate that expression."

"It was your husband you were waiting for?"

I sighed and felt foolish.

"I can make a quick exit out the back," said Sid.

"No, you can't." It was almost as if I had unconsciously planned the whole scenario.

Arnie entered and came over to the table glowing with post-yoga energy. Sid stood up and stuck out his hand, "Hi, I'm Sid."

"I'm Arnie." He dropped his bag on the floor, and shook Sid's hand. Then he rested his hand on my shoulder. "I see you've found good company. Let me get something, and I'll be right back."

When Arnie was at the counter, Sid located a chair and pulled it over to the table. "So who am I?" he said.

"The truth. You are who you are."

"Sid was a patient of mine a long time ago," I told Arnie when he came back to the table. "We ran into each other at the market."

"Yes. I was nine when I met your wife."

Arnie was relaxed and smiley as he always was after yoga. "Excellent. I imagine you had a lot to catch up on."

Arnie sat down with his mango iced tea infusion. "I need to hydrate. It was so hot in there today."

"Oh, do you do Bikram?" said Sid.

"Yes. Have you tried it?"

"A few times."

I watched my husband look at Sid. He was normally shy about staring when meeting strangers, but his curiosity slid over Sid's face, chest, and arms like a scanner.

"I've been doing it for six years now," said Arnie. "I love it. I know it's not for everybody."

He turned to me. "Did you pick up the asparagus, dear?"

"I'm afraid I got sidetracked."

"My fault," said Sid.

"We can get it afterward," said Arnie.

"They'll be closing up soon. We should probably go."

"I'll get this in a to-go cup then," said Arnie.

While Arnie got his cup, Sid and I exchanged information and promised to stay in touch. "Your husband seems nice," said Sid. "But he was totally checking me out."

"He's a doctor," I said, dismissing Sid's comment. "I mean, he's curious about people."

"I'm here if you want to continue this conversation."

"I do."

Arnie and I started up Trestle Glen with a pound of beautiful asparagus in the bag.

"That was kind of unusual," said Arnie.

"What?"

"You're normally so strict about not mixing professional with social."

"Oh, he was just a boy then, and we only had a few sessions. It was a long time ago."

"There's something special about him."

I didn't want to play the guessing game. "Yes, there is. He's a trans man."

"I had that feeling, not because he isn't convincing. Convincing is probably not the right word. He's a handsome young man. But I have several trans patients, mostly women but a few men as well. I suppose I'm sensitive to the little signs."

"He came to me totally convinced he was a boy. His mother, of course, wanted me to change his mind. I couldn't and didn't try very hard. She stopped the sessions. It was quite nice running into him and seeing how things turned out."

"You did the right thing in not trying to change his mind."

After getting home, we sat out on the deck with a pitcher of lemonade, made that morning with lemons from our tree. I tried to relax and just enjoy the yard. My mind had been on overload dealing with fatigue from the trip and the emotional trauma of the kidnapping. I hadn't even thought about the money. Of course it would take a lot more than a glass of lemonade and a beautiful yard to calm my brain.

"Is the money in the safe?" I asked. He had flown home with the backpack on Thursday.

"Oh, yes, my dear, completely safe behind that portrait of your parents. No one would think to look there," he chuckled. Yes, the house had an old style, behind-a-painting safe. We rarely kept things in it, but it occasionally came in handy.

"I guess we'll have to spend a good part of Monday redepositing the money." It had been taken out of multiple accounts at different banks so as not to draw suspicion. We didn't want to be flagged for funding terrorism or laundering money. "Did you count it?"

"I didn't even look at it. The zipper still had the zip tie on it. I just threw the dirty backpack in a plastic bag and put it in the bottom of my suitcase. When I got home, I put it in the safe."

"I suppose we should at least look at it," I said.

"Now? I thought you wanted to relax."

Arnie was still feeling peace after his yoga class, but I was antsy. "I'll get it."

I went to the safe with its old brass dial and put in the combination. I took the backpack out, and on my way back outside, stopped by the kitchen to get a pair of scissors to cut off the tie. I put it on the table between us and snipped the plastic. Arnie shook his head at my inability to relax. I opened the bag and stuck my hand in. I came up with a rolled-up magazine. "That's weird!"

"What?" said Arnie.

I dumped the contents of the bag on the table. Out tumbled about twenty rolled magazines. "No fucking way!"

Arnie's face, so calm a minute before, was struck with horror. "It's the same blue backpack we bought at the market in Puerto Vallarta. It still had the zip tie on it. It was probably out of our possession for less than an hour."

"I knew we shouldn't have trusted Tomas and his men," I said.

"You think it was them? He seemed so dedicated to helping us."

"I'm calling Lio. He was there the whole time. He must have seen something."

We weren't able to talk to Lio until he got back from Modesto that night. When he answered, I said, "Tell me exactly what happened from the time you and Flaco arrived at the gas station until we had the backpack in our possession again."

"Uh, hello to you, too. What's going on?" said Lio.

"The money is not in the backpack!"

"Wait. Wait. Wait. The hundred thousand dollars Tomas recovered is not in the fucking backpack?"

"Correct."

"Sweet sassy molassy! And you just discovered that now?"

"Did you at anytime see Tomas or his men open the bag?"

"No. After they knocked Flaco off his bike, they dragged him up from the ravine and gave the pack to Tomas. It sat on the seat between Tomas and me until we arrived at the hotel and he gave it to you. There's no way they could have taken the money."

"Okay," I said. "Let's go back to the gas station. Tell me exactly what happened."

"Flaco parked the bike behind the station. We climbed the hill and watched Augie arrive. As soon as he left, we went down and Flaco entered the station. He told me to wait outside."

"How long was he in there?"

"It seemed longer than he would need to pick up the bag. When he came out, I asked him why it took so long. He said he had to go to the bathroom."

"That is one smart son of a bitch. He must have left the money in the gas station. He could have cut off the tie, and then replaced it with another one."

"But what was in the pack?"

"Rolled-up magazines. He must have bought them in the store. We've been played royally. When Augie and I talked to Flaco, he acted the victim and he was sitting on a hundred thousand dollars. We insisted on letting him go. He must have gone back and collected the money. We need a family meeting. I'll call Augie and tell him."

"AJ's on a red eye out of Houston. Gets in at five in the morning. I'll go pick her up."

"Come straight here. We'll fix breakfast."

"God, I wonder if Chato knew about Flaco's plan. Or maybe Flaco did a Christian side hug on his own brother. Wouldn't surprise me."

"We need to talk to AJ and see what she knows."

Fog hung over the backyard, and the wind blew the papery cosmos flowers back and forth like metronomes. The atmosphere was equally glum inside as we sat around the dining table, the four siblings, Ruben, and Arnie. Everyone showed signs of a bad night of sleep. I had made a pot of strong coffee, and Arnie had whipped up a frittata. We had picked up bagels, lox, and cream cheese. So far, Ruben and Lio were the only ones eating.

Lio picked AJ up early that morning and informed her about the money on the way to our house. She had taken a quick shower before we all sat down, but she still looked mentally and physically exhausted. She sat quietly, her arms crossed in front of her chest as if daring anyone to ask her why she did what she did.

"I don't know if Chato was in on it," AJ blurted out before anyone had a chance to ask. "My feeling is that he didn't know Flaco's plan."

I didn't want to come down hard on AJ after everything she had been through, but her perception wasn't all that helpful. I wondered how much her opinions were still tied to her relationship with Chato. "I understand. But what we need are facts. How did this happen? Is there any way to get the money back?"

"I could call Tomas," said Ruben. "He might be able to find Flaco."

"Maybe we should just acknowledge that we fucked up," said Lio. "Got to hand it to the guy. We got jerked around."

"Arnie didn't fuck up," I said.

"I didn't say Arnie. I said 'we.' Any of us, you, me, Augie could have looked in the backpack that day, but we didn't."

"I don't like the idea of involving Tomas again," said Augie. "If they found him, I think they would really mess him up or even off him this time, and that would be on us. This guy is smart, as he has clearly shown us. My guess is that he is far away from Jalisco by now. I keep thinking of the time I sat with him at the clinic while he was awaiting treatment. I was mainly interested if he had any clue where AJ and Chato had gone. But we talked about other things as well. He whined about how much he had screwed up in his life. He even pretended to apologize, saying it was nothing personal against our family or *gringos* in general. They had been desperate, and people like them had so few options. All the while he was probably crazy to get up and go collect the money from where he had hidden it."

"I guess I should call Chato," said AJ. "Maybe he knows something."

"I don't think you should talk to him," said Lio.

AJ turned to her brother with a scowl. "You think he still has some power over me?"

"No. I never said that. If anybody talks to him, it should be me. If you call him, he might think you want further communication. From what you told me in the car, I'm gathering you don't."

AJ took a big sip of coffee and put the cup on the table with a thud, making some of it spill. "Look, I know everybody thinks I fell under the spell of a monster. Poor AJ, she just can't handle her men. She makes horrible decisions. I'm sorry if I'm an embarrassment to the family. I'm sorry if I just don't measure up." Her voice began to shake and gurgle. The tears started to flow. "And now I'm getting a divorce. I'm going to be the bad guy and everyone is going to hate me, maybe even my own boys." She was sobbing now. She grabbed a napkin and covered her face.

The rest of us were in shock. I had always known about her insecurity in the family, but I had perhaps been blind to what degree.

Augie jumped up. "Please, AJ. Nobody thinks you're an embarrassment. You are loved, and if we haven't made that clear, that's on us. You can't imagine how it feels when your little sister has been kidnapped, and you have no idea if you are going to get her back."

He walked over behind her chair and put his arms around her. "We all love you, AJ. We will support you in every way we can in your divorce."

I felt terrible. If anyone had treated AJ with less than the respect she deserved, it was me. I was like a mother who wanted her kids to achieve their best. I was disappointed at times. But when she and Lio were kidnapped, it was a stab in my heart. And I felt responsible just as every mother feels in some way guilty when something bad happens to her children.

I had to remind myself once again that Augie, Lio, and AJ were not my children but my siblings. They were adults. Their decisions were their decisions. "I reiterate everything Augie said," I said. "Plus I'm sorry if we weren't more supportive when you were struggling with Bart. We spent so much time ridiculing him or downright hating him, we forgot to focus on you, the person that mattered."

"You know you're my bestie," said Lio. "And I know it sounds weird, but you and Chato were kind of hot together."

AJ lowered the napkin away from her face. Augie was still behind her chair, but he had released his hug. "You don't have to say that," she said.

"What? The bestie part or the hot part?"

AJ laughed through her tears. "When you left on the bike with Flaco, I was overjoyed you were going to be free. I really wanted you to be the one to go. But at the same time, I felt an incredible emptiness like half of me had been torn away."

"I know we're upset about the money," said Augie. "But we're all here, alive. Our lives aren't perfect, but we'll be okay. Still we *can* do better with each other."

Ruben started sniffling like he was watching a sad movie. "Sorry," he said. "It's kind of amazing to watch you guys, the love you've got in your family.

Arnie looked out the window. "Doesn't look like the fog is going to burn off today," he said.

19: AJ

I tried calling Chato several times. I had to know if he was in on Flaco's plan. It seemed important to know if I had been a complete fool or a partial one. He didn't answer. Can't blame him for being angry since I left without saying goodbye. A number of times, I thought of his parting words at the restaurant in Mexico City, "I'm not giving up on you." At the time it didn't move me enough to stay, but in the midst of my emotional turmoil, it sounded sweet and sincere.

I had to recognize the possibility Flaco's clever maneuvering might have shut out Chato as well. He told me when we were in Mexico City he would return the money if it was possible. I hadn't told him we had recovered it because that would have entailed telling him Flaco had been beat up and was in danger. I believed his sentiment, though I did have to recognize he went along with the original kidnapping plot, and that negated any after the fact contrition.

We had decided not to contact Tomas. Augie was convinced Flaco would be a goner if Tomas's men caught him. None of us wanted to risk being responsible for a murder, even if it was someone who had done us harm and taken our money. When Mom's estate was settled, M and Augie would be paid back with enough left for each of us. It was a huge loss, and I was going to need every penny to start my new life. But as Augie said, we were all back home safe and sound, and that was what was really important.

A far bigger issue was how to tell the boys I was divorcing their father. I called Bart and told him I was coming down to Modesto on Sunday. I needed time alone with the boys. Then we could talk. Lio offered to come with me, but I told him I wanted to do it alone. Bart had never been physically abusive, so I wasn't afraid for my safety. The much greater fear was how Jason and Elijah were going to react.

On the way to Modesto, I listened to an Eighties station. It was the music M and Augie used to listen to when they were teenagers, so I knew a lot of the songs. A song, "Once in a Lifetime" by Talking Heads, came on. I remembered it particularly well because Augie would shout the lyrics every time it was on the radio, and M would tell him to shut up and slam her door.

I sang along in the car. I laughed and I cried. "My God! What have I done?" I shouted. By the time I pulled up in front of the house, the refrain was still in my head.

Bart's truck was in the driveway. Same as it ever was. The grass was brown, dotted with flowering dandelions a foot high. The house seemed a bit more drab than it had when I left for Mexico, not that it had ever been charming. The screen door was slightly askew. Yes, my husband worked in construction. I had asked him a million times to fix it. Same as it ever was. But I had changed.

I pulled in next to the pickup. I took a deep breath as I heard the aluminum screen bang. Bart stood on the porch. I started walking to the house.

"Why are you doing this?" he began.

I held up my hand and cut him off. "Stop. We'll talk later. I need some time with Jason and Elijah. Can you just…?"

"Don't worry. I'm leaving. I can't even look at you right now."

"Okay, go. Give me a couple of hours. Maybe your mom can come over later and take the kids. We'll talk."

"Fine." He slapped the ground with his flip-flops as he walked to the truck. He nodded in the direction of the house. "Good luck with that!" he said with a sneer.

As soon as I was in the house, Elijah ran down the hall and into my arms. "Mommy!" I squatted down to hug him. I looked over his shoulder down the hall.

"Where's Jason?" I said.

"I don't know," he said, meaning who cares? You've got me.

"Jason?" I said. "I'm home."

He came out of his room into the hall, maintaining his distance. "Are you staying?"

He was not going to let me ease into this. I wondered if his attitude came from someone telling him my intentions or something he intuited. "Come here, honey. Give me a hug."

He allowed me to hug him but didn't hug me back. "So?" he said.

"I'm going to spend the night here. Tomorrow I have to go back to Oakland to take care of some business. We're still sorting out grandma's affairs. Let's go in the living room." In truth, I had to go back to Oakland because I had an appointment with a divorce lawyer on Tuesday.

"Can I finish my video game?" said Jason.

"No, you can't."

I took Elijah by the hand and put my other hand on Jason's neck, leading them over to the couch. I had gone over the speech a thousand times in my head, though nothing came out the way it was supposed to. I thought I got the main points across: I love you now and forever; the problems Daddy and I are having have nothing to do with you; and I will always be as honest with you as possible. As expected, Elijah listened and wiped away tears. Jason stared at his hands. I had to add that if they ever had questions about something Daddy or Nana said, they should come and ask me.

"Jason said you weren't coming back from Mexico," said Elijah.

"Shut up."

I turned to Jason. "Did someone tell you that?"

"No. It was just weird Uncle Lio came here without you."

"Look. Here I am. I would never go away and not come back. Never ever. I love you guys."

"Where are you going to live?" said Elijah.

"I have to talk to Daddy. But this is what I hope. For now, you guys will stay here. I will be here half the time. When I'm here, your Dad can stay with Nana and Jimbo. Then when your Dad's here, I'll go stay at Grandma Burd's house in Oakland. We still have to work out the details."

"So, you and Dad don't even want to be in the same house?" said Jason.

"It's better that way. It's called a trial separation."

"Can we go to Grandma Burd's house with you?" asked Elijah.

"I don't want to go to Grandma Burd's house. She died there," said Jason.

"We're not going to worry about that now. For the time being, you'll just stay in our house like normal," I said.

"Except it won't be normal," said Jason.

"True. It won't be the same, but hopefully as normal as possible."

I took the boys out for pizza, and then texted Bart I would drop them at his parents' house. Bart and I could go to our house and work out the details.

Work out the details? he texted back. *It's a done deal? Fuck!*

On my way to drop off the boys.

No one would ever describe the drive from Modesto to Oakland as scenic. There was a brief respite from the boredom during the short section through the San Joaquin River Valley, particularly in the spring when the river flowed wide. I had done the drive a hundred times, and part of my penance for breaking up my marriage was to do it a couple hundred more. Bart had been petulant and combative at times during our talk. He claimed at one point he could deny me access to my sons based on no reason in particular.

He accused me of having an affair in Mexico. He couldn't have known that unless Lio had told him, and I was a hundred percent sure he hadn't. In the end, he agreed to split the week at the house with the boys. On his days, Wanda would take care of the boys while Bart was at work. I didn't like the boys spending so much time with her, but I had no choice until things were settled.

I spent the night on the sofa bed in the living room, insisting he sleep in the bedroom to avoid having to change the sheets. I doubt either of us slept much. I got up early, kissed my snoozing boys, and got on the road.

I had decided to stay at Mom's house while in Oakland, and Lio said he wanted to move back in there temporarily until we figured out what to do with it. It was worth a lot of money, but it needed some repairs before we could put it on the market. I asked Lio to meet me there.

The first thing I noticed when we opened the door was that it needed a good cleaning. We walked around opening up windows to allow the place to breathe.

"I'm sure hospice removed all the good drugs," said Lio.

I had to laugh. "That's what you think of when we enter the house the first time since Mom died?"

"They kill the pain, right?"

"We've got too much to do to be high. Besides I thought you were turning over a new leaf for Belle."

"I am. We had dinner. I'm going to take her on a little trip to Hawaii. Just the two of us."

"Not Puerto Vallarta?"

"Very funny. Actually, Kathy hasn't agreed to it yet, but she's got family there, so I'm hoping. Did you talk to Chato?"

"No. I'm sure he's pissed at me."

"I would be, too. It's so hard to keep a kidnap victim around these days."

When I was growing up, I often had a dream I would wake up and look out my upstairs window and see a man in a long coat standing in the yard, looking up at me. I would run downstairs to make sure all the doors and windows were locked. From the dining room window I would see he was no longer there, meaning he might already be in the house. I wanted to run back upstairs to tell my parents, but the stairway wasn't where it was supposed to be. I would keep searching for it in a panic.

Something woke me up from a deep sleep. At first I didn't know where I was. The room was semi-dark. I saw one of the collages I made in high school on the wall, so I was in my old room. I got up and went to the window. A sensation like molten steel ran through my veins. A man was stretched out on the garden furniture sofa close to the fire pit.

I ran into Lio's room and knelt beside his bed. "Lio, wake up. There's a man in the yard.

Lio groaned as he emerged from sleep. "You're dreaming," he said. When we were kids, I had told him about my dream.

"No. This is for real." I went to his window and looked out. "Come, look. He's still there," I whispered.

"Call the police then," mumbled Lio. With great effort he sat up, and then managed to crawl to the window. "Dubya-tee-eff! You're right."

"Watch him. I'm calling." I went into the bathroom and reported the prowler. "They said they'd send someone right out."

"Let's go downstairs and get a better look," said Lio. He grabbed his old baseball bat.

We had a good view from the dining room. It had just started getting light. I stared at the hand dangling over the edge of the sofa. "No! No way!"

"What?" said Lio.

"I've got to call the police back and cancel."

"Why? I don't think you can do that."

I raised the window. "Chato?" I called out in a low voice. He sat right up and looked around. "What are you doing?" I growled. "Come to the back door quickly."

"Well spank my ass and call me Charlie! Now what do we do? The police are on the way."

I unlocked the back door and a sheepish Chato walked in.

"I'm sorry," he said. "I didn't want to ring the doorbell until morning. Oh, hi, Lio."

"I don't even know what to say," I said. Having to deal with Chato was the last thing I needed, but there was no time to argue or discuss details. "The police are coming. You have to hide." I pushed him into the downstairs bathroom and closed the door.

He opened the door a crack. "Please don't send me back before I explain."

The doorbell rang. I took hold of the door and pulled it closed. "No one is sending you anywhere," I whispered. "Be quiet and stay in there."

"You answer it," I said to Lio. "I'm too nervous. No, wait. I'd better do it. I'm the one who called."

I apologized to the officers, a man and a woman, telling them the man jumped over the fence and ran down the street. When they asked for a description, I told them he was short and blond, wearing jeans and a hoodie.

"How did you know his hair was blond if he was wearing a hoodie?" asked the woman.

Lio jumped in. "The hood came off when he jumped over the fence."

They asked for a few more details, and then insisted on checking the backyard.

"I'm really sorry you had to come by for nothing," I said. I tried to hurry them out, but they kept asking questions.

"You're sure about the blond part?"

"Yes," said Lio. "Thanks again." He closed the door after them and collapsed in a chair.

"Go let Chato out. I'll make some coffee."

The three of us sat at the breakfast bar, my head spinning with a thousand questions. I wanted to yell at him, but I tried to stay calm. "How did you get this address?"

"Is the one on your license. I already tell you I look at your wallet."

I had never changed my permanent address to Modesto. That bizarre detail, showing my lack of full commitment to Modesto, plus his chance timing allowed him to find me. Last night was the Thursday I didn't have with the boys. "That is just so...so...wrong," I said.

"I know. You told me."

"Okay. Forget that. I have to clarify something. Did you know about Flaco's plan to screw us again?"

"What are you talking about?"

"That day when Flaco exchanged Lio for the money, some men, probably the same ones that came to the cabin, chased Flaco and recovered the money, at least that's what they thought. Flaco had the same blue backpack Augie delivered the cash in."

Lio jumped in. "I was there. They ran Flaco off the road. He was injured, but not badly. When we got home, there was no money in the backpack. Only rolled-up magazines."

Chato's wide-eyed astonishment couldn't have been faked. "I swear I know nothing. Wait. Nobody look in the backpack when you get it?"

"Nobody looked," Lio confirmed with a little chuckle. "It was still closed with the zip tie."

"Okay. Now I understand something. I have only one communication with Flaco since we leave for Mexico City. After you leave, he send me text to say there is money behind a stove in restaurant. I don't understand. I try many times to contact him, but he is disappear. I go home and yes is twenty-five thousand dollars behind stove. My mother she say he give her money too. She tell me I must go away like Flaco. Men come to her house looking for us. I think I must go to States...I *want* to go to States. I think you know why."

I held my coffee cup and felt the warmth. I stared out the window. Lio looked at me. Chato studied the countertop. "I told you this can't be," I said.

"When I get this money, I know I must come here and return the money I have. Only one problem—I must use a lot to cross the border. Every time more expensive. At least I can return fifteen thousand to you. But another problem. On the trip, they rob me everything except some dollars I have in the secret place of my belt. Anyway I can work and pay you back." He turned his head to look at me with those disarming eyes, his sweet smile. "I can't believe I'm sitting here talking to you."

I vowed I would not fall for his charm again. "I'm glad you're safe. But you can't stay here."

"I forget to ask how is your husband?"

Lio had just taken a gulp of coffee and he sprayed it all over the counter. I looked at Lio with murder in my eyes. "If you must know, we have a trial separation. Half the week I go to Modesto to be with my boys. But that's really none of your business."

"Of course. I am just curious."

He was still staring at me. Smiling. His hand was an inch away from mine on the counter. I stood up. "Excuse us a minute." I motioned for Lio to follow me. We went in the den and sat on the sofa.

"Help me," I said. "What do we do?"

"We need someone to do repairs on the house. He did construction, right?"

"Oh, that is so helpful. Are you insane? There are about a million reasons why he can't be here."

"Can you imagine M and Augie's faces if they knew he was here right now?"

"Are you enjoying this?"

"You obviously like him. I saw your face when he first walked in the door."

"He's a stalker!"

"Okay. I'll go tell him he has to leave," said Lio. He stopped at the doorway and turned around. "You're sure about this?"

"Yes."

He went back in the kitchen, but before I had a moment to reflect on my decision, I heard, "He's gone."

I ran in the kitchen. "What do you mean?"

"He's not in the bathroom or anywhere on this floor."

I would feel guilty about it later, but I flew up the stairs to see if my purse was still in my bedroom. It was. I looked in the other bedrooms, but no Chato.

We went out the front door and looked up and down the street. "You go toward College, and I'll go the other way," said Lio.

"I'm not running after him."

"Just do it."

I walked toward College Avenue, picking up my pace as I got near the intersection. My heart was thumping, but I told myself it was just from the exertion. I saw him walk into Hudson Bay Café on College. I followed him in. He turned around and saw me. He laughed. Bastard.

"What are you doing?" I said.

"Didn't you want me to leave?"

"I hate you."

"I know. I just come to get some breakfast. I'm hungry. What do you like? Something veggie?"

I took out my phone and sent a text to Lio. "We're at Hudson Bay. Come quick before I kill him."

He was still looking at me with raised bushy eyebrows. "Get a couple of bagels with cream cheese," I said. "You got any money left?"

"Yep."

We sat at a table by the window. "Did you have a plan when you decided to come here?" I said.

"Did you when you go to Mexico City with me?"

"That was different."

"Uh-huh. *Mira*...look, I don't want fight. In Mexico City, for maybe twenty-four hours, we don't fight. It is beautiful. Then you leave. I understand. You are afraid."

"Afraid of what? We had sex. It was nice. Our worlds are so far apart."

"I think we are in the same world. I can touch you. You can touch me."

He reached for my hand. I pulled it away. Lio walked into the cafe.

"We got you a bagel," said Chato.

I thought the "we" was interesting, as if we were a couple and had ordered for a late arriving friend.

Lio sat down and we all looked at each other. "Just like old times," said Lio. He turned to me with a laugh. "I think we should capture him and make him our sex slave."

At first, Chato didn't get the joke. "But you are not...?"

"No, he's not gay," I said. "Just has a weird sense of humor."

"Maybe we have fun," said Chato with a wink at Lio.

"No. No. No. You two are not ganging up on me," I said. "This is not a joking matter. I'm in the middle of a fucking divorce. Lio has no job. And..."

"I thought is trial separation," said Chato.

"Your comprehension is so fucking excellent when you want it to be," I said, regretting my slip of the tongue. "Yes, we are getting a divorce. And you played absolutely no part in that."

"Not even a little tiny bit?"

"No!"

20: Augie

Coming back from Mexico reminded me of pinball machines we used to play as kids that registered a tilt after too much jostling or nudging. Tilt would cut the power to the flippers, stop the music, and make the screen go dark. Life would stop for a moment. Some machines displayed a message. One of our favorites was "Cheating makes Baby Jesus cry." As a Jewish kid, I found it hilariously funny. The machine would reset itself, light up again, and the music would start. The playing environment would be the same, but you'd lose any bonus points and extra balls.

Our lives were restarted back on home territory with no lack of issues to deal with. AJ was going through with her divorce. Lio was unemployed and trying to be the father he had failed to be when Belle was younger. M refused to talk about how she felt or if she had revealed to Arnie what she shared with us in Puerto Vallarta. And I, with vast amounts of new material in my head, was unsure how I would get it all down on paper.

The last time the four of us got together, we agreed to stop whining about the tilt we had suffered in Mexico. We were all alive and safe at home. The music was playing, and we were back in the game. That didn't stop us from remembering how close we were to being safe at home and *not* out a hundred thousand dollars. Since the loss took a chunk out of our inheritance, we agreed to sell Mom and Dad's house.

Our agent told us we could list it for 1.2 million, and we nearly fell off our chairs. If we did a few repairs and some cosmetic upgrades, we could get even more. Selling the house where we all had so many memories was sad, but in a practical sense, it could also come in handy in situations like now when both AJ and Lio were temporarily living there. But who knew when real estate might again take a nosedive. Selling while the market was hot made sense.

AJ and Lio said they would handle contracting workers for the repairs. They had also sent me a text asking for another family meeting, but this time at Mom's house. They didn't give any details. M and I assumed it had something to do with the sale.

My dream of devoting myself full time to writing was about to become a reality. That would mean the pressure would be on to produce, but I was ready. I told Ruben what my part of the profits would be from selling the house. He looked at me and smiled. "Okay, you win." Our agreement was that I would return the money I had borrowed from Colton's college fund and double it once we sold the house.

Walking into the 1915 Carnegie-funded Mission branch of the library wasn't laden with the usual Monday morning back-to-work drudge. I already felt a certain nostalgia coupled with nervousness about my decision. On Friday, I had submitted my papers for a leave of absence, realizing it could be a permanent end to my job there.

"Hey, Josie." She was on the computer at the front desk.

"236," she shouted.

It was a nerdy game we played. Dewey Decimal System. "Eschatology," I shouted back.

"What's that? The study of shit?"

"Oh, Josie. It's religious doctrines concerning final matters."

"I knew that."

"Of course you did."

I got along well with all my coworkers and would miss them with the possible exception of Claudia, who had been my competition for the head librarian job at the branch three years before. The job should have gone to her. She was truly bilingual, having been born in Mexico and grown up in the Mission. She had developed the Spanish-English program at Mission branch. I worked at the main branch and just barely fulfilled the bilingual requirement, but I had much higher seniority. I thought about dropping out and letting her get the job, but Ruben said no. It was a significant increase in salary and walking distance from our house. I could drop Colton off at school on the way to work.

Claudia was at the reference desk and didn't look like she intended to look up when I went by. I stopped. "Claudia, just wanted to let you know I'm going to take a leave. I recommended that you take over."

"For how long?"

"A year. Maybe longer."

"Is everything okay?"

"Yes, everything's fine. I'm going to try writing full-time."

"Oh." She had a librarian's mistrust of detailed conversations unless it was a reference question.

When I left work, great billowy pillows of fog were falling over Twin Peaks and headed for the Mission. A group of tourists clad in summer wear, carrying expressions of shock that California could be so cold walked toward Valencia Street. Yes, the Mission had been discovered. It was summer in San Francisco.

Summer also brought the challenge of what to do with a ten-year-old's energy. In the last week of school, we were again called into the principal's office. Another fight. The boy Colton exchanged blows with didn't tease him about having two dads as might be expected, but rather had pointed out both his dads were white, and he was dark skinned. This incident brought up anew the sensitive subject of Colton's mother.

Ruben and I had a long discussion. The principal had suggested a summer camp or some team sport might be helpful, though his reasoning went right over my head. As soon as we mentioned it to Colton, he chose basketball. We also discussed getting in touch with Joy to see if she had an interest in meeting Colton. I was against basketball camp and contacting Joy, but I lost both arguments.

M and I arrived at Mom's house without our spouses. Ruben stayed home with Colton, and Arnie wanted to work in the yard, which had been showing neglect in the chaos of the last few weeks. Lio and AJ had set up lunch on the patio—cold cuts, cheese, bread, and prepared salads they had picked up at a local deli. Lio popped a bottle of rosé and poured four glasses.

I pointed to a fifth glass. "Is that set aside for Elijah?"

AJ's already tense face took a turn toward puzzlement. "My Elijah?"

"No, I was thinking of Passover Elijah. A joke."

"Not expecting either one."

"But someone."

"I'll get to that," said AJ.

Something told me the meeting was not about the house.

"I have some news," said AJ, serious, eyes cast down.

From the look on her face and Lio's twisted smile, I guessed it was not particularly good news. The first thing that came to mind was she was going to announce she was pregnant with a Mexican love child.

I had picked up M on the way over, and we had tried to imagine what the gathering was about. We both agreed we needed to be kinder to AJ, particularly during the difficult time of her divorce. We still felt the sting of her outburst the week before.

"You know we're behind you a hundred percent in your divorce," said M. "Anything you need, just let us know."

"It's not about that, though I would like to discuss matters with Bart later." She hesitated and looked at Lio.

"Just tell them," said Lio.

"We got word from Mexico that they found Flaco's body. It was by the side of the road near Sayulita. They don't know who did it, but one can assume that at least part of the motive was robbery."

My feelings about Flaco ran the gamut. At first I was angry at him for kidnapping my brother and sister, but that changed to near sympathy when I saw him battered and bruised. Then my feelings changed back to anger with a hint of respect when we found out how he had fooled us with the money. But learning someone I had spoken to face to face had met a violent death was nonetheless shocking. "Did you speak to Chato?" I asked.

Again AJ looked at Lio for support. "Yes," she said, drawing out the word to several syllables.

"Let me take it from here," said Lio. "If I leave it to AJ, this might take all day." It was a warm day, and the cold cuts and cheese were beginning to dry up. We all looked at the pasta salad that probably had mayonnaise in it. "A few nights ago, we found someone sleeping on the lounge chair over there." He pointed at the fire pit.

"Oh, no," I said.

"It was Chato. He had fled Mexico, but didn't know about Flaco yet. The other day he asked AJ if he could use her phone to call his mom to tell her he was all right. His mom gave him the news about Flaco."

"So he's here now?" I said.

"Yes," said Lio. He glanced at the house.

"In the house?"

"Yes," said AJ.

"You've got to be kidding me!" said M in outrage. Then she seemed to remember her promise to be nicer. "I mean..."

"Just hear me out, okay?" said AJ. "Sending him back to Mexico could possibly mean sending him to his death. He believes they killed Flaco in part for the money, but the local gangs were also angry the brothers were encroaching on their territory. He also said he didn't know about Flaco's trick to hide the money."

"And you believe him?" said M.

"Yes," said AJ.

I turned to M. "Do you think Tomas's men had anything to do with Flaco's death?"

I could see M's mind going. She was already several steps ahead. "I hope not," she said. "But there is nothing we can do about that. And I agree we don't want to be responsible for any more violence. And we certainly don't want to do ICE's work for them. Can we talk to him? We understand he just lost his brother. We'll be kind."

"He wants to talk to you," said AJ. "But I thought I should prep you first."

"I'll get him," said Lio.

Chato walked out in an aura of sadness. I tried very hard not to focus on the fact that he was stunningly handsome in a new salmon polo shirt and jeans. I knew AJ was watching my face, so I refrained from the wink I was dying to give her. I stood up and shook his hand. "*Mi más sentido pésame.* My condolences."

M also stood up and offered her hand to Chato. "Sorry for your loss."

I poured Chato a glass of wine and gave it to him.

"Can we sit down and eat?" said Lio. "The food is going bad."

Everybody put food on their plates and poured more wine. Chato cleared his throat. "Thank you for meeting me. I know you must think I am a terrible person. I think I am a terrible person in some things I do. I want to say I make my brother promise we don't ever hurt April and Lio even we don't get any money. Anyway, it was a stupid plan. I have no excuses. A disaster. And now my brother is dead. You can ask me anything you want."

I could only feel sadness listening to Chato talk. Each word was infused with melancholy, coming from a culture that swayed back and forth between intense joy and bouts of desperation. From the day Emilio arrived at our house to spend a year with us, I had been intrigued by the Mexican temperament. It was the first time I realized that different cultures had different views of the world.

I married a man of Mexican heritage years later, and though growing up in the States moderated his personality, his ancestry showed through in mysterious ways. In my travels through Mexico, time and time again I was impressed how much the American and Mexican ways of life differed, the most obvious being our dissimilar approaches to death. Once I was in Oaxaca for the Day of the Dead. I went to the cemeteries and saw the fantastic, joyful decorations, family members partying with their deceased relatives by eating their loved one's favorite foods, playing their favorite music. In my experience as an American, going to the cemetery was a rare occasion, heart wrenching and sad.

I wondered if AJ, like me, was fascinated by things she couldn't quite understand. Put that together with Chato's physical charms, and I could see why AJ had a strong attraction to him.

"How did you get here?" said M.

"Yes, well, this is a little bit difficult. My only communication with Flaco after I go to Mexico City, he text me he leave some money in a hiding place. It was twenty-five thousand. I know I need leave Mexico and is very expensive now. I pay coyote to bring me. I plan to return rest of money to you, but they rob me. I'm sorry."

It was hard not to feel sympathy for him. From what little I knew about him, his life had been pretty awful, a scene repeated millions of times all over Mexico. And despite all the odds and now an ever-increasing hostile government, the United States offered hope.

"He can work," said AJ. "He knows construction."

"Yes, I want to work," said Chato.

M and I both looked at AJ a bit incredulously. "You mean on the house?"

"I was a handyman at an apartment complex for a while and did some construction. I can do basic electricity and plumbing. Also I do gardening."

"We're not doubting your skills," said M. "It's just...there are so many questions. For example, where would you live?"

"We were thinking he could live here," said Lio.

A headline jumped into my head: Mexican kidnapper charms his way into the lives of his victims to work off his debt. "You can't make this shit up," I said.

"Maybe *you* can," said M. "AJ, it's up to you. You are adults. One word of advice. If Bart found out, he could use it against you."

"He doesn't know Chato exists. And I plan to keep it that way."

"What if Jason and Elijah come here for a visit?" said M.

"The current arrangement is for the kids to stay in Modesto. Bart and I will take turns being at the house with them. If for some reason they did come here, Lio said Chato could stay in his room in Montclair."

Because of Chato's obvious charms, having AJ and Chato under the same roof while she was going through a divorce seemed like a recipe for disaster. But M and I, knowing how sensitive AJ was to our opinions, were reluctant to criticize her.

"We're not sleeping together," AJ announced.

I couldn't help noticing the furrowed brow and sidelong glance Chato gave to AJ. He was obviously in love with her. I couldn't wait to get home and tell Ruben the newest plot developments.

We finished eating and AJ stood up, offering to make coffee.

"Before we have coffee, Chato, would you mind if we talked to AJ alone?" said M.

AJ sat back down. She grabbed a strand of hair and twisted it around her finger. Her eyes backed into her head.

"I go inside," said Chato. "No problem."

"I want to be clear. I'm not judging you," said M. "I just want to make sure you're okay. You're under a lot of stress right now. Taking on the responsibility of Chato could be overwhelming. You don't owe him anything."

"Believe me," said AJ. "I've thought a lot about this. When we were in Mexico City together, I got to see him for the decent human being he is. Yes, he is flawed, but aren't we all? Part of the reason for going to Mexico City was for him to apologize to his gay brother for the pain he caused him when they were growing up. I admired him for that. I know he went to great risk to come all the way here because he trusts me. And I believe he did intend to give back the money left after paying to get here. He even offered to work for free, but I don't think we should hold him to that."

"He could start with the yard," I said. When Mom got sick, no one paid the gardener, so he stopped coming. The back yard had turned into a jungle. "He should keep his shirt on though," I laughed. "Seriously, we'll probably need more people, but there's a lot he can do here."

"I guess I'm okay with it, too," said M. "And if we have to do any electrical or plumbing, make sure to get professionals. It should be to code. I'm glad Lio's here with you."

"I trust Chato," said Lio. "I'm not sure I should, but I do. Just a feeling."

I wondered if Lio and Chato would develop their own little special handshake or some such intimacy. I was back to my old tricks. I had promised myself when Lio was returned to us safe I would never again feel jealousy. Old habits die hard.

During a lull in the conversation, we heard a frail squeaking coming from above our heads. "What's that?" I asked.

Lio smiled. "We have a family living right above us, a whole life cycle going on in the trumpet vine."

"Another uninvited guest in the yard?" I said. "Sorry, I couldn't resist."

"There's a nest and babies. Mom and pop mockingbirds are constantly bringing worms and bugs to the screaming babies."

"The other day I guess I got too close to the nest," said AJ. "One of the birds dive-bombed me, came within inches of my head."

"It will be over soon. The baby birds are only in the nest two to three weeks," I said.

"Thanks, professor," said Lio. "It's cool, though. I like having a family here."

The squeaking continued. We sat quietly. A mockingbird with a bug in its mouth hopped from rooftop to tree to bush. It fanned its tail up and down. Deciding it was safe, it darted into the middle of the arbor. It left a few seconds later to forage some more.

"Amazing," I said. We all grabbed our wine glasses and took a sip.

"How is the divorce going?" said M.

AJ stared into her glass. "The petition will be filed this week, and I've gotten a tentative commitment through his lawyer that he won't contest. I'm not asking for alimony. Joint custody of course, and I do want something for the house. Unfortunately he doesn't have any money to buy me out, so there will be some negotiating. And then the six month wait."

"Where do you want to end up?" I asked.

"The Bay Area definitely. And I want the boys to go to school here. I'll have a fight over that, but he can have them weekends and holidays. I want them to be exposed to the environment we grew up in. Modesto is changing, but not fast enough."

"Yes, please. No more N-words!" I said.

"They could hang out with Colton more," AJ said.

"And Belle," said Lio. "Or maybe not. She might resist hanging with silly younger boys."

"We could revive our Sunday family gatherings," said M.

We talked about all the things we could do together, even the possibility of family trips. The conversation meandered, and we forgot all about Chato until AJ said, "Poor boy. He's probably in there cleaning the kitchen. He's been really helpful since he got here."

When I got home, both Ruben and Colton were smiling ear to ear.

"We have a surprise for you, Daddy," said Colton.

"Am I going to like it?"

"I think so. Close your eyes and take my hand." Colton led me to the garage. "Okay, open them."

They had cleaned out a corner where we stored junk near a window that looked out on the back yard. They had put down a rug and set up a folding screen so the area was sectioned off. There was a new desk and a lamp. I knew I would always remember that moment and the feeling of love and appreciation for the people I had in my life. I was overwhelmed with guilt I had sometimes blamed them for my lack of a writing career.

"Are you going to cry, Daddy?"

"I'm so happy. Thank you." I drew Colton into a hug.

"I know it's not your birthday for a few weeks," said Ruben. "But we couldn't wait."

21: Gloria

My children, my four calling Burds as I sometimes called you when the four of you were shouting "Mom" all at once, I know I was bothersome at times, ringing you in the middle of the day to tell you something I had read or seen on the Internet. Now I could wish for nothing more than to hear you calling, or maybe I can if I listen closely enough. It's ironic, isn't it? I have so many things I want to tell you now that the lines of communication are gone. I especially would like to clarify some things about my last days.

In the very last few days, the days when my eyes were closed and my mouth was open, my semi-comatose state, I heard the question swirling about as to if I could hear you or not. I *could* hear you, though I couldn't respond despite my greatest desire to do so. I heard loud and strong your declarations of love, your sweet words of gratitude, and the little stories you remembered from childhood. I also heard in those few minutes each of you was alone with me your secret mumblings and desires. Since I was incapable of reacting at that point, perhaps you felt safe, thinking you were speaking to nothing more than an image of me, thinking you were free from my usual motherly feedback. But I heard you.

I also heard you in the days before that when I could still open my eyes, utter words, put my withering cold hands in yours. I know some of the things that came out of my mouth sounded bizarre. The problem was that I could still think in complete sentences, but when I tried to speak, half my phrases would be lost. I had already started to leave my body.

Separating myself from the emaciated confines of the flesh was peaceful and alluring. In the middle of a sentence, some magical thing of beauty would distract me. Unspoken words would dissipate into the air. Then I would realize as you all sat leaning forward expectantly, that something was incomplete. In my head it *had* been complete. By the time I realized what had happened, the thought was gone, replaced by a glorious image or a dazzling light drawing me.

One evening, you were all talking about the day-to-day while I contemplated the universe of stars. Out of the blue, I said, "Your father wants me to…" It was almost comical how the conversation in the room immediately stopped and all heads turned toward me, waiting for me to finish the sentence. But it was not to be. I had seen Ira in a flash of light, and he wanted me to tell all of you he loved you. The last half of the phrase floated away, and I left you hanging. I'm sorry.

Your father loved all of you dearly, even if it wasn't always obvious. He was a quiet man, an introvert, enjoyed being alone, felt most comfortable in his study. I'm sure he never imagined having four children, and yet he was so excited each time I got pregnant. I think it both made him feel more of a man, and he was leaving a legacy. He would often tell me how amazed he was at the way each of you turned out. Even if he didn't check in with you the way I used to, he was aware of everything you were going through and would discuss the day's events when we went to bed at night, things as simple as a bruised knee or a good grade on a test.

Perhaps the biggest misunderstanding of those semi-lucid days sounded quite awful and not surprisingly fell on Augie. It was the end of the day, maybe three days before I passed. I was exhausted. Augie came to my side to say goodnight. He had to drive back across the bridge to San Francisco and work the next day.

"Goodnight, mommy dearest," he said.

It hit a nerve in some dark place of my brain. I'm sure he wasn't referencing the Joan Crawford movie, but I did wonder. I remember that play he wrote as a little boy called, "Mean Mother and Jimmy" where the mother figure did things like pull the chair out from under her son, Jimmy, when he went to sit down.

It was amusing how he got his siblings to play the parts, but I couldn't help feeling a little unsettled. Had I done cruel things to you children that would provoke such a creative endeavor? You were always telling me, Augie, not to read too much into your stories. Yet it is the onus of your loved ones always to be looking for a bit of themselves in your fiction. All of that somehow became jumbled in my head, and I replied, "You're mistaken. I'm not your mommy…" and then the phrase fell off. What I meant to say was that I was not your mommy dearest like the one in the movie, or that mean mommy in the play.

After a moment of shock, my dear Augie, you took it quite well and said, "That's okay. I love you anyway." And then he joked with the rest of you that he always knew he was adopted. I could have died right then and there. And though I lasted another two days, those ended up being the last words I said to my son. Of course I was your mommy, August. Of all my children, you were the most like me.

Oh, August, I'm sure I didn't tell you enough when you were growing up how much you were appreciated and loved. Possibly because you were the one with whom I shared the most, I didn't think it necessary. I hope I made up for it later when we were able to confide our mutual love of books and literature. And, of course, you learned to speak Spanish fluently. How can I forget the Neruda poem, *"Para lavar a un niño,"* you read to me in Spanish one of those nights before my death? I could have a conversation about anything with you, even the Dewey Decimal System. I even made a pact with you to never utter his name, that one with the orange skin and yellow hair.

Still, you weren't all that lovable at times, with your need to make snide comments and constantly show how much you knew. I was afraid you would push people away, even though I know it was your way of protecting yourself. And then you met Ruben. You blossomed. And when you and Ruben decided to have Colton, all the love bottled up inside you for so long came rushing out. So when you said to me in the last couple of days, when I could not even respond in partial sentences, that you wanted to be a writer, all I could think was of course you did.

And you went on to say Ruben and Colton were keeping you from your dream. You weren't sure if your love for them was more powerful than your desire to finally pursue your dream. I didn't believe you for a minute. I couldn't tell you the only thing keeping you from being a writer was you. I know you will figure it out. You aren't smarter than you think, but you're stronger than you think. Words aren't adequate to say how proud I am of you.

My dear Julio, it wouldn't be fair if I said I loved you more than the other three. A mother can't do that. But our love had a different quality. I would look at you and feel a passion for life. It was similar to the inexplicable passion I had for learning Spanish, so I gave you a Spanish name.

From the moment you were born, you were the adorable, cuddly puppy everyone loved. So full of life. Unfortunately, being the adorable puppy can't sustain itself into adult life. I watched you struggle with your marriage, finding your way with your daughter after your divorce. I knew you would figure out partying your life away can't bring happiness. And you did find your way. I might have chosen a higher course for you than managing a dental office, but you did it well. You loved to remind me I used to say to all you kids it didn't matter if you were a ditch digger as long as you did it well. Thank God none of you became ditch diggers.

When you whispered in my ear that you were determined to have a relationship with your daughter, you probably couldn't see my smile. I don't remember if I told you Belle came to visit me after I got sick. She is a lovely girl and has the same sparkle in her eyes that you do. She thanked me for introducing her to the world of books. When she was very young, I used to read to her and always gave her books for her birthdays. She told me it changed her life. It brought me to tears. So yes, you must be as much of a father to her as you can.

The other thing you told me was you still wanted to be an actor. I can only wish you the best. I actually think you could be a fine actor though I'm not sure it's a career you can pursue at the age of forty. You were pretty good in the productions your brother used to put on. Follow your dreams, *querido.*

Dearest May, my springtime child, my first and most accomplished offspring. You came into the world ready to climb the highest mountains, swim the widest seas. So intelligent and driven. Where did all that energy come from? Perhaps you were able to find some answers in your study of psychology. But I doubt the biggest mystery of you, the male force within, has an answer. I remember you telling me when you were a teenager you might be lesbian. Other athletic girls like you were considering that option. But when I asked if you were attracted to other girls, you answered, "Not really." I knew your struggle would have no easy solution.

And then that day when we were alone, you told me about the young patient you had had, how he had been born a girl, but was absolutely convinced he was a boy. You couldn't stop thinking about him, wondering if that was where you should go. I could give you no advice from the almost other side.

Did I wrinkle my brow with worry? You are a headstrong woman, and I know you will do what you want, but I kept thinking of Arnold. In your work, you must know how lucky one is to find a partner in life. I watched you two grow together and it warmed my heart. He was the gentle brake to your fast-moving train. I don't want to speak against transitioning to the gender you feel inside. For some I understand that it is the best option. The force must be strong if you would even consider doing that, but I wonder if it is strong enough that you would risk everything, your marriage, your career.

You have accomplished so much being the wonderful person you are. I want nothing more than your happiness. In your dilemma, I was almost glad I couldn't speak. How does one address an issue so complex and so personal? Though your personality has always been a mystery to me, you know I love a good mystery, particularly the one that is you.

My baby girl, April June, you are both spring and summer. You were always determined to pursue your own course, to escape the shadow of your three older siblings, perhaps to a fault. It caused you to make some strange choices. When you told me you wanted to divorce Bart, it was the least surprising of any of my children's revelations. You doubted your strength to do it though. You didn't know how you would manage. You were worried about the boys.

If I could have said something, I most certainly would have spoken against it, thereby ensuring you would do it. As in the case with marrying Bart, it was almost as if your family being against something made you decide to go through with it. The thing I could never say to you is that you would never be as driven as May, as intelligent as August, or as charming as Julio. But you always had a natural beauty and self-assurance people were attracted to. It was so important for you to have that beautiful house in the hills, showing us you had made something of your life. But unlike May's home, a logical result of a high-paying professional career, yours fell into your hands and just as easily slipped away. It wasn't your fault, but I hope it was a lesson.

I know your desire to divorce stems from a realization Bart is so different from you, and that difference became blaringly obvious when you moved to Modesto. You grew up in the Burd household in the Bay

Area's bastion of progressive values, open hearts, and critical thinking. That is in you, and I have a feeling you will return to that both in full acceptance of those ideas and in location. I hope and pray you will be able to instill those same values in your boys without too much interference from Bart.

It may take a trauma or unfathomable episode to wake you up, make you realize your life is speeding by and you're married to a man you have nothing in common with. I believe with all my heart you will find your path after the dust has settled. And at the end of that path will be a man who will give you the love you deserve.

From where I am, I wish I could impart to all of you some special knowledge to help you on your journeys. As a parent, I guess you are given a certain amount of time to do what parents do. I feel confident that something worked because of, or in spite of, my mothering. You are all decent human beings and you genuinely seem to like and support each other. What more could a mother ask for? Farewell, my darlings. My job is done, and you are truly on your own now.

Acknowledgements

I would like to thank Jerry Wheeler for editing this book. He has learned all my bad habits and gently corrects them. Mary Hardcastle spent months working through this book with me, offerings suggestions and corrections. My other siblings, Bill Meis, Michael Meis, Monica Wellman, and Marcia Meis, have always been supportive of my writing. They have also taught me all the ways siblings can have distinct and wonderful relationships, which was essential to this book. I must also thank my mother, Virginia C. Meis for her hours of listening to me read from the manuscript. Her health was failing, but her mind remained sharp and her comments appreciated. I would also like to recognize Richard May and Wayne Goodman for their tireless support of Bay Area writers as well as LGBTQ writers across the country. Wayne recently featured me in a queerwords.org podcast where I read a selection from this novel. Gilberto Leon helped me with the Spanish phrases found throughout the book. Erik Pihel assisted with some technical matters. Divij Anderson-Santibañez showed me the beautiful and challenging aspects of growing up in these times in an alternative family. And to the beautiful and resilient people of Mexico, I apologize if some of the incidents in the book add to the narrative traveling in Mexico is unsafe. It was a plot device and nothing more. I never hesitate to visit this always-fascinating country. And last but not least, thanks to my husband for putting up with me when I'm in one of my manic writing phases.

About the author

Vincent Meis has published four previous novels, *Eddie's Desert Rose, Tio Jorge, Down in Cuba,* and *Deluge.* He has also published various articles and short stories in publications and anthologies. He lives in San Leandro, California with his husband.